# TRIPLE THREAT

Arabella's still attractive, recently widowed mother, Lady Ann, was under the spell of a local doctor who was devilishly determined to cure her loneliness.

Arabella's unworldly sister Elspeth was in the seductive hands of a suspect French aristocrat who was molding her into his sensual plaything and sacrificial pawn.

Arabella herself was faced with the menacing mystery of a suddenly brutish and immodest husband whom she could not bring herself to loathe.

*Three rogue males were loose on the fields of love—and Arabella had to tame them all. . . .*

# Lord Deverill's Heir

## Catherine Coulter

A SIGNET BOOK

## NEW AMERICAN LIBRARY

A DIVISION OF PENGUIN BOOKS USA INC.

NAL BOOKS ARE AVAILABLE AT QUANTITY DISCOUNTS
WHEN USED TO PROMOTE PRODUCTS OR SERVICES.
FOR INFORMATION PLEASE WRITE TO PREMIUM MARKETING DIVISION,
NEW AMERICAN LIBRARY, 1633 BROADWAY,
NEW YORK, NEW YORK 10019.

SIGNET, SIGNET CLASSIC, MENTOR, ONYX, PLUME, MERIDIAN
and NAL BOOKS are published by New American Library, a division of
Penguin Books USA Inc., 1633 Broadway, New York, New York 10019

First Printing, May, 1980

7   8   9   10   11   12   13   14

PRINTED IN THE UNITED STATES OF AMERICA

*To*
*Anton*

# Lord Deverill's Heir

# MAGDALAINE

### 1

*Evesham Abbey, 1790*

Magdalaine lay alone again, waiting patiently for the opium to still the ravaging pain in her body. She could scarce make out the high vaulted ceiling and the dark oak-paneled walls in the dim winter-afternoon light.

*At last the pain is lessening, soon I will be freed from that terrible gnawing. Please, let the opium last. God, why did he wait so long to give me the opium?*

*My little Elsbeth, my poor baby. But yesterday you toddled to my outstretched arms. Oh, my child, so soon, so very soon you will forget your mama. If only I could hold you to me one more time. Dear God, you will forget me, strangers will take your love, and he will be there, not I.*

Silent tears slid from the corners of Magdalaine's dark almond eyes and coursed unchecked down her cheeks, for there were no wrinkles or aged hollows to impede their downward flow. They rested briefly against the raised fullness of her lips before she licked away their salty wetness. There seemed so much to regret, so very little to give meaning to her short life.

*Come, Magdalaine, savour the small triumphs, the fleeting moments of pleasure. Remember the victories. Why can I not? It is ridiculous to be so helpless, so alone. A cry. It is Elsbeth. Please, Josette, take her from her crib, hold her close. Flow my love into her small body. Comfort her, protect her, for I cannot.*

The piercing, angry child's cries ceased, and Magdalaine calmed. She tilted her head back onto the lacy pillow and focused her gaze at the darkened oak beams overhead. Elsbeth and Josette were just above her in the nursery. They were so very close to her, just minutes away. Such a short time ago she could have flown up the stairs, her step light and sure, at the sound of her baby's cries.

*No, not a short time ago . . . centuries ago. You will only know my tomb, my little one. Only a carved plaque with your mother's name. I will be but cold gray stone and a simple name to you. Aged, lifeless stone pressing down upon me, shrouding me forever.*

Magdalaine shifted her weakened eyes to the large gilt-framed painting of Evesham Abbey, hung above the mantelpiece so proudly by the last Earl of Strafford. As if in a trance, her eyes unwavering, Magdalaine gazed at the painting. It was as if she was standing in the green undulating park that surrounded the red brick house. The magnificent lime trees that lined the graveled drive shaded the bright sun from her eyes and the hedges of yew and holly were so vividly alive that she felt she could reach out and touch them. How very English were the gables and chimney stacks that rose up the walls and towered beyond the slate roof. Forty gables; she had counted them. And just beyond the house were the old abbey ruins, crumbling with eloquent dignity for over seven hundred years. Time had etched inexorably into the mortared walls, tumbling countless stone hulks into characterless heaps. Each stone with a past so dark and mysterious that she had at first been afraid to draw near to them. One of those stones would be hauled to the Strafford cemetery to mark the earth where she would lie.

Magdalaine's opium-clouded mind drew her eyes away, to the wall opposite the bed, to seek out the bizarre carved oak panel—*The Dance of Death*, it was called. A grotesque skeleton, a blunted sword held high in its bony grip, held dominion over an eerie host of demonic figures, the gaping hollow of its mouth chanting soundless words.

*I am so very cold. Why does not someone build up the fire? If only I could snuggle down into the covers.*

Once again Magdalaine's eyes swept the room, more slowly now, for an uncontrollable lassitude was dragging down on her lids. A slow smile spread its way over her face, creasing her smooth cheeks. It was a precise smile, a triumphant smile.

*I have won a final victory over you, my lord husband. I will defeat you with my death.*

The smile froze on her lips into a ludicrous jagged line. An infant's cry rent the silence.

The bedroom door burst open. "Await me outside. I wish to speak to my wife."

The doctor straightened slowly. A tall man himself, he drew up to his full height, but the Earl of Strafford seemed to dominate the room. His tone was abrupt, his breathing rasping and sharp. The doctor did not release the countess's wrist from between his long fingers. He said evenly, "I am sorry, my lord, but that will not be possible."

"God damn you to hell, Branyon, do as I tell you! I want to be alone with my wife! It is my right!" the earl shouted. As he advanced in jerky steps toward the bed, the doctor saw that his regular features were distorted into a strange mask of fear and anger.

The doctor gently lowered the countess's hand under the covers at her side. The simple movement gave him time to control his pique at being thus spoken to. He answered softly, "I am sorry, my lord, but her ladyship is beyond words. She is gone, my lord, but a few minutes ago."

"No!" the earl cried, and rushed at the doctor to fling him away.

The doctor quickly stepped aside from the earl's onslaught. He stood silently as the earl gazed mutely down at his wife's calm pale face. Dr. Branyon placed his hand firmly upon the earl's arm. "The countess is dead, my lord. There is naught either of us can do for her now."

The earl stood motionless by the bedside for a long while. Finally he turned and said more to himself than to the doctor, "It is . . . unfortunate." Without again looking at his dead wife, he turned abruptly and left the room.

# ANN

## 2

*Evesham Abbey, 1792*

Four people stood around the writhing naked woman on the sweat-soaked sheets. The doctor had negligently thrown his coat to a tabletop many hours before, his full white shirt now loose about his neck and wrists. Fine lines of fatigue drew his mouth taut, and beads of perspiration stood out on his smooth forehead. The bleary-eyed midwife and housekeeper kept silent vigil at the foot of the bed, their hands dangling helplessly at their sides.

It was ghastly hot, so stifling that the woman in her ceaseless misery had thrown off the covers, uncaring that her swollen body was exposed to these people. She was beyond thinking, almost beyond the searing pain that receded quickly, only to explode with greater ferocity within her belly, tearing hoarse screams from her parched throat.

She lay now gasping for breath, her senses momentarily returned to her, as the agonizing pain waited for its next inevitable onslaught on her body. She gazed up at the doctor, her large blue eyes glazed with fear and suffering.

He leaned over her and wiped rivulets of sweat from her brow. "Lady Ann," he pleaded softly, "you must try harder.

You must bear down with all your strength when I tell you. Do you understand me?"

She licked her tongue over her cracked lips and whimpered helplessly. She wanted desperately to detach herself from her gross child-filled body. She sought his steady dark eyes and wished herself a part of him. So intense was her longing that he felt that part of her that was the laughing, gentle girl burn into the very depth of his being. His voice faltered as he knelt beside her and clasped her limp fingers in his hands. "Lady Ann, please, you cannot . . . you must not give up. Please, help yourself . . . help me."

A horrible croaking shriek tore from her throat, and she was lost to him, consumed back within her body as the vicious contractions tore through her belly.

He shouted at her. "Push! Now, bear down!" He hesitated only the briefest moment, splayed his fingers over her belly, and pushed downward with all his strength.

The doctor trod softly into the library and stood wearily in the dim curtained room, waiting for the earl to speak. The earl brushed careless fingers over his immaculate waistcoat, eyed the blood-flecked white shirt of the doctor with distaste, and said indifferently, "A girl, eh, Branyon? Ah, well, 'tis but her first. She still has many years of youth to bear me sons."

Angry bile rose in the doctor's throat. He managed to exert his calm professional demeanor and say with outward civility, "I am afraid that it will not be possible, my lord." He paused, seeing the earl's face darken. "You see, Lady Ann very nearly lost her life birthing your daughter. She will be unable to bear you further children."

"The devil you say! Why, the girl is but eighteen years of age!" the earl shouted.

"Unfortunately, my lord, the lady's years make very little difference," the doctor said evenly, his jaw tightening in anger. *God, how I hate this man. I am the keeper of life, yet I could kill him gladly. Poor Ann . . . you are nothing to him, just as Magdalaine was nothing.*

The earl turned abruptly away from the doctor and cursed long and fluently. He did not hear the doctor leave the library.

# ARABELLA

⬥◯◯◯ 3 ◯◯◯⬥

*London, 1810*

Sir Ralph Wigston peered over the top of his spectacles and droned his mournful phrases of condolence. He had painstakingly commited the brief message from the ministry to memory, believing that he owed the mental effort required not only to the earl's lovely widow, but also to the Earl of Strafford himself. He was a fine loyal man of unquestioned intelligence and bravery, and had died as befitted a leader of men. Proud he was, to be sure, and a determined autocrat, demanding unswerving obedience. But, of course, that was as it should be.

"We do, however, regret to inform you, my dear Lady Ann, that the earl's . . . remains have not as yet been recovered from the conflagration that ensued."

"Then it is possible that my father still lives."

The words were spoken with a cold flatness, and underlying them, Sir Ralph sensed a flicker of hope, almost a challenge to his authority and position. He carefully stored away his few remaining phrases and bent his myopic gaze upon the Earl of Strafford's daughter. "My dear young lady, let me hasten to inform you that I would most certainly not be executing this most unhappy mission were your father's demise not a proven fact." He had spoken too harshly, and hurried to soften his tone. "I am truly sorry, Lady Ann, Miss Arabella, but there were trustworthy witnesses whose word cannot be gainsaid."

"I see." Again that cold, emotionless voice. Sir Ralph disposed of his remaining phrases neatly and quickly. "The prince wishes me to assure you, Lady Ann, that there is no question of the speedy disposition of the earl's estate, in view of the reliability of the witnesses. I will, if you wish it, notify your advocate of this tragic circumstance."

"No!" The earl's daughter bounded from her chair, her hands clenched in front of her.

Sir Ralph stiffened and frowned his disapproval at this unbecoming impertinence from the earl's daughter.

Lady Ann interposed, "Arabella, my dear, surely it would be best if Sir Ralph—"

"No, Mother," Arabella declared with implacable hardness. She turned cold gray eyes to Sir Ralph's flushed face. The earl's eyes, he realized with a start.

"We appreciate your kindness, Sir Ralph, but it is for us— my mother and me—to make whatever arrangements are now necessary. Please extend our gratitude to the prince for his most kind display of condolence."

The stiffly spoken words barely cloaked a tinge of irony and an inescapable note of dismissal. Sir Ralph tugged off his spectacles and raised his ample bulk slowly from the chair.

Arabella rose also, and to Sir Ralph's discomfiture, her wintry gray eyes were on a level with his. She extended a slender hand. "Thank you, Sir Ralph. As as can see, the news has been quite a shock to my mother. If you will forgive us, I really must see to her needs now."

"Yes, yes, of course," he said hurriedly, not wishing to appear churlish. "My dear Lady Ann, if there is anything . . ."

The countess had averted her face and did not rise. Only a slight nodding of her fair head acknowledged his words.

"Good-bye, Sir Ralph," Arabella said with clipped finality.

He thought regretfully that he would have liked to clasp the small trembling hands of the countess in his own, to assure her that he would shoulder her burdens, share her grief. He was not, however, in a position to carry out his wishes with the earl's dragon of a daughter standing so militantly by the open parlour door. He looked unwillingly away from the beautiful countess into the set, unsmiling face of her daughter.

As the parlour door closed with a snap behind him, he was again struck with the thought that the earl's daughter was molded in his very image. Their physical likeness was striking—the same coal-black hair and dark arched brows set above haughty, arrogant gray eyes. But it was not simply their physical similarities. How very alike in temperament they were! Proud, autocratic, and most damnably capable. Even though Sir Ralph was displeased at being so peremptorily dismissed from his selfless errand of comfort, he felt it rather a pity that Arabella could not have been born a boy. Damn, but she could have most ably filled her father's position!

The Countess of Strafford raised wide blue eyes to her daughter's finely chiseled face. "Really, dear child, were you not a bit harsh with his lordship? You must know that he meant well."

"My father need not be dead now," Arabella stated coldly, disregarding. "Such a stupid waste! Stupid, stupid war to appease the ridiculous greed of stupid men! Dear God, could there be anything more unjust?" She flung away her mother's open arms and pounded her fists impotently against the paneled wall.

*My poor foolish child. You will not let me comfort you, for you are too much like him. You grieve for a man whose very existence made mine an endless misery. Is there no part of me in you? Poor Arabella, to shed tears is not to be despicable and weak.*

"Arabella, where are you going?" The countess rose quickly and hurried after her daughter.

"To see Brammersley, father's advocate."

"Yes, but surely, you are in no fit condition to—"

"Do not be ridiculous, Mother," Arabella said sharply over her shoulder. She was consumed with bitter, raging anger and boundless, helpless energy. She was suddenly pulled from her own pain at the sight of her mother's pale, pinched face. "Oh, God, I am such a beast," she said shakily, dashing a hand across her forehead. "Mother, you will be all right without me, will you not? Please, it is something I must do. I could not bear that father not be given a proper service before there is any disposition of his estates. I will make the arrangements to leave London. We must return to Evesham

Abbey. I will see to it . . . I must see to it! You do understand, do you not, Mother?"

The countess held the stormy gray eyes in a steady gaze and said slowly, with only a hint of sadness, "Yes, my love, I . . . understand. I shall be quite all right. Go now, Arabella, and do what you must."

The countess felt immeasurably older than her thirty-six years. It was with an effort of will that she dragged herself to the front bow window and sank down into a chair. Thick gray fog swirled about the house, twining itself about tree branches and obscuring the green grass in the small park opposite her view.

She saw John coachman holding the skittish horses. And there was Arabella crossing the flagstone in her long, sure stride. Arabella would arrange everything and no one would know that her determined, implacable energy cloaked a despairing grief.

*Perhaps it is better that she will not even seek comfort from me. For then I too would have to feign sorrow. She can not even see that his death means only the end of my imprisonment. Her furious energy will burn out her grief. It is just as well. . . . Dear Elsbeth, innocent elfin child. Like me, you are now to be freed. I must write you, for now you belong at Evesham Abbey. Now you may return to your home.*

The countess rose from her chair with such a spurt of activity that the silken blond curls trembled about her face. She threw back her head and walked purposefully to a small writing desk in the corner of the parlour. It was a curiously odd gesture, one of confidence, reborn as if by instinct after eighteen years. With crisp, almost cheerful movements she dipped the quill into the ink pot and plied her hand to a sheet of elegant stationery.

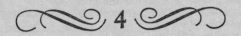

## 4

Lucifer's massive hooves sent loose gravel careening from the lime-bordered drive. His rhythmic, powerful pounding brought some comfort to his rider.

Arabella turned in the saddle and gazed with stonily calm eyes toward her home. Evesham Abbey stood proudly in the hazy morning light, its sun-baked red brick walls extending upward to innumerable chimney stacks and gables. There were forty gables in all; she had counted them. As a child of eight she had eagerly announced this arithmetic feat to her father, received a startled look, a hearty laugh, and a powerful hug that had left her small, sturdy ribs bruised until Michaelmas Day.

They had buried an empty coffin in the marbled family vault. After the women, save for Arabella, had left the cemetery, four of her father's farmers heaved a huge stone slab over the coffin and the local smithy set about his laborious job of chipping and hewing out fragments of stone, leaving in the indentations the earl's name and the years that marked his life. The empty coffin rested beside Magdalaine's, the earl's first wife. It chilled Arabella to see the empty cavern to the other side of her father's coffin, destined for her mother.

She had stood in quiet command, stiff and cold as the marble wall behind her, until finally the smithy's ringing hammer and chisel ceased their monotonous echoing.

Arabella guided Lucifer off the graveled drive onto a narrow footpath that wound through the home wood to the small fish pond that nestled like an exquisite circular gem set amidst the emerald forest. The day was too warm for the heavy velvet riding habit, and the morning sun baked through the stark black material, plastering her shift against her skin. Only a splash of white about her neck broke the somberness of her dress. She thought with mild irritation that even the soft lawn ruffles about her throat made her skin itch vexatiously.

Arabella slid off Lucifer's muscular back and tethered him to a low sturdy yew tree. She lifted her skirts from the encroaching morning wetness and walked slowly about the edge of the still water to the far side, careful not to tread on the long, silken water reeds.

What a blessed relief to escape from all those black-garbed visitors, with their long, unsmiling faces, nodding and bowing and reciting in low, doleful voices their mechanical phrases of sympathy. She marveled at how graciously her mother moved among them in her black rustling widow's weeds, seemingly tireless.

Arabella paused a moment to listen to the baleful croaking of a lone frog, hidden from her view in the thick reeds. As she bent down with a graceful swish of her black skirts, she chanced to spot a patch of black, quite at variance with the steady shades of green, in a cluster of reeds but a few feet away from her. She forgot her small croaking companion, and with a frown of inquiry furrowing her brow, moved stealthily forward.

She carefully parted a throng of reeds and found herself staring down at a sleeping man, stretched out his full length on his back, his arms pillowed behind his head. He wore no coat, only black breeches, black top boots, and a white frilled lawn shirt that was loose and open about his neck. She looked more closely at his face, calm and expressionless in sleep, and started back with a swallowed cry of surprise. It was as though she were looking at herself in a mirror, so alike were their features. His curling raven hair was cut close above his smooth brow. Distinctive black brows flared upward in a proud arch, then sloped gently toward the temples. His mouth was sensually full, as was hers, and his high cheekbones accentuated his straight roman nose. She was certain that his nostrils flared when he was angry.

"Hellfire and damnation," she swore with thoughtful precision, pronouncing each syllable.

His heavily fringed black lashes parted slowly, and she found herself gazing, mouth now agape, into her own upward-tilted gray eyes.

"My word," the man said slowly, his voice smoothly resonant. He did not move, but narrowed his eyes against the glare of the sun to take in the face above him.

"I declare, it is a *lady* I see. But where, I wonder, is the tavern wench who spoke such . . . picturesque language?"

She continued to search his face, unmoved. There was a deep cleft in his chin that she did not have, and he was sunbaked, with a pirate's swarthy face. "Who the devil are you?" she demanded finally.

Still he did not shift his position (at least he could stand up like a gentleman!), but parted his lips in an insolent, lazy smile that revealed strong white teeth. She saw that his eyes were of a lighter shade of gray than were hers, and flecked with pale gold lights.

"Do you always talk like a slut off the streets?" he asked amiably, bringing himself up to rest on his elbows.

"The way I choose to talk to an insolent ruffian lazing about on Deverill land cannot be questioned by the likes of you," she said coldly. She brought her riding crop up from her side and slapped the leather thongs lightly against her gloved hand. "I asked you a question, but it occurs to me now your reason for not answering." She stared at him thoughtfully and felt a sickening tightening in her chest. "You are obviously a bastard—my father's bastard. You cannot be so blind as not to notice the great similarity between our features, and I am the very image of my father." She averted her face, unwilling to let him see her pain. Poor father, he had not the good fortune to beget a son in wedlock. In but a moment she turned wintry eyes back to his face and said bleakly, "I wonder if there are others like you. If there are, I only pray that they do not all so closely resemble him as do you."

"It would seem unlikely to me. But you appear to be in a

better position to know of such matters than I. What, however, does seem likely is that if the earl sired children out of wedlock, they would have the good sense not to show their faces here." He spoke with calm matter-of-factness, sensing her hurt. He rose unhurriedly to his feet to face her.

"But you are here," she said sharply. She was forced to look up as she spoke. "Damn you to hell!" she swore suddenly. "You are even of his size. Dear God, how can you come here at such a time? Have you no sense of honour?"

"A great deal, I daresay."

She felt a terrible urge to slash his face with her riding crop. He stepped toward her, looming over her head, blocking the sun. Her nostrils flared and her eyes darkened, mirroring her violent intent.

"Don't, my dear," he said softly.

"I am not 'your dear,'" she said angrily, backing away from him. Her eyes narrowed and she said with cold cruelty lacing her words, "You need not tell me your purpose for being here. I am a fool not to have guessed sooner. My father's bastard, come for the reading of his will! What a scurrilous knave you are! Do you think to be acknowledged, to be given some of my father's money for your despicable use?" Impotent frustration welled up inside her.

She sensed insolent disregard as he leaned down, brushed twigs and grass blades from his breeches, and picked up his coat. "Yes," he affirmed finally with slow precision, "I am come for the reading of the earl's will."

"God, you are a damned unspeakable cur!" she hissed.

"What venom from such a lovely mouth," he observed as he shrugged into his coat. "Tell me, gentle lady, has no man yet beaten you senseless? I vow I could most easily be persuaded to do so."

"How dare you, you whore's son! You come near me and I shall slash your face to ribbons!"

"Whore's son?" His left eyebrow shot up in a sleek inquiry. "If I am a whore's son, my dear, then you must be the ill-begotten daughter of a fishmonger. As to my coming near to you, why, I can think of little else that would give me lesser pleasure."

"Then I may add cowardice to your other sterling qualities," she said with such an air of perversity that his left eyebrow shot up again and lines of amusement creased his tanned cheeks.

"One would almost think that you wished me to wrest that riding crop from you and give you a sound thrashing," he mused aloud, his voice dropping suddenly lower.

"I will see you in hell first," she spat with deadly contempt. It dawned on her with something of a shock that she no longer held the reins of control, and she knew a moment of uncertainty about herself. Because she could not bear to feel the weaker, anger at this arrogant man twisted and knotted inside her. She clutched the riding crop in her hand so tightly that a stab of white fire shot up her fingers into her arm.

"Get off my land," she said finally, reverting to the unreasoning, autocratic command used only rarely by her father.

"*Your* land?" he asked, cocking his head wonderingly. "Though you have the manners and tongue of an ill-bred, spoiled young man, you surely cannot mean to lay claim to the earl's title?"

He unwittingly struck at the festered wound deep within her, laying it raw and ugly. She was filled with the despair of failure, with the old hatred of herself for not being born a boy, her father's heir, her father's pride. A stinging retort lay leaden on her tongue. She whipped back her head, drew upon a reserve of strength unique to herself, and said with a quiet dignity that took him off his guard, "I suppose it is now my mother's land. Unfortunately, my father did not have a . . son, nor did his brother, Lord Thomas. It grieves me as it must have grieved him, for his title must become extinct. My father did not seem to be blessed in the . . . sex of his offspring."

Admirable, he thought. Aloud he said smoothly, "Do not reproach yourself for being a woman. Surely you cannot imagine that the fault somehow lies within you. Your father was more proud of you than he would have been of a dozen sons." He felt uncomfortable at a stirring of compassion for her.

"You could hardly know what my father felt." Hardness entered her voice, and her eyes turned icy cold.

"As you will," he said quietly, with a sort of odd finality to his voice.

Arabella stiffened at the hint of dismissal, sensing in him the long habit of command, the ingrained assumption of authority. She said with frigid formality, "I will bid you good-bye. I only hope that your sense of honour will prohibit your presence at Evesham Abbey. It would cause my . . . mother great pain were you to intrude upon her grief." She turned from him abruptly and strode with swift determination away from him. She tasted fleeting victory at having beaten him to the last word.

He stood in thoughtful silence, staring after her retreating figure. "No," he said with a deliberateness she would have abhorred, "my presence will not cause your mother pain. Only you will suffer, my proud, arrogant Miss Deverill."

As he voiced his insight to no one in particular, there was no response save for the gentle rustling of the thin-armed water reeds.

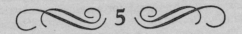

## 5

Lady Ann sat between her daughter and Elsbeth, her shoulders hunched slightly forward and her ivory hands clasped lightly in her lap. The heavy black veils hung about her face, obscuring the smooth plaits of blond hair and weighing down her back so that she could no longer sit board-straight. She was stickily hot and wished only that it could become evening so she could be alone in the curtain-drawn coolness of her room, out of the wretched black clothing that swathed her from head to toe.

George Brammersley, advocate to her late husband and only yesterday arrived in one of the earl's crested carriages, arranged himself with portentous dignity behind the great oak library desk. Lady Ann watched as he dallied, first polishing the small circles of his glasses, then setting them with practiced ease on the bridge of his vein-lined hawk nose. He slowly spread a sheaf of papers before him on the desktop, arranging them first one way and then another. His rheumy old eyes assiduously avoided the three women. Lady Ann longed for a brush to smooth down the unruly wisps of gray frazzled hair that stood about his scalp at odds angles.

She could feel a mounting intensity in Arabella's slender

body even though only their black gowns touched. She knew that her daughter viewed the reading of her father's will as the irrevocable recognition of his death. She wondered if Arabella's stern self-control would crack under the strain of the advocate's delay. She sought for soothing words to whisper to her daughter.

Lady Ann was too late. Arabella sprang from her seat and cannoned to the desk in two long strides. She leaned toward Mr. Brammersley, her hands splayed on the desktop to support her.

She whispered with ferocious calm, "I do not wish you to delay further, sir. I do not know your reason for tarrying in this ridiculous manner, but I will not have it! My mother grows weary, if you have not sense enough in your head to see it. Read my father's will now, else I shall relieve you of the responsibility!"

The red veins on Mr. Brammersley's nose quivered and seemed to grow like a fine-webbed network to his wizened cheeks. He sucked in his breath, affronted, and cast an outraged glance at Lady Ann. She nodded to him wearily. He assumed a dignified position, thrusting his receding chin out over his shirt points, cleared his throat, and said repressively, "My dear Miss Deverill, if you will please to be seated, we will begin the reading."

" 'Tis about time," she snapped, turned abruptly, and stiffly resumed her chair. Lady Ann had not the energy to remonstrate with her. She felt a flutter of apprehensive movement at her right, and turned a gentle smile to Elsbeth. Taking a small hand in hers, Lady Ann squeezed it reassuringly.

George Brammersley, seated behind the large desk, twitched an impressive document into his line of vision and began in a mournful monotone. "It is an unhappy occasion that brings us together this day. The untimely demise of John Latham Everhard Deverill, sixth Earl of Strafford, has touched us all—his family, his friends, those in his employ, and above all, his country. His courageous sacrifice of his life, so selflessly and gallantly offered to preserve the rights of Englishmen . . ."

There was a flutter of movement, and Arabella felt a light brush of air on the back of her neck. She was disinterestedly aware that the library door opened and closed. She did not notice that the aged advocate's tone took on a new crispness.

Lady Ann shifted with unobtrusive grace in her chair and gazed from the corner of her eyes toward the library door. She turned back, drew a determined breath, and straightened perceptibly in her chair.

". . . and to the faithful Deverill butler, Josiah Crupper, I bequeath the sum of five hundred pounds, with the hope that he will remain with the family until such time as . . ."

He droned on and on, mentioning, it seemed to Arabella, the name of every servant in her father's employ. How she itched for all of it to be over and done with!

Mr. Brammersley paused in his reading, raised thoughtful eyes to Elsbeth, and allowed a tight smile to tug at the corners of his mouth. His voice softened and he read more slowly, enunciating each word. "To my daughter Elsbeth Maria, born of my first wife, Magdalaine Henriette de Trécassis, I bequeath the sum of ten thousand pounds for her sole and private use."

Well done of you, Father, thought Arabella. She turned at the gasp of surprise from her half-sister and saw her lovely almond eyes widen with disbelief, then barely suppressed excitement.

Mr. Brammersley chewed furiously at his lower lip, guiltily aware that he had violated a professional trust. But the final statement the earl had written about his gentle eldest daughter had seemed so malevolent, so cuttingly cruel, that he could not bring himself to mouth the words. What had the earl meant in any case—"that she, unlike her mother and the rapacious de Trécassis family, will honestly and freely bestow this promised sum to her future husband?"

Arabella pulled her attention back to the advocate's face and waited, impatiently tapping her fingers on her lap. She assumed that now would come her father's instructions for holding his estates in trust for her until her twenty-first birthday. She hoped her mother would be named her primary trustee.

George Brammersley looked down resolutely at the finely written script in his hands. Dash it all, he had to get it over and done with. He read, "My final wishes I have weighed with careful deliberation for the past several years. The conditions that I attach to them are binding and absolute. The seventh Earl of Strafford, Justin Everhard Morley Deverill, grandnephew of the fifth Earl of Strafford, through his brother, Timothy Popham Morley, is my heir, and I bequeath to him my entire worldly fortune, whose primary assets include Evesham Abbey, its lands and rents . . ."

Arabella felt the room spin unpleasantly about her. The *seventh* Earl of Strafford! Some sort of grandnephew of her grandfather! Why, no one had ever told her that any such grandnephew existed! God, there must be some sort of mistake! But he wasn't even here. Suddenly there was a stirring in her memory of the opening and closing of the library door. Almost reluctantly she swiveled in her chair and met the cool gray eyes of the man she had seen only that morning by the fish pond. Her absolute astonishment quelled any anger or embarrassment she might have felt now at her utter lack of civility toward him. He merely nodded to her politely, nothing in his calm countenance to betray that he had even met her.

"Arabella, Arabella . . ." Lady Ann gently shook her daughter's sleeve. "Come, child, attend."

Arabella turned back in her chair, gazed with dumb shock at her mother and then at the advocate, whose lined cheeks had taken on a sudden purplish hue. He read with faltering voice, "The following stipulations are binding to both my heir and to my daughter, Arabella Elaine. It has always been my fondest wish that my daughter, through her body, would continue the proud heritage of the Deverill line. To encourage her in my wishes, I stipulate that she must wed her second cousin, the seventh Earl of Strafford, within two months of my death in order to retain her wealth and position. Should she refuse to follow my wishes within this stated time, she is to forfeit any and all monetary claims to the Deverill estates. If the seventh Earl of Strafford disinclines to wed with his second cousin Arabella Elaine, he will take claim only to the earldom and Evesham Abbey, as all other lands, rents, residences, etc., are unentailed and mine to do with as I deem fit. In this event, my daughter Arabella Elaine shall take possession of my entire worldly estates, excepting any entailed property, upon her twenty-first birthday."

"No!" Arabella sprang shakily to her feet, her face ashen. She shook her head back and forth. "No, it must . . . it *must* be a mistake! My father would never have—"

"Arabella, be seated!" Lady Ann spoke with firm authority,

and Arabella turned stricken eyes to her, then slowly sank back into her chair.

"Miss Deverill," Mr. Brammersley said with prim formality, "your esteemed father's instructions, as I have detailed them, are binding. I wish to add that the earl left a sealed envelope for you. I assure you that no one save your father is aware of the contents." He rose as he spoke, and skirted the large desk. Arabella automatically extended her hand to receive the letter, then surged up from her chair and gazed at the blurred sea of faces around the room. Clutching the envelope to her breast, she whirled about, toppling her chair to its side on the carpet, and sped to the door. Long iron-hard fingers closed about her arm as she wrenched at the ivoried knob.

"Your dramatic reaction does you little credit," the earl said with cold disapproval.

She looked up at him with blank misery, read grim censure in his gray eyes, and felt as if all the demons in hell were breaking loose within her. "Take your hands off me! God, how I hate you!"

She jerked violently away from him, and as his grip did not loosen from her sleeve, she felt the harsh rending of material. She looked down stupidly at the gaping tear, snarled her fury, for she had no more words, and flung from the library, slamming the door behind her.

A delicate Dresden shepherdess trembled, then toppled from its precarious perch on the mantelpiece and shattered onto the marble hearth.

Arabella rushed to her bedchamber in tumultuous confusion, unheeding of the shocked silence she had left in the library, and kicked the door shut behind her. She ground the key into the lock, and cursed it for its stubbornness before it succumbed to sheer force and clicked into place. She stood for a moment, panting heavily, trying to gain some sort of understanding, of meaning. As she could not find it within herself, she stooped, grasped a brocade-topped stool by a spindly leg, and hurled it with all her strength against the wall. It thudded with breaking force and dropped, now two-legged, to the carpet. Suddenly she felt drained of all anger. She looked down at the stool blankly. What an incredibly stupid thing to do, she thought. She gazed now at the crumpled envelope she held fisted in her hand. With a sense of calm purpose she crossed to her small writing desk, seated herself, and with steady fingers gently drew out a white sheet of paper. She felt a tightening in her throat at the sight of her father's meticulously fine handwriting. She formed her letters in exactly the same economical manner, for he had taught her.

She gave her head a tiny shake and began to read. "My dearest child," her father wrote, "that you are reading this letter means that I am now gone from you. If I know my Arabella, you are in a confused rage. No doubt your grief at my death is distorted by anger and misunderstanding of my instructions. As I pen this letter to you, you and your mother prepare to go to London for your first Season." Arabella stared at the paper, suspended in surprise. Why, he had written his will but five or six months ago! She gazed back at the letter and read with grim rapidity. "I myself prepare to leave for the Peninsula to assume the command of an area that is noted for the brutality and bloodiness of its conflicts. If I am fortunate enough to return from this assignment, you will not be reading this letter, for I will tell you of my wishes in person. I ramble. Forgive me, child. You have by now met your second cousin and my heir, Justin Deverill, or, more appropriately, I should write *Captain* Justin Deverill, for he is a brave and intelligent military man himself. Either rightly or wrongly, I kept you from meeting him, indeed, even knowing of his existence, until you reached a marriageable age. Do not blame your mother for not telling you that there was a male heir to the earldom, for I forbade her expressly to do so. Evesham Abbey is *your* home and I could not bring myself to inform you that there was someone who could possibly usurp your position. Forgive me, my child, for what I believed to be a necessary deception. As to your second cousin, I have been in close contact with him for some eight years now, critically following his career, to determine in my own mind if he were indeed the man I wished to sire my grandsons. I assume that you have found the physical resemblance between you to be striking. I conclude that you cannot think him ill-looking, for to do so would be to insult your own fine features. He is much like you and me, Arabella: fiercely loyal, proud, and possessed of the Deverill stubbornness. I beg you do as I have instructed. Evesham Abbey is your home. If you do not wed your second cousin, you would forfeit your birthright. You have much to think about, my child. If you decide to follow my wishes, you will have given my life meaning. Adieu, my dearest daughter."

Late-afternoon sunlight sent shafts of dazzling gold from between lazy clouds to blend with the forty stalwart red brick gables, colouring them a deep titian. Arabella walked swiftly across the undulating green lawn, unmindful of the gay parterre with its crisscrossed walks hedged by yew and holly, and the sprightly daffodils that clustered about the middle in colourful profusion. Nor did she give prideful recognition to the great cedar on the lawn, said to have been planted by Charles II.

She walked to the south of the old abbey ruins, where the ground rose gently, and turned off the avenue into the neat-plotted Deverill cemetery. She made her way through the straight rows of Deverills from generations past to the very center of the cemetery to where her father had erected his own Italian marble vault. The archangel Gabriel hovered overhead, his white stone wings spread protectively over the heavy oaken Gothic doors. Arabella tugged open the wrought handles and slipped into the dim-lit chamber. She sank wearily down to the cold stone floor beside the earl's empty coffin. Her long slender fingers, with infinite sadness, slowly traced out the letters of his name.

Dusk was shadowing the season-faded names on the gravestones when the earl eased open the vault doors and stepped noiselessly inside. His eyes widened to adjust to the dim light, and he made out Arabella curled up like a small child, asleep, her feet tucked up beneath her skirts and her arm resting gently atop her father's coffin. How very vulnerable and helpless she looks, he thought.

He moved soundlessly to her side and dropped to his knees. His eyes followed the unremitting black of her gown to where it cut a severe line at her throat, casting a dark shadow over her pale cheeks. Pins had worked themselves loose and her dusky hair fell in silky raven waves over her forehead and across her shoulders. It seemed a pity to awaken her. Even as he shook her slender shoulder, he knew the gentleness of sleep would flee from her and unforgiving hardness would enter her eyes and her voice.

She awoke slowly, with a soft whimper, as if loath to part from her dreamless state. She opened heavy black-fringed lids and looked straight into clear gray eyes. The dim light and her drowsiness clouded her sight and she gasped, "Father!"

"No, Arabella, it is not your father," the earl said gently. "It is I, Justin, come to fetch you. I am sorry to have frightened you."

Arabella flung out her arms, nearly unbalancing him, and scrambled to her feet. "How dare you come here! How dare you . . . make me think you were my father!" She felt fury at herself for showing him her pain. "You did not frighten me," she added with a harsh snap.

The earl rose leisurely to his feet, looked searchingly down at her, and saw the furiously pounding pulse in the hollow of her throat. "We seem to have an affinity for meeting in the most peculiar places. First the fish pond and now the cemetery. Come, Miss Deverill, it is chilly and dark in here. Let us return to the house. It is a long walk, but it is just as well, for I believe we have much to say to each other." His dispassionate voice echoed with unnerving resonance off the stone walls.

"We have absolutely nothing to say to each other, *Captain* Deverill," she said coldly.

"Miss Deverill, you wish me to forcibly remove you? Perhaps tear your other sleeve?" He did not pause for her to reply, but continued in the same intolerably calm tone. "I am most willing to make . . . allowances for your behavior because of your bereavement, but stupid childishness I will not tolerate."

Unconsciously she moved her hand to the rent sleeve and rubbed her arm. "Yes," she said finally, moving away from him, "it is rather chilly here. I will most willingly remove myself, Captain Deverill." Her dignified reply was belied by the angry words that still lay within her.

He merely nodded and followed her from the vault, pulling the oak doors closed behind them. They walked in silence through the cemetery until they gained the avenue. Arabella studied his profile, still strong-lined and distinct in the fading light, and felt indignation grow within her. She finally spoke, layers of accusation heavy in her voice. "You . . . you knew of this . . . arrangement, did you not? Even this morning, you knew!"

"Yes, of course I knew. The earl approached me some years ago, after the death of my own father. I must avow, he was most thorough in his examination of my character and prospects."

"And if my father had not died, he would have presented you to me as my future husband?" she pressed baldly.

"That is true." He halted a moment and looked down at her agitated countenance. "After making your most interesting acquaintance, Miss Deverill, I now applaud your father's decision to defer our meeting until you were of . . . marriageable age."

"Marriageable age!" she repeated angrily. "Why you . . . you . . ."

"Whore's son, Miss Deverill?" he supplied smoothly.

She stared at him more in incredulity than in anger. " 'Marriageable age' is what my father wrote in his letter to me. I think it a strange coincidence, sir, that you use the very same words."

"Of a truth it is, but I assure you that I did not read the contents of your letter. Surely you realize that your father and I discussed the matter at great length."

"You would be willing to . . . to follow my father's instructions?" she asked, incredulous still.

"You are not exactly stupid, Miss Deverill. You must see that marriage with you would be to my great advantage." He continued with smooth irony, "Were you not attending to the details of your father's will?"

"You mean that you wish to wed me for the . . . wealth I would bring to you?" He did not hear the forlorn catch in her voice.

He shrugged his broad shoulders and nodded. "It is certainly a powerful motive, and not one to be despised. But of course, you would gain also by such an alliance." Her eyes flashed with sudden anger, and he continued harshly, "If you do not wed me, Miss Deverill, I am afraid you will find yourself quite penniless. As I imagine that the term 'penniless' has little or no meaning to you, let me tell you quite frankly that in spite of all the young lady's accomplishments I am certain you possess, you would not survive in our proud and just land for more than a week." He paused and looked down at her with cool appraisal. "Though with your looks and figure, and with some luck thrown in, you could perhaps become a rich man's whore."

"You sicken me," she spat contemptuously.

A somewhat cynical note entered his level voice. "You disappoint me, Miss Deverill. Your language was much more colourful this morning. Though I may sicken you, I speak but the truth. If you do not wed me, you will leave Evesham Abbey in two months' time."

As if her body wished to prove her words true, Arabella suddenly felt quite sick. Her stomach was tied into knots, and nauseating bile rose in her throat. Her well-ordered, quite satisfactory world as the favoured daughter of the Earl of Strafford had crumbled, like the old abbey ruins, leaving her most secure thoughts in jagged, meaningless confusion. Unable to help herself, she dropped to her knees in the soft grass lining the drive and retched in violent, racking spasms.

The earl drew up in astonishment, looked within himself, and saw a good deal lacking. He cursed himself in far more descriptive language than had ever made its way into Arabella's vocabulary. He had mistakenly read her bald confident bravado as vain, prideful arrogance. Her father's death, his own unexpected entry into her life, the terms of the earl's will—all had been a great shock to her. He had blundered, he had ridden her too hard. God, but she was young and wretchedly confused. He bent over her and steadied her, closing his long fingers protectively about her heaving shoulders. He gently pulled black clouds of hair that hung loosely about her face. She seemed unaware of him. When she quieted, he drew a handkerchief from his waistcoat pocket and handed it silently to her. She clutched it in her hand, and without looking up, wiped her mouth.

"Miss Deverill, can you rise if I assist you? It is nearly dark, and your mother will be quite worried."

*How calmly he speaks, as if we had stopped to admire the daffodils! Come on, Arabella, stand up. See how dark it becomes; he cannot see the shame etched in your eyes.*

She drew a shuddering breath and with an effort of will locked her knees to support her weight.

The earl slipped his hands beneath her elbows and held her swaying body.

"I do not need you!" The naked pain in her voice sliced through the still evening air. Her hands clenched into fists, and in a swift, totally unexpected movement she whirled in his arms and smashed at his chest with all the fury of an enraged, trapped animal.

He dropped his arms and sucked in his breath, more from sheer surprise than from any pain she caused him. "You little devil!"

She flew from him, thick masses of hair streaming out about her shoulders and down her back.

*I do not need your help, I need no one save myself. Oh, Father, what have you done to me!*

Sharp gravel bits dug into the thin soles of her kid slippers, sending stabs of pain up her legs. Blind, unreasoning panic blurred her vision, yet she ran on as if death itself pursued her. A gently rising slope rose before her, but her mind did not tell her legs to adjust for the abrupt unevenness. She went hurtling forward, clutching frantically at the empty air to balance herself. Instinct brought her arms in front of her face to cushion the impact as she sprawled facedown onto the drive. Sharp-pointed stones cut into her arms, tearing mercilessly at her gown to dig into her slender body. One sharp cry exploded from her throat as the pain in her body seared through to her mind, unleashing the unshed tears for her father. They coursed down her cheeks, salty burning tears that had not touched her face since her father with grim resolution had put his pistol to her pony's head and pulled the trigger. Years of stoic discipline, of scorn for such despicable weakness, were stripped from her.

The earl loomed above her shaking body within an instant of her headlong plunge. *It is becoming quite a habit with me,* he thought almost inconsequentially as he knelt down beside her. Her gown was grimy and rent with small jagged tears; blood welled up and spread, blending into and encrusting the black material. He knew with an uncanny sense that the deep rending sobs were not from her fall; nor, he guessed, did tears come easily to her. He did not attempt to speak to her or soothe her. Rather, with practical efficiency he grasped her about the waist, hauled her upright, and swung her into his arms.

She went rigid, and he thought wearily that she would lash out at him again. He tightened his grip and strode on, not looking down at her.

It did not occur to Arabella to fight him. She had tensed with shock at the touch of a man's body, for no one save her father had ever held her. She felt the strength of his arms about her, and for a fleeting instant sensed an inner strength in him, a calm self-assurance that heightened the stark emptiness deep within her.

The earl halted a moment at the edge of the front lawn and stared thoughtfully at the bright candlelit mullioned windows. "Is there a staircase to your room through the west entrance?" he asked briefly, scanning the giant edifice.

He felt her head nod against his shoulder.

As the earl turned to skirt the front doors, they were suddenly flung wide and Lady Ann waved frantically to him. "Justin, you have found her!"

He leaned his face close to Arabella's and whispered, "I am sorry, Miss Deverill, but there seems to be no hope for it."

"Yes, Ann, I have found her," he called, changing his stride toward her.

Lady Ann did not shriek or fall back into hysterics. Her wide blue eyes fastened with disbelief on her daughter's ravaged face. She saw the tear streaks trailing through the dirt and blood down her white cheeks. "Dear God," she managed to say.

The earl felt Arabella clutch at his coat as if she wanted somehow to disappear inside of him. He sensed her deep mortification and hastened to say matter-of-factly, "She is not hurt, Ann, merely cut up a trifle from an accidental fall. Is Dr. Branyon still about? I think it wise that he see her."

Arabella gathered scattered remnants of pride and struggled in the earl's arms to face her mother. "I do not wish to see Dr. Branyon. Mother, I am perfectly fine . . . I simply took a stupid fall and . . . stubbed my toe. If you will please to let me down, sir."

"As you will, Miss Deverill," he said indifferently, and dropped her to the ground.

She staggered against him and would have fallen had he not slipped his arm around her waist. She drew from her sadly depleted supply of dignity, placed her hand upon his arm, and walked stiffly beside him into the house.

Dr. Paul Branyon straightened over a well-scrubbed, nightgowned Arabella and said with his charming smile, "Well, my little Bella, though you were a rare mess to be sure, I can find nothing in particular wrong with you that your bath did not cure. You will be a trifle sore here and there for a couple of days, but nothing of consequence. I do, though, insist that you have a good night's sleep."

This evening the lurking twinkle always present in Dr. Branyon's brown eyes failed to elicit a smile from her. She felt confoundedly sore from the top of her still-damp head to the soles of her bruised feet. She eyed him suspiciously as he carefully measured out several drops from a small vial into a glass of water. Like her father, Arabella hated sickness, the earl having convinced her over the years that weak persons used various illnesses to gain attention. Succumbing to idiotish complaints showed lack of character. She said stiffly, "I absolutely refuse to be quacked, so you can take your vile potion and dump it in Mrs. Tucker's tea!"

"Always my little tyrant," Dr. Branyon responded cheerfully, disregarding her outburst.

Lady Ann stepped forward and said with a new firmness that Arabella found unnerving, "Hush, child. It has been an extraordinarily trying day. There is much change . . . and much for you to think about. I will not have you bleary-eyed and out-of-reason cross, all for the want of a good night's sleep.

"Mother, really," Arabella essayed in a tone of voice that normally reduced Lady Ann to a sighing silence.

"No more nonsense, child," Lady Ann replied with an edge of sharpness to her gentle voice. "Come, drink your medicine. You have far more need of it than poor Mrs. Tucker."

With little grace Arabella downed the liquid and screwed up her face in such an expression of loathing that Lady Ann could scarce restrain a chuckle. "I will send Grace to you now, my love. Just ring if there is anything you desire." Lady Ann bent swiftly over her daughter and kissed her lightly on the cheek. She said softly, "Forgive me, child, for not telling you of Justin's existence. I have grown more and more concerned about your not knowing, yet it was a promise I made to your father."

"I . . . I think I understand, Mama," Arabella replied uncertainly. She could not fault her mother, for she knew her father's strength of will.

"Good night, little Bella." Dr. Branyon smiled and patted her hand.

Cobwebs of drowsiness had begun to cloud her eyes as she watched the doctor and her mother walk from her room.

There was a distinct quizzing look in Dr. Branyon's brown eyes as he escorted Lady Ann down the wide staircase into the large entrance hall. He remarked in a light bantering voice, "If I were a superstitious man, my dear, I would begin to think that you are a sorceress." Lady Ann raised a beautifully arched light brow in silent query.

"Sapping that indomitable will from your daughter," he finished. "I think I shall spend some time searching for a lone black cat that acts as your familiar. Never before have I observed you having the last word."

Lady Ann paused a moment, digested this piece of insight from her oldest friend, and queried him mischievously, "Why, Paul, you picture me in a most unflattering light! Am I, or was I, really such a Milquetoast?"

He responded seriously, "No, not that, precisely. It is just that the earl and Arabella . . . well, they seemed somehow to smother you with their vitality, their boundless energy. I could never quite feel Lady Ann's personality in Evesham Abbey."

"They are terribly alike." Lady Ann sighed. "Sometimes, Paul, I think you are far too acute in your perceptions." She frowned a moment and gazed almost unwillingly down at the huge Deverill family ring on her third finger. Somehow it did not seem to weigh so heavily as usual on her hand. She drew a deep breath and looked up with absolute trust into a face whose every expression she had memorized. "Many times I have felt that I am the child and Arabella, the fond, yet dominating mother. I have felt sometimes very out-of-place with her, as if she regarded me with a sort of affectionate condescension. You know, of course, how the earl felt." She found, surprisingly, that she spoke without bitterness.

Dr. Branyon fought down the familiar unreasoning anger that had clutched at him so many times during the past years. "Yes, I know," he said quietly, the firm lines of his jaw tightening.

Lady Ann stopped in the middle of the entrance hall and looked dispassionately about her. There were grand Renaissance screens, with two archways divided by fluted pilasters and enriched with elaborate paneling of splendid craftsmanship. All the trappings of war were displayed on and about the walls—hand breastplates and morions, buff leather jerkins, matchlocks, and many other articles of equipment worn or used by the foemen of the Civil Wars. Faded Flemish tapestries depicting scenes of battle shimmered in soft glowing patterns. Ancient flambeaux sent spiraling threads of blue-black smoke upward to the smoke-seared beamed ceiling.

"It is really quite strange, you know," she mused aloud, "but I have always hated Evesham Abbey, though I cannot deny its incredible beauty. The history of England still lives in this hall, yet I have no pride in it, no flights of fancy for its grandeur. You said, dear friend, that I am drawing upon Arabella's strength. I will tell you that if she were forced to leave Evesham Abbey, I would dread to think of what would happen to her." Lady Ann waved her hand out about her. "Every panel, every armament, shield, every nook and cranny of this house is a part of her. Much of her indomitable will, as you call it, is tied up with this house. So, you see, I must be firm with her, temper her impulsiveness . . ."

"So that she will marry the new Earl of Strafford as her father demanded," Dr. Branyon finished for her.

"Yes, Paul, she must marry Justin."

"Judging from the events of the day, I should say that you have your work cut out for you," he said wryly.

"Arabella cried, Paul," Lady Ann said softly. Before Dr. Branyon could seek clarification to this unusual remark, Lady Ann nodded to the footman who held open the door, and walked into the Velvet Room.

"Justin, Elsbeth," she greeted them in her gracious way. "I trust we have not kept you waiting overlong."

"Oh, no, dear ma'am," Elsbeth exclaimed. She moved forward to her stepmother and asked in her shy voice, "Is Arabella all right, ma'am?"

Dr. Branyon replied, "By now, Elsbeth, she should be sound asleep. On the morrow she will be quite restored to her usual self."

" 'Tis a pity," the earl remarked somewhat obscurely to no one in particular.

Lady Ann silenced a chuckle and turned kindly to Elsbeth. "Have you become acquainted with his lordship, my dear?"

The earl looked taken aback with his new appellation.

"Oh, no, not as yet, Lady Ann. His lordship had to change his clothes, you see. He had been with me but a moment before you and Dr. Branyon," Elsbeth said artlessly.

"We have the evening to remedy that, Miss Deverill," the

earl interposed gallantly as he assisted her to one of the small crimson velvet-and-gold chairs near to the fireplace.

Lady Ann disposed herself neatly in front of the ornate tea service. "Do you take cream in your tea, Justin? We must accustom ourselves."

"Just as it comes from the pot, Ann," he replied.

"No frills, hmm, my lord?" Dr. Banyon observed, nodding approvingly. As teacups were passed around and sips taken, he gazed covertly at the new Earl of Strafford. He was not displeased with what he saw. The earl was a large man, much like his late relative, and carried his size with loose-limbed grace. Though his bronzed face looked more suited to rugged adventuring, his elegant fitted evening clothes were not at all out of place on him. He looked to be as at ease in the drawing room as on the battlefield. The earl sensed eyes upon him and turned to face Dr. Branyon, an inquiring smile spreading over his countenance. It softened his features.

Dr. Branyon could observe none of the hardness of self-indulgence or the cold arrogance that he had always despised in the late earl. He was beginning to think that Ann was quite correct in her hope. The earl might be just the right husband for Arabella.

The earl shifted his attention to Lady Ann and remarked approvingly, "I must compliment you, Ann, on your furnishing of this room. The Velvet Room, I believe it is called?"

"I shall most willingly accept your praise, Justin, even though this room has not been touched in years. The crimson velvet has lasted beautifully, has it not?"

The earl glanced about the room and nodded. The crimson velvet and gold furniture produced a peculiarly rich effect that was enhanced by the white columns about the room and the white marble mantelpiece delicately supported by Ionic columns.

"Do you plan to make your home at Evesham Abbey, Miss Deverill?" the earl asked presently, turning to include Elsbeth in the conversation.

"Oh, no, my lord!" she exclaimed, turning quite pink. "That is . . . I do think it most *kind* of your lordship to extend such a gracious offer, but now I can afford to have quite *different* plans."

The earl remembered the ten-thousand-pound legacy from

her father and smiled. "What do you intend to do with your fortune, Miss Deverill?"

Elsbeth shot an imploring glance to Lady Ann. With the utmost composure Lady Ann replied, "It is not yet altogether decided, Justin. But I think that Elsbeth would greatly enjoy a prolonged stay in London. I would, of course, accompany her." She paused a moment and met his gray eyes squarely. "After you and Arabella are wed, we shall firmly settle our plans."

The earl's left eyebrow flared upward to his temple in ironic surprise, but he did not reply.

After Crupper had cleared away the tea tray, Dr. Branyon moved closer to Lady Ann and chided her gently, "Don't rush your fences, my dear. Though the earl did not give you a rousing set-down, you undoubtedly ruffled his feathers."

"Oh, pooh," Lady Ann replied placidly. "Justin knows quite well what is at stake. He will do his best to drag Arabella to the altar, just you mark my words."

Dr. Branyon did not reply but looked meditatively toward Elsbeth, who was making painstaking conversation with the earl. "I did not know that you intended to leave with Elsbeth," he said finally.

Lady Ann felt a sudden quickening of her pulse and looked away from him in confusion. A long-buried memory rose in her mind, and she said unexpectedly, "Do you remember, Paul, when I was birthing Arabella? I have never told you, but I know that you were with me for all of those long agonizing hours. I know that you saved my life."

Dr. Branyon regarded her, quite astonished. "No, Ann, I did not think you remembered." She could not guess the hours of torment he had experienced at her side. He decided she was but being polite to an old trusted friend. "It grows late, Ann, and I should stop by and check on Mr. Crocker's stomach pains." He rose abruptly, feeling saddened and somewhat downcast.

I have made him uncomfortable, Lady Ann thought, rising reluctantly. She planted a winsome smile on her face. "Do come by tomorrow, Paul, if for no other reason than to pronounce Arabella fit as a fiddle."

"Of course."

Lady Ann placed her hand upon his arm and again felt a strange tingling course through her. She said shyly, "It would give me . . . give us great pleasure if you would stay to dinner."

You do not owe me your gratitude, he wanted to shout at her. "As you wish, Ann," he said instead, with a coldness that caused her lovely eyes to cloud in confusion. Through long years of controlled practice, he assumed his jocular professional demeanor and patted her hand. "Tomorrow, then, my dear."

Lady Ann stood silently at the door of the Velvet Room until Dr. Branyon had accompanied Crupper out of her hearing. "I am behaving in a most ridiculous manner," she said half-aloud. "Acting like a romantic schoolgirl . . . and here I am with a grown daughter!"

She turned an absurdly youthful face to find the earl's eyes upon her in a most uncomfortably penetrating stare. Because she was not a young, inexperienced girl, she was able to meet his gaze with nonchalant composure. "My dear Elsbeth," she said in a heartening tone, crossing to where her stepdaughter sat, "if you do not retire to your bed soon, I shall have to fetch some match sticks to keep your eyes propped open."

Elsbeth yawned with the unrestrained candor of a child.

"Have I been such a boring companion, Miss Deverill?" the earl asked pensively.

"Oh, no, my lord!" Elsbeth disclaimed, blushing fiercely and instantly snapping her mouth closed. She felt terribly gauche. Why could she not be more like Arabella, so confident, so very sure of herself? "It is just that I am so very tired. It has nothing to do with you, my lord," she finished hastily.

Lady Ann rescued her stepdaughter. "Pay no attention to his lordship, my dear, he is but funning you. Now, off to your bed." She added conspiratorially, "We have much to discuss tomorrow, my love."

Elsbeth's dark almond eyes glowed. "Oh, yes, Lady Ann, to be sure," she breathed happily. She turned and sketched her best curtsy to the earl. "Good night, my lord. Indeed, sir, I did not find you at all boring!"

"I shall now sleep well, Miss Deverill, with that assurance." The earl smiled and took her small hand.

"You should have been a diplomat, Ann," the earl remarked, breaking a comfortable silence that had lasted some minutes after Elsbeth's departure.

"Ah, that mission seems to be reserved for you, brave, courageous men," she replied lightly, pulling her gaze almost unwillingly away from the orange crackling fire. She tried to banish Dr. Branyon from her thoughts.

"True, but I cannot imagine that it will always be so." His gray eyes took on a keen, searching look, narrowing so that the thick-black-fringed lids nearly met. "Dr. Branyon seems a charming man. Most . . . devoted to the Deverill family."

She felt a slight catch in her throat, and not trusting herself to speak, merely nodded.

The earl tucked away her reaction and changed the subject. "I knew your husband for nearly eight years, Ann. I find it quite strange that he never once mentioned that he had another daughter. She is a charming girl, but . . ." He paused hesitantly.

"But what, Justin?"

"Do not, I pray you, Ann, think me forward, but I would say that she is starved for love, for attention."

"I daresay that you are right, Justin," she said slowly. "The earl, her father, did not allow her to live with us. She was but a small frightened child when he packed her off to Kent to make her home with his older sister, Caroline. I have maintained a constant correspondence with the child all these years, but of course it cannot be the same thing. I am certain that Caroline did her best by Elsbeth, but as you said, she is starved for love." Lady Ann drew a deep breath of resolution. "I fully intend to remedy all the past ills Elsbeth has suffered."

"But why did the earl treat her so?"

"Because he loved Arabella so very much," Lady Ann said sadly. "And for some reason that I could never discover, he bore some sort of grudge toward the de Trécassis family. The earl was never a very forgiving man, you know."

"Does it not seem rather curious to you, then, that he bequeathed her ten thousand pounds?"

"Yes. I fear that we shall never know his reasons for doing so. I myself was quite surprised." Lady Ann paused a moment, mentally constructing an apology. She said earnestly, "Do forgive me for being so very blunt, Justin . . . about you and Arabella, that is. Dr. Branyon accused me of rushing my fences," she added with a chuckle.

The earl rubbed his chin in a rueful manner. "Let us just

say that you did not leave me a great deal of latitude on the subject. Though I made up my mind several years ago that I would marry Arabella, it still comes as a shock to be thrust so baldly into the caldron. You know, Ann, that I shall try to do my best by her."

"If I had believed otherwise, my dear Justin, I would have fought the entire proposition with the ferociousness of a mother lion. Although I felt some trepidation about the earl's deception, I thought his decision to be the best solution. You know, it was all I could do to keep quiet while George Brammersley dallied about before you arrived. I spoke briefly to Arabella this evening. If naught else, I believe she begins to understand her father's motives as well as my silence over the matter."

"You are a remarkable woman, Ann."

"No, Justin," she replied quietly, "merely a very realistic one. Years of life do that to one, you know. Perhaps it was wrong of the earl to wish to protect Arabella. You know how he felt."

"Yes. If Arabella had known that there was an heir to the earldom, she would have been terribly upset at the thought of her eventual dispossession."

"Well, 'tis over now." She paused a moment, then asked the earl brightly, "What do you think of your new home, Justin?"

He laughed. "I feel somewhat daunted by such grandeur. Only this evening I noticed the truly vast number of gables and chimney stacks."

Lady Ann chuckled as a piquant memory rose in her mind. "You must ask Arabella the exact number of gables." She shook her head fondly. "Do you know that when she was but eight years old she came rushing into the library and proudly announced to her father that there were exactly forty gables on Evesham Abbey. She was such a sturdy little girl, her hair always a tumbled mess and her knees invariably scratched. Oh, I don't know, but even then she was so full of life, so inquisitive . . ." Lady Ann paused and said ruefully, "Do forgive me, Justin. I do not mean to bore you. I cannot imagine why I thought of this."

The earl said brusquely, "Don't be a widgeon, Ann. How could I possibly be bored with stories about my . . . intended wife?"

"Do you always answer so . . . admirably, Justin?" she countered.

"Always," he affirmed cheerily. "Now, my dear, please continue."

"Very well. Back to Arabella's forty gables. A short time later, her father sent her to Cornwall to visit her greataunt Grenhilde. No sooner had she left than he commissioned carpenters and bricklayers to construct another gable to the abbey. When Arabella returned and bounded into his arms, he held her away and said in the most stern voice you could imagine, 'Well, my fine daughter, it seems that I will have to hire a special mathematics tutor for you! *Forty* gables indeed! You have disappointed me gravely, Arabella.' She said not a word, slipped out of his arms, and was not to be seen for two hours. Her father was beginning to grow quite anxious, nearly to the point of berating himself, when the little scamp comes running in to him, completely filthy and utterly frazzled. She stood right in front of him, her little legs planted firmly apart, grubby hands on her hips, scowling, and said in the most scathing voice, 'How dare you serve me such a trick, Father! I forbid you to deny it! I have brought your bricklayer to be my witness that there were indeed forty gables.' As I remember, from that day on the earl ceased to pine about not having a son. He kept Arabella with him constantly. Even in the hunt, he bundled her in front of him on his huge black stallion, and they would go tearing off at a speed that made my hair stand on end!"

The earl grinned, then threw back his head and roared with laughter. "So are there forty or forty-one gables, Ann?"

"Under Arabella's glowering instructions, the earl had the forty-first gable removed. Such a little commander she was!"

The earl rose, stretched his long frame, and leaned against the mantelpiece, hands thrust into his pockets. "There is still quite a lot of scamp and commander in her, I daresay."

Lady Ann turned in her chair, her black silk skirts rustling softly. "True," she admitted with a smile, "but it is part of her charm. Poor George Brammersley, though, I fear her treatment of him sent the dear man to his room with a *tisane* to soothe his ruffled nerves."

"But recall, Ann, what a shock the conditions of her father's will were to her." He thought about his first meeting with Arabella earlier that morning, but said nothing of it.

"Well, this is progress indeed!" Lady Ann teased. "Already you defend her . . . high spirits!"

He retorted with a wide grin, "Her spirits can soar as high as the gables, just so long as she does not send mine plummeting!"

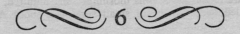

# 6

Arabella walked slowly down the stairs early the next morning, feeling quite subdued. It was an unusual state of mind for her, and she did not particularly like it. She had been placed in a situation where she had only two choices—one of course being totally unacceptable (she could not bear the thought of leaving Evesham Abbey), and the other, holding no visible pleasure. It was simply not fair. It was rather like being afflicted with a stomachache when one had not even stuffed oneself with an overabundance of food.

She walked through the large entrance hall, under the great arch, to a narrow corridor that led to the small breakfast parlour. Only she and her father ever breakfasted so early, and she looked forward now to being alone.

"Miss Arabella!"

Arabella turned, her hand on the doorknob of the breakfast parlour, to see Mrs. Tucker balancing a large pot of coffee near one dimpled elbow and a rack of toast near the other.

"Good morning, Mrs. Tucker. I am glad that you have prepared my breakfast as usual. 'Twill be a lovely day, do you not agree?"

"Yes, yes, of course, Miss Arabella." Two chins bobbed nervously about a ruched white collar. Mrs. Tucker twitched her nose to prevent the downward slide of her spectacles. "You are feeling better this morning?" she inquired, focusing her faded eyes on several small scratches about Arabella's chin.

"Tolerable, Mrs. Tucker," Arabella replied. She pushed the door open and stepped aside to allow the housekeeper's voluminous black bombazine skirts to brush through without incident to either the coffee or the toast.

She turned to follow her through the open doorway, looked up, and froze where she stood, a ludicrous expression of surprise and dismay flooding her face. The earl sat at the head of the table, in her father's chair, plates of scrambled eggs, bacon, and a haunch of rare beef arrayed in front of him, his eyes upon a London newspaper. He glanced up at the sound of a sharp intake of breath, took in Arabella's flushed countenance, and rose politely. "Thank you, Mrs. Tucker, that will be all for now," he said to the wheezing housekeeper. "Compliment Cook on a most delicious breakfast," he added kindly.

"Yes, my lord." Mrs. Tucker achieved a fairly creditable curtsy, fluttered her short sausage fingers about her netted cap, and retreated from the room, avoiding Arabella's eyes.

"Will you join me, Miss Deverill?" the earl offered, pulling out a chair beside his own at the table.

"You!" she breathed, her nostrils flaring. What wretched luck that he should be up so early! No wonder Mrs. Tucker was so discomfited to see her this morning! Arabella gulped down her rising anger. She managed to ask with tolerable calm, "Are you always at breakfast so early?"

"Yes," he replied, still holding her chair. He grinned, noting her riding habit, and said pointedly, "I always like to ride early after my breakfast. It would seem, Miss Deverill, that you are in the same habit."

"Yes," she said in a clipped voice. She accepted his assistance into her chair and began to dish eggs and bacon onto her plate before he had again eased back into his place.

"Would it not be simple politeness to wait for your . . . host?" he asked smoothly.

Her hand tightened involuntarily about the handle of her fork, and she shot him a smoldering glance.

He sighed, picked up his paper, and lowered his head.

"Would you please pass the coffee?"

The earl's curling black head emerged from the newspaper. "Certainly, Miss Deverill. Here you are."

"And a section of the newspaper, if you please."

"Of course, Miss Deverill. Any particular section?"

"Since I would not wish to deprive you, you may give me a section that you have already read."

"Here you are, Miss Deverill." As she twitched the pages from his outstretched hand, he noticed angry scratches on the back of hers.

"You are feeling just the thing this morning?" he asked significantly.

"Of course." Her eyes traveled to her hands, and she whipped them from his view.

"I am relieved, but not surprised. Dr. Branyon assured me last evening that you would be restored to your *usual self* today."

She ground her teeth at the amused irony in his voice and resumed her breakfast in disdainful silence.

"Would you care to ride with me, Miss Deverill?" he inquired presently.

It was on the tip of her tongue to refuse him, but she harked to her situation, recognized the inevitable illogic of such an action, and replied with scarcely a tremor to betray her agitation, "As you will."

"Excellent. You can conduct me upon my first tour. Which horse do you ride, Miss Deverill? I shall send word to the stables."

"The earl's horse," she said without thought.

"Oh? Do you not think it will be a trifle uncomfortable riding pillion?" He added with an amused grin. "Not, of course, that I would mind sharing my horse with you."

"I did not mean *your* horse!" she said hotly. "I mean the earl's . . . that is, my father's . . ."

"You mean Lucifer," he supplied kindly.

"Yes," she snapped.

"Of course, you have my permission."

"You are all kindness!" Her biting sarcasm appeared to be lost on him, and she shoved back her chair in a motion reminiscent of her violent display in the library the afternoon before.

"I would that you take better care of . . . *my* furniture, Miss Deverill," the earl remarked pensively.

She glared at him in speechless fury.

"Come, my dear Miss Deverill, I believe we have fenced enough for one morning. I, for one, would not particularly care to have my breakfast disagree with me." At her continued silence, he added with a smile that displayed his strong white teeth, "I will make Lucifer a gift to you. Soon we shall rename him the countess's horse."

Arabella thought that her brains were becoming quite as scrambled as the eggs she had just consumed. His blatant reference to their marriage left her momentarily speechless.

The earl drew out his watch and consulted it. "Coming, Miss Deverill?"

"Yes," she said slowly. "I am coming."

Dr. Branyon was granted a brief yet quite pleasing view of Lady Ann's finely shaped ankles as she lifted her skirts to step daintily over a tiny blossoming rosebush. She wore no bonnet and her thick blond hair shone with a golden sheen in the bright midday sun. A handful of cut daffodils bespoke her activity. It seemed to his prejudiced eye that her face glowed with a new health and vitality.

As Lady Ann was carefully stepping over a rosebush, she was wondering where in heaven's name Dr. Branyon could be. It was growing quite late, and he had not even sent a message. She clasped her daffodils more securely and looked up, a tiny frown puckering her alabaster forehead. She saw Dr. Branyon standing but a few feet away from her, silently regarding her. She flushed to the roots of her hair, felt an uneasy weakness afflict her knees, and stammered, "Paul . . . however did you find me?"

"Crupper is very observant, my dear."

Lady Ann used the few moments of this speech to roundly chide her rubbery knees and assume what she thought to be a matronly demeanor. "I thought that perhaps you were too busy with your patients to come to us today."

"Only the imminent birth of triplets would have prevented me. May I carry those murderous-looking cutters for you, Ann?"

"Yes, thank you, Paul." She relinquished the flower cutters and found that the mundane action brought back balance and perspective. Everything between them was back into focus, and he was again her old friend of many years. Still, she could not recall having ever found his dark brown corduroy suit so terribly smart. His eyes were very nearly the same colour, with gentle, amused lights.

Dr. Branyon matched his stride to her shorter one as they walked through the ornamented parterre back to the front lawn. "How is our Arabella getting on?" he asked.

"Do you mean her physical health or her relationship with Justin?"

"Well, knowing my little Bella, she is as healthy as that black beast she persists in riding. Justin, though, is another matter, I think."

"In the first case, you are quite right, as usual. As to Justin, I am not so very sure. They rode together this morning, you know. Neither of them looked any the worse for it at luncheon. If Arabella was not quite her usual voluble self, she was not, at least, rude to the earl. If I am not mistaken, I think the both of them are in the library pouring over the Evesham Abbey accounts. Arabella knows as much as her father about running the estate. Poor child, I remember him drumming fact after fact into her young head! Dear Mr. Blackwater, the earl's agent, was so terribly put out when Arabella issued her first orders to him at the advanced age of sixteen."

Dr. Branyon chuckled, a deep rich sound that made the daffodils tremble for a moment in Lady Ann's hand.

He asked, "How do you think the earl will adjust to Bella's most unwomanish competence in a traditional man's domain? To boot, the chit is even ten years his junior!"

"To tell you the truth, Paul, he seemed to me to be rather pleased. I think he will come to admire her tremendously."

Dr. Branyon paused and dropped a hand on Lady Ann's shoulder, gripping it an instant. "Perhaps you are right, Ann. Though I can easily picture some ferocious ragtag fights between them, they are perhaps better suited than most. Arabella needs a partner of great strength, else she would render the unfortunate's life miserable. As for Justin, I vow that, given an obliging, meek spouse, he would become a household tyrant."

"How very tidily you wrap up all my concerns! You are a most complete hand, Paul." She gaily plucked a daffodil from her bunch and with a mock curtsy pulled its stem through a buttonhole in his coat.

"And now a dapper dog as well," he said, smiling tenderly down at her upturned face.

Lady Ann gulped, then gave a guilty start. "Oh, dear, I forgot about Elsbeth. She will think I've strayed and fallen into the fish pond! Let us join her, Paul. It is nearly teatime."

Dr. Branyon pulled up short in his tracks and gave a shout of laughter.

"Good heavens, Paul, whatever have I said?"

"It just occurred to me, my dear Ann, that you will soon be the *Dowager* Countess of Strafford! How very ridiculous, to be sure!"

"I . . . I am quite matronly, Paul," she managed to say, herself overcome by such an awesomely aged title.

"But not quite yet in your dotage." He grinned and took her arm. "Come, my dear dowager countess, let me assist you. Perhaps I can prescribe a cane."

"Paul, really!"

Elsbeth had not drawn the conclusion that Lady Ann had succumbed to some unfortunate accident. She was not thinking about Lady Ann at all. Rather, she was staring off at nothing in particular, her small hand poised above her stitchery, her colourful creation for the moment forgotten. She was thinking about all sorts of pleasurable dissipations that awaited her in London. Balls, routs, even plays in Drury Lane! She had heard of the Pantheon Bazaar all of her life, where one could find literally any colour ribbon and myriad other gewgaws. And there was, of course, Almack's, that most holy of inner sanctums, where young girls spent untold hours dancing with charming, dashing young men. Her ten thousand pounds would ensure her foothold in London society. With Lady Ann, the widow of a peer and military hero, she could not imagine any door being closed to her. So excited was she at the prospect that her natural shyness and hesitancy in mixing in polite society dimmed in importance.

She frowned, thinking of Josette. How she wished that her old servant would cease with her dark mutterings against every Deverill! After all, had not her father proven his love for her? Such a vast sum he had bequeathed to her! Elsbeth sighed. Josette was just getting old and crotchety. Her wits were becoming clouded, too. Just this morning, Josette had called her Magdalaine.

Quite clearly she had said, "Come closer to the window, Magdalaine! How can I mend this flounce with you fidgeting about so!"

Elsbeth had chosen not to remind her faithful old servant that she was not her mother, Magdalaine. Docilely she had moved to the window.

It was then that she espied the earl and Arabella. "Oh, just look, Josette," she cried, moving closer to the window, "there come Arabella and the earl!" Two great plunging stallions were cannoning across the drive onto the front lawn. "They are racing! There, Arabella has won! Oh, my, just look how her horse is plunging and rearing!" Elsbeth shivered. Horses seemed quite unpredictable to her; they were nasty, jittery beasts, and not to be trusted.

Elsbeth heard Arabella's shout of victory and watched her alight from her horse, unassisted. Josette drew closer, narrowed her watery eyes against the glare of the morning sun, and muttered disdainfully, "Just like her father she is! Brash and conceited. Not a lady like you, my little pet. Leaping off her horse as if she were a man! And look at the new earl—encouraging her!"

Elsbeth did not particularly attend to Josette's strictures. She was thinking with a slight twinge of envy that she was older than Arabella, yet she felt so terribly . . . unfinished.

Elsbeth drew her thoughts back to the present. Her hands were still poised motionlessly above her stitchery. It was quite ridiculous, she decided, to be at all jealous of Arabella. After all, it was she, Elsbeth, who had the ten thousand pounds. If Arabella did not comply with her father's instructions, she would have nothing. Arabella would have to marry the new earl. Elsbeth shivered. She found the new earl almost as terrifying as the huge bay stallion he rode. He was so large, so overwhelming. He seemed to fill the room with his presence. She felt a fearful tremor that caused her small hand to tremble. It was a delicious sort of fear that somehow caused her cheeks to burn. She grasped her needle firmly between her fingers and quickly set a stitch of bright yellow silk.

She did not look up until Lady Ann and Dr. Branyon came strolling into the Velvet Room, side by side, their heads close in quiet conversation. She sensed something about them that was somehow different, something that she did not quite understand.

"Bravo, Elsbeth! You play Mozart beautifully," Dr. Branyon cheered.

The earl readily concurred. He thought it strange that the shy, painfully quiet Elsbeth should play the pianoforte with such passion.

Elsbeth rose from the piano stool and blushed pink with modest pleasure. She had played particularly well, losing herself upon several occasions in the thrilling tempo, the deep resounding chords.

It was drawing near to ten o'clock in the evening and Lady Ann was on the point of excusing herself when the earl turned to Arabella and asked politely, "It is now your turn, Miss Deverill. Will you play for us?"

Arabella went into a peal of laughter. "Were I to play, you would most certainly suffer for your gallantry!"

"Now, Arabella, that is not *quite* true," Lady Ann objected. She thought of all the torturous hours she had stood behind Arabella at the pianoforte, and the woeful result she had achieved.

"Oh, Mother," Arabella said mischievously, "it is time *you* faced the truth. Despite her inexhaustible, heroic efforts," she said over her shoulder to the earl, "I could never even execute a simple scale without falling over my fingers!"

"But, Arabella, you do everything so very well," Elsbeth bravely protested. "I cannot believe that you do not—"

"Dear little goose," Arabella said fondly to her half-sister, "you have every scrap of talent in the Deverill family. I would much rather listen to you than have everyone howling at me with their hands over their ears!"

Lady Ann was hard-pressed not to smile. She threw up her hands in mock defeat.

"Excellent, Mama! You have saved everyone from a most trying experience!" Arabella felt the earl's eyes upon her and became suddenly absorbed in a wrinkled pleat in her skirt. If he is disappointed that I do not have a young lady's accomplishments, he can go to the devil, she thought with unusually tepid annoyance.

"Well, my lord," Dr. Branyon addressed the earl, "how did you find your first night spent at Evesham Abbey?"

The earl sat forward in his chair and clasped his hands between his knees. "It is strange that you should ask, sir," he began slowly, "for I spent a somewhat unusual night."

The company's attention was upon him, and he looked around, a rueful grin upon his lips.

"I am inclined to think that it was all suggestion and my own imagination. In any case, all of you are familiar with that most unusual paneling in my bedchamber—*The Dance of Death*."

"It is horrible!" Elsbeth exclaimed with a delicate shudder.

The earl said kindly, "It is certainly out of the ordinary. I was examining it before I retired to bed, trying to determine its theme. I could discover no plausible explanation, and I was still dwelling upon it when I fell asleep." The earl paused and glanced at Dr. Branyon. "I pray you will not have me committed to Bedlam, sir, for what I am about to tell you."

"Come, get to the point," Arabella interrupted impatiently.

"Do not rush me, Miss Deverill, you interfere with my dramatic introduction. It was very late, well into the early hours of the morning, when I awoke suddenly, certain that I was not alone. I lit the candle at my bedside and lifted it to look about the room. I could see nothing save that hideous grinning skeleton on the paneling. I was beginning to feel particularly foolish when I heard a strange thudding sound near to the fireplace. I raised the candle but saw nothing. Then I swear I heard a high wailing cry, like that of a newborn infant. Before I could even react, there came, quite close to me, it seemed, another cry. Not a babe's, but a woman's cry—piercing and somehow incredibly anguished. Then there was nothing. I am still not certain in my own mind that I did not imagine it."

The earl looked around at the sea of startled faces.

Lady Ann was the first to regain her composure. "You did not imagine it, Justin. You have made the acquaintance of Evesham Abbey's ghosts. What you have described happens on rare occasions, and only in the earl's bedchamber."

"Surely you jest, Ann," the earl said, astonished and somewhat unsettled at the thought of sharing his room with unearthly occupants.

"No, it is true," Arabella continued. "My father heard just what you recounted at least four or five times. It seems that well over two hundred years ago, before Evesham Abbey came into the Deverill family, a lord named Favill lived here. He was reputed to be viciously cruel, and a wild, unstable man. The story goes that one stormy night a servant arrived at the cottage of the local midwife and ordered her to accompany him. She was afraid and refused, but he forced her. She was blindfolded and driven many miles. At last the carriage halted. She was dragged up a long flight of steps, through a large hall, up a straight staircase, and led to a bedchamber. When the servant removed her blindfold, she saw a lady, huge with child, propped up in a great bed. A large, broodingly silent man stood by the fireplace. The lady began to scream, and the midwife rushed forward to help her.

"After a long and difficult labor, the child was finally born. To the horror of the midwife, the man rushed forward and grabbed the babe and hurled it wailing into a roaring fire. The lady screamed and fell in a faint back on her pillow.

"The servant grabbed the midwife, tied the blindfold back on, and hurried her back to her cottage." Arabella felt gooseflesh rise on her arms even though she had heard the story many times before.

"Good God," the earl said finally.

"There is a just ending, though," Lady Ann said in a heartening tone. "It seems that the midwife remembered certain sounds, and even counted the number of stair steps. She was able to lead the magistrate to Evesham Abbey. Though the magistrate could find no conclusive proof of violence, and thus Lord Favill escaped lawful punishment, it did not end. It was reported that late one night, Lord Favill came bounding out of his bedchamber, his face contorted with sheer terror. He raced to the stables and threw himself upon one of his half-wild stallions. No one is certain what happened then, but the next morning Lord Favill was found under his horse, crushed to death, just beyond a small knoll behind the old abbey ruins. To this day, the drop is called Favill's Jump."

"How dreadful." Elsbeth shuddered. "Josette told me about Lord Favill, but I did not believe her."

Lady Ann said in a lighter voice, " 'Tis a gruesome story, to be sure, but it was hundreds of years ago."

Dr. Branyon shook his head. "I fear all of you will be hearing strange noises tonight."

Lady Ann rose. "Well, I for one intend to do nothing save

sleep." She turned to Elsbeth. "Come, love, I will accompany you to your room. You are looking quite fagged."

Arabella was somewhat discomfited to find herself alone with the earl a few moments later. She eyed him as he rose and strolled to the sideboard. "A glass of sherry, Miss Deverill?"

"Yes, thank you." She tucked her knees up under her and balanced her chin on her hand. "You are certainly calm about all this," she observed.

He handed her the glass, grinning ruefully. "Believe me, I would gladly ask Dr. Branyon for a sleeping potion if I thought it would not lower me in your estimation."

"Oh, fie! How absurd you are!" She tossed down several gulps of the rich deep sherry. "You know, another couple of glasses of my father's sherry, and you will sleep quite as soundly as a log."

"Then by all means, let us drink up! To your health . . . Arabella. 'Tis a beautiful name, you know. I hope you do not mind my using it. 'Miss Deverill' is so terribly impersonal."

"I am not certain that I do not mind," Arabella replied bluntly. " 'Tis far easier to keep you at arm's length with 'Miss Deverill.' "

"But I would prefer being much closer."

His caressing tone made her untangle her legs and start up from the sofa. "You . . . you move too quickly, sir."

"Justin," he corrected softly.

"Sir!" she snapped. "It grows late. Good night."

"So craven, Arabella?" He set down his glass and walked purposefully toward her.

"I swear, if you come one step farther, I shall dash this sherry in your face!" She assumed a militant stance and watched him carefully.

To her surprise and only partial relief, the earl appeared to take her threat quite seriously. He disposed his large frame in a spindly chair that groaned under his weight, and sighed soulfully. "You abandon me to my fate in the haunted bedchamber."

Arabella knit her brows a little over this admission and said in a more conciliatory voice, "I suppose I cannot blame you, after that hair-raising experience. I have always felt uncomfortable in that room."

"How glad I am to hear you say that," the earl said, relieved. "Is your bedroom large enough for the both of us?"

His question evoked a series of very intimate images in her mind, and Arabella drew back, embarrassed colour flooding her cheeks.

"Not missish, are you, my dear?"

"You are really quite impossible and . . . provoking!" she said scathingly, and flung out of the room.

An expectant, confident smile passed over the earl's lips. So very obstinate and headstrong she was! Yet, he did not think that he would wish her to be any other way. He was beginning to think that he had not made such a bad bargain after all.

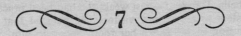

## 7

The earl drummed long fingers impatiently on the most recent pages of the estate account book. Damn, he was not used to the endless rows of numbers to be tallied and retallied, all the details of what to do with this or that investment, or the juggling of rents of his tenants to secure the best income. He would just as soon that all the numbers would magically disappear and stay gone, just as had the ghost of Evesham Abbey a week ago. He sat back in his chair and dropped his pen on the open page. He had passed his adult years soldiering—a leader of men, not numbers! Ah, Cuidad Rodrigo—there was a battle, and a decisive one. Yet, he thought glumly, Napoleon still holds Europe fast in his Corsican hands. England was suffering from the French blockade, and if rumour had it correctly, Napoleon was now casting greedy eyes to the east, to Russia. Here he was, far from the thick of things. With a frustrated grunt the earl shook his head and returned his concentration to the page of entries. What he needed was Arabella. The one afternoon she had spent with him explaining such things as rents, market prices, crops, and the like, she had spoken concisely and knowledgeably, and he had achieved at least some rudimentary insights. Blackwater, his agent, had been far less helpful. The studious little man seemed to have difficulty in focusing his fading wits on the new century.

Arabella. During the past week, she had been practically as nonexistent as his ghostly visitors. He guessed that she was breakfasting very early in her room, to avoid him. She rode out alone on Lucifer, and on many days did not return until the sun was fading behind Charles II's cedar in the front lawn.

Wisely, he left her alone. At least he thought he was acting wisely. On many occasions it was Arabella who maneuvered circumstances so as not to be alone with him. He would have felt totally at sea had he not several times felt her wide gray eyes upon him while he was in conversation with someone else.

He started at a distant clap of thunder. Finally a diversion from his wretched task. He rose and walked to the windows. Dark, mottled rain clouds hung low and threateningly to the east.

Layers of chill, heavy air swirled about Arabella, announcing the imminent arrival of the storm. Yet, she did not move from her perch on the highest outjutting gray stone in the old abbey ruins. How strange it was that her father had always hated the ruins. Even as a child, he had forbidden her to go near them. This was the only instance she could ever remember where she had defied him. She glided her fingers over the smooth, lifeless stone, capturing and lovingly reliving some of her cherished childhood adventures.

A rain pellet struck her cheek and dripped off her chin. She rose reluctantly and looked toward Evesham Abbey, now almost obscured in the gathering darkness. It seemed unlikely that Lady Ann and Elsbeth would venture from Talgarth Hall with the storm brewing up so quickly. She had watched them sally forth a couple of hours before with only John coachman in attendance. She wondered why the earl had not accompanied them.

The earl stood, hands on his hips, under the protection of the columned entrance. "Miss Arabella did not take Lucifer?" he grimly asked James, the head groom. Heavy rain fell in sheets in front of them, and a chill wind whipped at the earl's full-sleeved shirt.

"No, my lord," James answered worriedly, his thin legs trembling with cold.

"Very well, thank you, James. Fetch a cloak before you return to the stables."

Damnation! Did she find his company so distasteful that she preferred catching a chill? In a very short time his worry for her safety had worked its way to savage anger. God, he would throttle her for being such an idiot to remain out in such weather!

He was furiously contemplating wringing her neck when through the thick blanket of darkness and rain he made out the vague outline of someone running full tilt up the front lawn. The figure drew closer, and he saw Arabella, skirts held above her knees, racing toward him. She took the front steps two at a time and drew up panting in front of him.

"Where the devil have you been?" he exploded angrily.

Arabella swept her soaked hair from her forehead, lifted an inquiring eyebrow, and replied instructively, "I think it obvious even to one of the meanest intelligence that I have been running in the rain. Now, if you will stop glowering at me in that ridiculous way, I would go change my clothes."

He gazed with momentary longing at her slender neck, and pictured his fingers tightening about it.

"Oh, for heaven's sake, you look as though you'd just lost a battle, or something. You really should not stand out here, you know, it is quite chilly, and you might catch an inflammation of the lung!"

"Arabella!" he thundered, but she had already swept past him into the front entrance hall.

He wished that her soaked gown did not cling so revealingly to her breasts and hips. It quite made him forget his anger.

"We shall dine in thirty minutes in the Velvet Room, madam," he shouted after her. "I refuse to have my dinner delayed any longer!"

She turned on the stairs, pools of water forming at her feet, regarded him steadily, and replied in the voice one might use to soothe an upset child, "Yes, of course. Do not fret further, sir. I shall be with you presently."

The earl felt a grin tug at the corners of his mouth, and sternly repressed it.

He prided himself on being immune to female charms, and

thus was taken aback at the entrance of Arabella, precisely thirty minutes later, in the Velvet Room. She glided gracefully into the room, still dressed in severe black silk. It was her hair that quite unsettled him. Still damp, it hung in waving clouds of glossy black down to her waist, a simple narrow ribbon securing it back from her forehead. He stilled the desire to gather the silky masses into his hands and press them against his face.

"Well, I hope that we do not have to summon Dr. Branyon to prescribe for you," he said irritably, quelling his momentary lapse.

"I am blessed with my father's good health," she said affably, walking to where he stood by the fireplace. She drew up dangerously close, and for once the earl found himself a trifle daunted. He found her cool confidence rather annoying, and turned sharply away from her.

"Justin."

He whirled around and stared at her incredulously. Surely he had not heard her aright!

"You have a charming name too. Do you mind if I use it?"

There was a distinct husky quality to her voice that made a quite pleasant sensation course through his body. "You cannot be Arabella Deverill," he said firmly. "Perhaps you are her twin sister, long kept in hiding."

She replied, quite unperturbed at the scowling set of his mouth, "No, it is I, Justin. I have no twin sister. Now, if you would come out of your sullens, I should like to speak to you of serious matters."

The earl's black brows snapped together. Why, the little chit—here she was suddenly wooing *him!*

"Not before I've had my dinner," he growled.

"To be sure, I cannot expect you to be reasonable without sustenance," she said kindly, and tugged at the bell cord.

"Ah, here you are, Crupper," the earl said upon the butler's entrance several moments later. At least he would take command of his own dinner!

"Yes, my lord, roast pork and fresh garden peas, just as Miss Arabella ordered."

"I do not particularly care for roast pork, Crupper. Have you other dishes as well?"

"Of course there are other dishes," Arabella interposed

graciously. "Cook always prepares roast pork for me on Thursdays," she added with a distinct twinkle in her eyes.

"Leave the damned pork, Crupper, and forget the other dishes. This will do admirably."

Lord, but the earl was in a twitchity mood, Crupper thought nervously. He waited until he had very nearly bowed himself out of the Velvet Room before giving his important message. "Begging your lordship's pardon, but a footman arrived from Talgarth Hall. Lady Ann and Miss Elsbeth will remain for dinner, not wishing to venture out in this weather, my lord."

"Thank you, Crupper," the earl said, a scowl still creasing his forehead. He was not so certain at this moment whether to be sorry or gladdened by their absence.

"Is the pork to your liking?" Arabella asked cordially after observing the earl's hearty appetite.

"It is passable," he replied grudgingly. He realized he had just heaped another portion onto his plate, and became uncomfortably aware that he was behaving in a churlish manner. He dropped his fork to his plate and sat back in his chair, his arms folded over his chest. He had inadvertently given her the upper hand, and she had rolled him up, foot and guns! He was obliged to laugh. He remembered thinking that she was admirable upon one occasion. He could not but admit to it again.

Arabella glanced up at his unexpected display of mirth and cocked her head to one side. She sensed he was trying to regain his mastery over the situation, cudgeled her brain for a suitable rejoinder, and said provocatively, "You know, Justin, the cleft in your chin is really quite attractive. I do not have it."

"Would you care to examine my attractive cleft more closely, Arabella?" he asked audaciously. "There is also a great deal more of me that I trust you will find equally attractive."

"I trust you will find the same true of me, Justin," she replied with a saucy smile.

"After seeing you in your drenched, very clinging gown, my dear, I cannot in all truth imagine being disappointed."

Although she did not overtly acknowledge his thrust, her expressive eyes widened appreciatively.

The earl grinned, then abruptly became serious. "Come, let

us sit by the fire and discuss your serious matters." He directed her to a small sofa and sat himself purposefully close to her.

"I will marry you," she announced baldly, looking at him squarely in the eyes.

"You render me the happiest man in the world, ma'am," he said promptly.

"Oh, hell and damnation, Justin! Would you be serious! You know very well why we must wed. I pray you not make more of a mockery of it than is necessary."

"I begin to think that our marriage will be no mockery, Arabella," he said slowly, his eyes resting hungrily upon the masses of thick raven hair. "I like your hair loose. It is so very silken and smooth." He wrapped a waving tress about his fingers, released it, and watched it spring into a soft curl.

"Justin, really, I . . . I . . ." She ground to a tangled halt, silenced by a peculiarly pleasant sort of feeling that seemed to afflict her tongue.

Tentatively she placed her hands upon his chest and with a hesitant gesture brought her fingertips to touch the deep cleft in his chin.

"That is a devilishly well-cut coat, Justin," she murmured quite unnecessarily, not lowering her eyes from his chin.

"You have excellent taste, Arabella."

"Weston?" She named her father's tailor.

"Yes, my dear."

Arabella felt in that moment that the wretched uncertainty that had engulfed her since her father's death was slowly blurring away from her thoughts. "Justin . . ." she whispered, and to his delight, slipped her arms trustingly about his neck.

The earl willingly enfolded her in his arms. He lightly rested his chin upon her hair and let his hands rove slowly up and down her slender back. He gave an insistent tug at her hair, and when she raised her face, cupped her chin in his hand. With a naturalness that she did not question, Arabella parted her lips. His tongue explored her mouth, and she felt a new, quite tantalizing need grow in her body. For the first time in her eighteen years she became aware of her womanhood, of her breasts pressed hard against his broad chest, of an insistent yet undefined ache deep within her. She was not at all embarrassed at the invasion of her mouth, and met the demands of his tongue with an eagerness that matched his own.

The earl drew a shaky breath and gently released her. "God, Arabella," he groaned close to her ear, "I have never before desired a woman as I do you." He grasped her hands and drew her out of the circle of his arms. "Do not tempt me further, my dear, else we will consummate our marriage before it occurs."

"But you tempt me too, Justin," she protested, her voice husky.

He moaned, and with great strength of will held her at arm's length. He could not trust himself to kiss her again. Her eyes clouded with disappointment and she gazed at him with bewildered longing.

"Could you not kiss me again, Justin?" she asked with ingenuous innocence. "I . . . I find it most pleasurable."

Justin gazed at her full lips, parted slightly and most invitingly, and felt his resolution fast fading.

"I too find it most pleasurable, my dear. But I cannot, I must not take advantage of your innocence."

"I suppose I am not much . . . experienced, but I am certainly not an innocent," she retorted, bridling at his male condescension to her maidenhood.

Justin smiled down at her with tender amusement, but had no time to answer, for the door flung open, and Lady Ann and Elsbeth entered, laughing, their cloaks glistening with raindrops.

"How vexatious the rain is! What a miserable night, to be sure. I hope that you two have enjoyed a good dinner!" Lady Ann ceased her monologue as she swiftly and with impeccable accuracy reconstructed the romantic scene that had just occurred. Arabella's colour was high and her hair tumbled about her face in a disheveled profusion of damp curls.

"Lady Ann, Miss Deverill," Justin managed to say with a modicum of calm. He knew with rueful certainty that he could not as yet rise and greet the ladies as was expected.

Lady Ann was enjoying the awkward situation quite as much as Arabella was cringing in embarrassment. She smiled with twinkling understanding at the earl and said to Elsbeth, who was gazing with blinking confusion at the strangely silent couple, "Come, my love, let us go to our rooms and change our gowns."

"Yes, ma'am," Elsbeth concurred with vague disappointment, and followed Lady Ann to the door.

"If it pleases you, my lord," Lady Ann said with a wicked grin over her shoulder, "Elsbeth and I will join you for tea. In about half an hour, Justin?"

"Just so, Ann," the earl replied wryly.

Upon their judiciously timed return to the Velvet Room, the earl placed a sparkling glass of champagne in their hands and announced grandly, "Do wish us well, Ann, Elsbeth. Arabella has done me the honour of accepting my hand in marriage."

"Oh! So that was why you were so very . . . that is, you seemed a bit—"

"Yes, yes, Elsbeth," Lady Ann interrupted her quickly, seeing Arabella cringe from the corner of her eye. "It is only proper for people to become . . . better acquainted when they become engaged. To your health and happiness, my dears!"

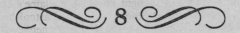

## 8

"Then it is settled. Arabella and I shall be wed Wednesday next." The earl grasped Arabella's cool fingers and gave them an affectionate squeeze.

"You see, Mother, he must needs threaten to break my fingers unless I agree." Arabella sighed mournfully, her eyes alight with mischief.

Lady Ann was not deceived by her daughter's banter. There was an air of complacency about her that made Lady Ann regard the earl with bemused admiration.

"I am so very happy for you, Arabella," Elsbeth said softly, a momentary twinge of undefined envy shadowing her thoughts.

The library doors opened, and Crupper, his back stiff with age and dignity, stepped into the room, cleared his throat, and announced, "My lord, Lady Ann, there is a young gentleman just arrived."

"How very early in the morning it is for visitors," Lady Ann exclaimed, somewhat vexed.

"Who is this young gentleman, Crupper?" the earl inquired.

"He informs me his name is Gervaise de Trécassis, my lord, cousin to Miss Elsbeth." Crupper's inherent distaste for

foreigners, particularly the French, was apparent in his man-
gling of the gentleman's name. "Calls himself the Comte de
Trécassis," he added with suspicious emphasis.

"Good grief! I had thought all of Magdalaine's family per-
ished in the revolution!" Lady Ann turned astonished eyes to
Elsbeth. "My dear, he must be your mama's nephew."

"By all means, Crupper, show the comte in," the earl said
calmly. He released Arabella's hand and rose slowly. Crupper
ushered into the room a strikingly handsome young man of
medium height and slender build, elegantly dressed in buff
pantaloons and gleaming black hessians. Arabella readily forgave his affectations of dandyism—a large jewel-encrusted
fob, several heavy rings, and shirt points that touched his
smooth chin—when she met his flashing black eyes, set
beneath delicately arched black brows and stylishly disar-
rayed black locks. How very dashing and romantic he looked,
she thought, regretting that she had not seen the devastatingly
handsome Lord Byron to draw a comparison.

"The Comte de Trécassis," Crupper announced. The young
gentleman, certainly not of many years more than Elsbeth,
surveyed the present company with a half-apologetic, yet
somehow supremely confident smile upon his well-formed
lips.

"Monsieur le comte, what an unexpected surprise!" Lady
Ann rose gracefully and extended her hand. Rather to her
surprise, the comte clasped her fingers and gallantly brushed
his lips over her palm, in the French style. "The pleasure is
indeed mine, my lady. I pray you will forgive my intrusion in
your period of mourning, but news of the earl's death just
reached me. I wished to express my condolences in person."
He spoke with a soft, lilting accent that made the three
females in the room most readily forgive any supposed
intrusion.

"You are the Earl of Strafford, my lord?" he inquired respectfully of Justin as he released Lady Ann's hand.

There was a brief moment of silent appraisal on the part
of both gentlemen before the earl remarked with negligent politeness, "Yes, I am Strafford. Lady Ann informs us that you
are nephew to the late earl's first wife."

The comte bowed in assent.

"Where indeed are my manners! My dear comte, do allow
me to present you to your cousin, Elsbeth, and my daughter,

Arabella." Lady Ann was not at all surprised that the charming young man was greeted even by her normally stand-offish daughter with genuine pleasure. Elsbeth drew back a moment, allowing Arabella to speak first.

"Although we are not related, Comte," Arabella assured him with a dimpled smile, "I am deuced glad to make your acquaintance."

The comte smiled at her engagingly and inquired with endearing simplicity, "I am not familiar with your 'deuced,' mademoiselle, but I trust that it carries a pleasant meaning." He turned to Elsbeth and murmured softly, "Ah, my dear little cousin, I count it my good fortune to at last meet the only remaining member of our esteemed family."

"I, too," Elsbeth said shyly. Instead of taking her hand, the comte gently placed his hands upon her shoulders and lightly kissed her on each cheek. Elsbeth flushed scarlet with embarrassed pleasure.

The comte stood back from Elsbeth, beamed at the assembled company, and said, embracing them all with outflung arms, "You are so very kind to me, a stranger. Though my little cousin is my only blood relation, I think already you are like my family," He paused with an expectant look of charming inquiry.

The earl, clearly seeing his duty from all three eager female faces, said a trifle too coolly, Arabella thought, "Monsieur, your solicitude at this time does you honour. We trust that you will remain at Evesham Abbey for a time, if, that is, you have no other pressing business matters."

"Oh, no, my lord," the comte hastened to disclaim. "Of course, my first duty is to my cousin. I accept your kind invitation, Monsieur le Earl."

Arabella went into a peal of laughter. "Dear Comte, you must not call him 'le Earl,' but rather Justin."

"In that case, you must call me Gervaise. Unfortunately, my title is only that—a title. You see before you a simple émigré, torn from his home by that Corsican upstart!"

"Oh, how very awful for you, sir!" Elsbeth cried with unwonted emotion.

"You are too kind, *ma petite cousine*."

The earl's eyebrow shot up at the caressing tone in the young man's voice. He thought he read an almost imperceptible calculating gleam in those flashing black eyes as they rested on Elsbeth, and thought cynically about Elsbeth's ten thousand pounds. The comte was certainly dressed smack up to the nines, and the earl wondered uncharitably if Evesham Abbey would be descended upon by irate tailors.

"My dear boy . . . Gervaise," Lady Ann said gaily, "it is nearly time for luncheon. Let me ring for a footman to take up your luggage. We can spend the afternoon getting better acquainted."

The comte bestowed upon her a boyish grin, calculated, Justin thought dryly, to appeal to Lady Ann's maternal instincts. "I am your slave, my lady!"

By evening's end, the earl concluded with a certain sour admiration that the young comte was no one's slave. Indeed, it seemed that all the women had quite fallen under his compelling charm. Even his Arabella appeared to accept the comte's presence with unquestioned acceptance that left the earl scowling into the darkness of his bedchamber.

During the next several days, the earl was left to wonder if he was not betrothed to a whirlwind. If Arabella was not in long fittings with the seamstress and Lady Ann for her bridal clothes, she was riding with the comte, fishing with the comte, exploring the countryside with the comte, all in all treating her affianced husband with an insouciance that bordered on the cavalier. The earl did not even at his most disagreeable fault her with being a flirt; it was just that her natural exuberance and vitality seemed to blossom in the comte's presence. That Elsbeth accompanied Arabella and the comte on all their jaunts did little to soothe the earl's sense of injustice. He fell back upon an outward appearance of cool detachment, on occasion treating all three young people with an avuncular kind of indifferent tolerance that made Lady Ann arch her fine brows at him, and Arabella grind her teeth.

The earl found his only ally to be Dr. Branyon. It was the doctor who said in a very measured voice one evening as Lady Ann and the three younger members of the group were playing lottery tickets, "Undoubtedly the young comte is innocuous enough, though I do find his sense of *timing* to be almost suspiciously flawless, shall we say. I ask myself why he did not make himself known years ago. After all, the late earl was his uncle by marriage."

The earl said slowly, watching the young man adroitly lose

a fish to Lady Ann, "Perhaps the comte's . . . prior activities bear closer examination."

The comte threw up his hands in mock despair at that moment and exclaimed, "I am all done up! *Violà, j'ai perdu touts mes poissons!*"

"You were too careless, Gervaise," Arabella chided, laughing. "And I suspicion that you lost your fish on purpose to mother!"

"I presume we shall be invited to join tea, doctor," the earl remarked dryly, and rose to join the high-spirited group.

The earl was pleasantly surprised the next morning to find himself sharing breakfast with only Arabella. "Good morning, my lord," she greeted him with a happy smile.

"You are up and about early this morning, Bella."

"Uh-huh," she said only by way of reply. She grabbed a slice of hot toast, downed a quick gulp of coffee, and without even sitting down at the table, prepared to hurry out of the room.

"Arabella!"

There were toast crumbs on her chin that made her look utterly adorable, but the earl said gruffly, "At least take the time to wipe your mouth. You would not want the comte to think you a messy eater."

Arabella touched her fingers to her chin, whisked away the offending crumbs, and said gaily, "I really must hurry, Justin. We do not wish to be back too late this afternoon."

"And just where are you going today, my girl?" he inquired in a peevish voice.

Arabella drew up and smiled at him with amused affection. "Why, I am taking Gervaise, and Elsbeth of course, to see the Roman ruins at Bury St. Edmunds."

"And why was I not invited?" he asked, immediately wishing he had not.

"But, Justin, you have already visited the ruins. Do you not remember? You told me that when you were kicking up your heels before coming to Evesham Abbey you toured the countryside."

"Arabella, we are to be wed in two days' time," he said, knowing himself to be not at all to the point.

Gentle colour touched her cheeks and she said shyly, "It is most certainly a date that I would not forget." She added quickly, "Would you care to join us, Justin? It is just that I would not wish you to be bored."

The earl rose from his chair, walked to his betrothed, and lightly placed his hands upon her shoulders. "My little Bella, it is just that I have not had you at all to myself these past days." His fingers gently caressed her. He felt a quickening response in her and pulled her roughly against his chest.

She sighed and nestled her face against his shoulder, her arms moving around his back. "I thought you did not wish to be . . . tempted," she murmured, her voice muffled in his waistcoat.

He laughed shakily and pulled her back. "You are a vixen, madam," he said huskily.

She rose on her tiptoes and kissed the cleft in his chin. "There is so very much of you to kiss, Justin, I vow it will take me years."

He groaned and kissed her fiercely, savouring the soft, sweet taste of her mouth. Arabella pressed herself against the length of his body, and felt such aching pleasure that she quite forgot the Roman ruins.

"Be off with you," the earl said thickly, mentally calculating that less than forty-eight hours remained before his dishonourable intentions would magically be proclaimed honourable.

She hugged him again, then whisked herself out of the breakfast parlour.

The earl returned to his breakfast and roundly chided himself for entertaining any jealous suspicions of Arabella. He tried to concentrate on his rare sirloin instead of the exquisite pleasure he knew awaited him on their wedding night.

He planned a regimen designed to keep body and mind thoroughly occupied for the remainder of the day. He met with Blackwater in the morning, shared luncheon with Lady Ann and Dr. Branyon, who, the earl observed, was now almost a daily visitor to Evesham Abbey, and made the rounds of several of his tenants throughout the afternoon. It was late in the day when he returned and stabled his horse. Since there was still sufficient daylight, he decided to make a brief inspection of the farmyard. The cows had not yet been brought back for their evening milking, and only a few desultory chickens pecked lazily about their graveled pen. He neared the large two-story barn, and stopped for a moment to inhale the sweet smell of hay. To his surprise and delight, he saw Arabella come around the side of the barn, slowly pull open the front doors, and disappear inside.

He stood struggling with himself for several minutes, his body very much demanding to follow her, and his mind quickly reviewing all the pitfalls of such an action. "Oh, the devil!" he said aloud, throwing his mind's logical arguments to the winds. As he stepped forward, he chanced to see movement from the corner of his eyes. He turned and saw the Comte de Trécassis striding purposefully toward the barn, his natty cloak billowing out behind him.

A deep foreboding, something he could not explain, swept over him. The earl did not move forward to greet the comte; instead, he remained firmly planted where he was, his eyes fixed on the elegant, slender young man.

The comte paused a moment before the barn door, glanced quickly around him, tugged at the handle, and as Arabella had done, disappeared into the dim interior.

In a swift military motion the earl clapped his hand to his side where his deadly sword had hung for so many years. His hand balled into a fist at finding nothing more deadly than his pocket. He drew a deep breath, stilled his violent compulsion, and remained standing stiffly, his eyes never leaving the barn door. He felt a black, numbing misery. He felt he was losing a part of himself, a precious part, one not yet fully understood or explored.

Time passed, but he had no sense of it. From the meadow just beyond the farmyard came the insistent mooing of cows. The sun was fast fading, bathing the barn in gentle golden rays of dusk. The day was coming to a close much the same as any other day, yet he felt no part of it.

Even as his eyes probed the barn door, it opened and the comte quickly emerged. Again he gazed about him with the air of one who does not wish to be discovered. In a gesture that left the earl trembling with sudden black rage, the comte swiftly adjusted the buttons of his breeches, brushed lingering straws from his legs and cloak, and strode with a swaggering gait back to Evesham Abbey.

Still the earl did not move, his eyes fastened to the closed barn door. He had not long to wait, for just as the last light of day flickered into darkness, the door opened, and Arabella, her hair disheveled and tumbling about her shoulders, ventured out, stood for a moment executing a languorous stretch, then turned toward the abbey, humming softly to herself. Every few steps she leaned over and picked bits of straw from her gown. He saw her wave gaily to the farmboys who were busily herding the cows toward the barn for their evening milking.

A gruesome kaleidoscope of images whirled through the earl's mind. He saw clearly the first man he had killed in battle—a young French soldier, a bullet from the earl's gun spreading deadly red fingers across his bright coat. He saw the leathery, grimacing face of an old sergeant, run through with his sword, the astonishment of imminent death written in his eyes. He wanted to retch now, as he had then.

The earl had no romantic illusions about killing; he had learned that life is too precious, too fragile a thing to be dispatched in the heat of passion.

He turned and walked back to his new home. The proud set of his shoulders and his precise military gait were belied only by the staring emptiness of his gray eyes.

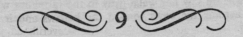

## 9

"It is a joyous and sacred ceremony that brings us together today. In the presence of our Lord, we come to join two of his children, his lordship the seventh Earl of Strafford and Arabella Elaine Deverill, daughter of the late esteemed Earl of Strafford, in the holiest of earthly bonds."

Arabella gazed up at the earl's finely chiseled profile. She silently willed him to look at her, but he did not, his gray eyes remaining fastened intently upon the curate's face. He had seemed rather withdrawn, even standoffish with her the previous evening, and now she suppressed a giggle, deciding that he was having a final attack of bachelor's nervousness.

"If there is any man present who can state objection to the joining of this man and woman, let him rise now and speak."

Lady Ann felt a brief catch in her throat and swallowed quickly. She had always abhorred emotional mothers loudly sniffing at their daughters' wedding after they had plied their matchmaking talents so assiduously to bring it all about. Perhaps it was the calm radiance of Arabella's lovely face that brought tears to her eyes. The yards of white satin and lace became her so well, enhancing her dark hair and brows as the dismal black gowns of mourning had dampened them.

And Justin, standing so straight and proud, as if he were preparing to go into battle. He had been unswerving in his pursuit of Arabella. She wondered if Justin had any regrets now that the portentous day had come.

"In the presence of God, and by his laws and commandments, I now ask you, Justin Morley Deverill, do you take this woman, Arabella Elaine Deverill, to be your lawfully wedded wife . . ."

Elsbeth strained to hear the earl repeat his vows, his voice deep, yet somehow strangely quiet. She saw Arabella gaze up at him while he spoke, a bemused smile on her lips.

It was in a loud, clear voice that Arabella spoke her vows after the prompting of the curate. "I, Arabella Elaine, take you, Justin Morley Deverill, to be my lawfully wedded husband, to love, honour and obey . . ."

Obey—Lady Ann's mind clutched at the simple word. That is quite a concession from my headstrong independent daughter, she thought. She heard herself repeating the same vow to another Earl of Strafford, as if it were only a moment of time ago, her voice unsteady and barely audible in the large cathedral. Obey. He had hurled the word at her on their wedding night, when she had cringed away from his feverishly mauling hands. She had obeyed, had submitted, her fear and pain heightened by his harsh demands. She had always submitted, knowing she had no other choice, and when he did not curse her for lying passively beneath him, he avenged himself on her body in other ways, cruelly demeaning ways that made her nights a conscious nightmare. Lady Ann brought her mind back into focus to see Justin, after a peculiar brief hesitation, slip a gold band upon Arabella's third finger.

"By the authority vested in me by the Church of England, I now pronounce you man and wife." The curate beamed his protruding teeth at the couple and whispered to the earl, "You may now kiss your bride, my lord."

The earl felt his jaw tighten, and it was with a stiff, unnatural movement that he forced himself to lean down and brush his lips against Arabella's proffered lips. The radiant glow on her face sickened him. He turned quickly away and gazed with hopeless intensity at the golden cross behind the curate's left shoulder.

Lady Ann found herself praying silently that Justin would

be gentle with Arabella. But that wish brought a wry smile to her lips. Only that afternoon, as she had bustled about Arabella, enumerating her new articles of clothing, scolding her for her inattention as her maid toweled her damp hair, she had thought it time to do her duty as a mother. Nervously she had dismissed the maid and faced her daughter. "My love," she began slowly, "tonight you will be a married lady. I think you ought to know that there will be certain . . . changes. That is, Justin will be your *husband*, and—"

Arabella interrupted her with a shout of delighted laughter. "My dear mama," she gurgled, lightly tapping her mother's arm, "are you by any chance referring to the imminent loss of my virginity?"

"Arabella!"

"Now, Mama, I am sorry to have shocked you! But you must know that Father most superbly detailed the entire *process*! I am not afraid, Mama, indeed, I can think of nothing more pleasurable than making love with Justin."

"Oh . . ." Lady Ann managed in a fading voice.

"I hope you do not think me a fallen woman, but I do think it utterly ridiculous that ladies should not enjoy lovemaking! And when I think that many girls are taught to regard it as a most disagreeable duty . . . well, it quite puts me out of patience!"

"Are you certain, my love, that there is nothing I can tell you?" Lady Ann asked, now rueful.

"No, dear ma'am. But I do love you dearly for your concern." Again, as Arabella scooped her mother into her arms and gave her a fond, reassuring hug, Lady Ann had the dampening yet inescapable feeling that she should have been the daughter.

As Lady Ann tried with valiant calm to array Arabella in her nightgown, she was sensitive to her daughter's suppressed excitement, her sparkling gray eyes devoid of shyness or fear. She stepped back finally and placed the hairbrush on the dresser.

"Justin will be delighted, my love," she said gently. Indeed, Arabella presented a most lovely picture, her black hair brushed and flowing loosely down her back. Though her white maidenly gown covered her from her throat to her toes,

Lady Ann could not but believe that her daughter would not at all have minded dispensing with the traditional garment.

She forced a complacent smile on her lips and kissed her daughter on the cheek. "I shall fetch Justin now, my dear. Oh, Arabella," she cried suddenly, flinging herself into her daughter's arms. "I do hope that you will be happy!"

"In matters regarding me, Mama, Father never erred in his judgment."

Arabella spoke softly, and Lady Ann looked up quickly. Perhaps it was her imagination, but she thought she detected a briefly sad awareness in her daughter's voice. She gave her head a tiny shake and turned abruptly away. "I hope you are right, Arabella. Good night, my love."

After her mother had left her, Arabella paced the bedroom with the eagerness of pleasurable anticipation. She delighted in discoveries, and tonight . . . well, tonight . . . She hugged herself with excited impatience. She chanced to look at *The Dance of Death* panel, stuck out her tongue at it in amused dismissal, and let her eyes rove to the large bed. She was beginning to wonder, an impish smile on her mouth, if Lady Ann was endeavoring to give instruction to Justin, when the door opened suddenly and her husband appeared. How magnificent he looked in the dark blue brocade dressing gown! Her pulse quickened at the sight of him.

The earl closed the door, fastened his fingers over the key, and clicked it into place.

"I am glad you did not leave me awaiting too long, my husband," Arabella said mischievously, and proffered him a mock curtsy.

He stood by the door, unmoving, his eyes taking in her appearance. "How very . . . virginal you look, Arabella."

"Indeed, I trust so," she returned with a smile, too filled with the excitement of the moment to hear anything amiss.

Still the earl did not move toward her, and Arabella, with a light, dancing step, skipped to him, her bare feet soundless on the thick carpet. Trustingly she laid her hands on his shoulders, rose to her tiptoes, and offered him her lips.

His hands moved to her arms, and suddenly, with wrenching force, he shoved her away from him. She staggered back, clutched the back of a chair, and stared at him, mouth agape, stunned with confusion. "Justin, I . . . I do not understand—" she began, her voice bewildered.

"Take off your nightgown," he said savagely.

"Justin, if you have been drinking, I would just as soon that we did not . . ." She stopped and drew back as he advanced toward her. She saw the taut, angry cords standing out in his neck.

"Do as I tell you, you little slut, else I shall rip it off you!"

His words cut through her. "Dear God, Justin, what is the matter with you? Why do you speak to me like that? How dare you call me a slut!" Her moment of sudden, indignant anger turned to numbing fear as she read savage fury in his flaring nostrils, saw implacable menacing resolve in his gray eyes. He stalked her, cornering her momentarily behind a large wing chair near the fireplace. "Dear God, Justin, will you stop this!" she panted, fear clogging her throat.

His arm shot out to grab her, and with a rasping cry she whirled about and raced to the door. With sweaty palms she clutched frantically at the knob, but it did not open. She felt him standing behind her, watching her futile efforts. Suddenly he grabbed a thick mass of her hair and wound it about his hand, pulling inexorably, until she cried out in pain and stumbled back against his chest. He jerked her about with his other hand to face him.

"Now, madam, you will do as I tell you," he hissed.

Instinctively she realized that she could not reason with him, that he would not respond to her. She gritted her teeth against the stabbing pain in her scalp and brought her knee up and forward with all her strength. She connected with muscular thigh, as he quickly turned to avert her blow.

His eyes blazed with such fury that she thought he would strike her, and her body tensed, awaiting the blow. Instead, he drew a deep breath and jerked savagely at her hair, bringing her face to within inches of his own. He met her eyes with a gleam of derisive amusement and sneered, "A trick I presume your esteemed father taught you. It would have been the worse for you had you succeeded, you know."

"Justin . . ." she whispered, her mind emptied of other words.

In a swift, violent motion he released her hair, dug his fingers into the ruffled lace about her throat, and pulled with a force that doubled her forward. The sharp rending of satin filled the silence of the room, and Arabella looked down stupidly at her gown, torn from her throat to her ankles. Before she could react, he ripped the gown from her shoulders, tearing apart the small buttons from her wrists. She saw the satin-covered buttons bounce and roll about the carpet near the remnants of her nightgown. She felt his eyes sweep over her naked body and was shocked into action at the awareness of her vulnerability. With explosive fury she balled her hand into a fist and with all her might struck at his face.

He blocked her arm before it reached his jaw. He snarled, "You wish to fight me, do you, madam!" He grasped her about the waist and flung her over his shoulder.

Arabella pounded impotently at his back, her blows falling on hard muscle. He hurled her away from him, and she fell sprawled on her back atop the bed, the breath momentarily crushed out of her. Even as she gasped painfully, she thought only to escape him, clutching at the covers to scramble to the far side of the bed. She cried out as his hand grasped her ankle and gave it a wrench, flipping her again upon her back.

"Lie still!" he commanded. "That is much better. Now, I think it only fair that I examine my purchase."

Dear God, he was mad, quite mad! She screamed at him, "God damn you to hell! Stop your madness and let me go! Let me go, do you hear?"

His lips curled disdainfully, and he flicked his eyes over her with taunting precision. "You have the language of a tavern wench, madam. I should have known then that it denoted a deeper streak of vileness in you."

Appalled, she again tried to jerk away from him. "Move again and I shall tie you down," he said coldly. "I have paid dearly for your favors, my *dear* Countess of Strafford."

"Why are you doing this, Justin? Please, listen to me! What have I done to you?" Arabella hated the pleading in her voice, but she could not help herself.

Disregarding, he seemed to study her body with calm detachment. "How very lovely you are, indeed. All that raven hair spilling wildly about your shoulders. Did I not tell you that I desired you above all other women?"

His eyes were upon her breasts, and she tried vainly to stop their heaving upward-and-downward movement. Dear God, this could not be happening to her! She closed her eyes so tightly that burning lights exploded against her lids.

His hand touched her breast. "Oh, God, no." She whimpered the words.

"You are perfectly right, madam. I would not wish to stir your wanton passions."

Abruptly he stood back from the bed and with deliberate movements untied his dressing gown and shrugged it from his broad shoulders. He stood naked before her, carefully watching her face, a marked sneer playing about his mouth.

Arabella could not prevent her eyes from traveling the length of his lean, muscular body. She had never before seen a naked man, and her eyes widened with shock and fear at his huge, swollen manhood. Instinctively she pressed her thighs together and brought her hands over her body to cover herself.

"God, what an actress you would have made," he mocked. "Well, my dear *virgin* bride, I trust my proportions do not disappoint you."

She could only stare at him and mutely shake her head back and forth. He leaned over her, wrenched her legs apart, and straddled her. She began a silent struggle, scratching at his face, kicking up at his groin with her knees. Efficiently he pinioned her hands over her belly and held down her legs under his own. She felt his hand move purposefully between her thighs, and froze with numbed shock. She recoiled from his foreignness, from his brutal, probing fingers. Even as she struggled, trying to break his hold on her hands, she felt his fingers part her. Mindlessly she thrashed from side to side, whirling masses of tangled hair into her eyes, blinding her. She gasped aloud as he forced his swollen manhood into her.

He paused an instant, grasped her hands, and jerked them over her head. With an almost tender motion he pulled the strands of hair from her eyes.

"God, I cannot believe that you have done this to me!" he cried, and drove with all his might into her. Even as the dry, ripping pain brought a cry to her lips, she felt him pause within her, momentarily arrested by her taut maidenhead. There was a brief flicker of surprise in his eyes.

"Justin!" she cried piteously.

He growled deep in his throat, released her, and digging his fingers into her hips, jerked her upward. He drove ferociously into her, tearing through the thin barrier and beyond.

She let out a rending animal cry, and knew a pain that seared deep in her loins and plummeted her mind into burning, senseless agony. Still he drove deeper and deeper inside her, thrusting with savage force, until with a moan of release his seed burst from him, flooding her.

Arabella was drained of fight, of courage. The pain was like the numbing sharp thrust of jabbing needles, and when he pulled himself back through the torn small passage, she could not help herself, and cried out again.

The earl drew up over her, panting, his fury exhausted. He met her eyes, enormous pools of shocked pain, and for an instant, doubted. It was the memory of the comte's swaggering gait, as meaningful as a man's crow of victory, and of her own disheveled, tumbled appearance, that hardened his soul against her. He rolled away without a word to her and rose. He could not prevent his eyes from gazing at her body, and drew back at the sight of her blood and his seed slowly flowing to her thighs and onto the bedcover. He felt sickened and disgusted at what he had done to her.

He grabbed a towel from the washbasin and threw it at her. "Here, clean yourself."

Arabella did not move, her legs still sprawled apart as he had left her. Her eyes were still fixed with glazed shock upon his face.

He said to her with empty bitterness, "It seems that I was wrong about your virginity. How very noble of your lover to leave you intact for your wedding night, to grant me the honour of deflowering you." His gray eyes narrowed with bleak appraisal. "But, of course, there are certainly other ways, are there not, madam? Did he sodomize you? Or perhaps you pleasured him with your lovely sensuous mouth?" Still she gazed at him mutely, and he flung at her with harsh, cold finality, "Now that your *husband* has claimed your maidenhead, you can take your lover in more conventional ways. My thanks, *dear* Arabella, for this mockery of a marriage."

She felt his deadly fury, winced at his damning words. Yet, they were meaningless sounds to her.

Her silence was a confession of guilt to him. Infuriated, he grabbed up his dressing gown, flung it on, and rapped out, "That you could be such a wanton trollop sickens me. You have made me pay dearly for my inheritance, an inheritance that you wanted for yourself! I only ask, dear wife, that in future you conduct your affairs with more discretion!"

He turned on his heel, and without looking back, strode

into the small adjoining dressing room and slammed the door behind him.

The gilt-edged ormolu clock on the mantelpiece ticked away its minutes with time-honoured accuracy. The orang-ish-yellow embers in the fireplace crackled and hissed in their final death glow, finally succumbing to the invading chill of the room. The hideous grinning skeleton, mouth agape, eternally suspended on *The Dance of Death* panel, taunted the motionless figure on the bed with scornful silence.

Lady Ann broke her habit and took Mrs. Tucker quite by surprise by appearing at the inordinately early-morning hour of eight o'clock at the breakfast-parlour door. It was really rather a foolish thing to do, for in all likelihood the newly wedded couple would not emerge for hours. Yet, Lady Ann had awakened with a vague sense that something was not quite right, and in spite of the comforting warmth that tempted her to snuggle down in her bed, she swung her feet to the floor, rang for her maid, and dressed with more speed than was her usual habit.

"My lady!" Mrs. Tucker exclaimed, her dimpled chins rolling agitatedly above her white starched collar.

"Good morning, Mrs. Tucker," Lady Ann replied with an air of charming ruefulness. "I suppose that I am the only one to demand breakfast at such an untimely hour."

"Oh, no, my lady. His lordship has been in the breakfast parlour for a good half-hour, though I can't say that he's quite done justice to Cook's kidneys and eggs!"

Lady Ann experienced a sudden sinking in the pit of her stomach. "If that is the case, Mrs. Tucker," she said with outward calm, "Cook will not have to prepare additional kidneys and eggs for me."

The door to the breakfast parlour was slight ajar, and as Lady Ann stepped into the room, she was able to observe the earl before he was aware of her presence. His plate was un-touched. He lounged sideways in his chair, one leather-breeched leg thrown negligently over the brocade arm. His firm chin rested lightly upon his hand, and he appeared to be gazing out onto the south lawn at nothing in particular.

Lady Ann straightened her shoulders and walked com-posedly into the parlour. "Good morning, Justin. Mrs. Tucker tells me you are sadly neglecting Cook's delicious breakfast."

He turned quickly to face her, and she saw tense, haggard lines about his expressive eyes and mouth. The lines smoothed out in a trice, replaced by his normally calm impassivity.

"Good morning, Ann. You are certainly up and about early! Do join me, else I will be in Cook's black books."

Lady Ann eased herself into a chair beside him. She wanted desperately to question him, but she found herself at a loss as to how to proceed. His face grew rather forbidding, as if he guessed her thoughts. She began to methodically butter a slice of warm toast, and without raising her eyes again to his face, she said airily, "How odd it seems that you are now my son-in-law. Dr. Branyon most unobligingly pointed out that I can no longer escape my new appellation of Dowager Countess of Strafford! How very ancient it makes me feel!"

"How absurd, to be sure. Are you planning to marry Paul Branyon, Ann?"

"Justin, what a question!" she exclaimed, totally taken off her guard. Her hand was shaking so that her toast slipped from her fingers and fell atop her marmalade.

"An impertinent one that perhaps you do not wish to answer. Do forgive me, Ann. Questions such as that tend to place the person being asked in a rather difficult position, do you not agree?"

"Just so, Justin," she replied after a brief pause. What an elegant set-down he had given her!

"If you will excuse me, Ann, I have many matters to attend to this morning." The earl rose rather stiffly from his chair and strode in his firm manner from the breakfast parlour.

"Yes, of course, Justin," she murmured to his retreating back. She gazed morosely down at the array of dishes. Dear God, whatever could have happened? Arabella had been so very happy and excited the night before—not at all the terrified young bride! Arabella. She must go to her. Her concern made her small feet fly up the stairs to the earl's bedchamber.

The door stood partially ajar, and she tapped on it perfunctorily as she entered.

"Oh," she said in surprise at the sight of Grace, Arabella's maid, standing alone in the room, the tattered remnants of a nightgown held in her hands.

Grace quickly dropped a curtsy, her doe brown eyes darting quickly away from Lady Ann's face.

"Where is Miss Arabella?" She could not help walking forward to affirm that it was Arabella's once-beautiful nightgown that the maid held.

Grace gulped uncomfortably. Miss Arabella, or rather her ladyship, since she had wedded the earl, had given her strict orders to straighten the room before anyone was about. "Her ladyship is in her room, my lady."

"I see," Lady Ann said, her eyes taking in the dried bloodstains on top of the bedcover, the red-tinged water-and-blood-flecked towel on the washbasin. She felt sick with apprehension. "Thank you, Grace," she said, turning hurriedly. "Do finish with your work."

Lady Ann found that her stride became slower and slower as she neared her daughter's bedroom. She could not help remembering her own terrifying wedding night. But it simply could not have been like that! Justin was so very different from her late husband. Her hands were clammy as she knocked lightly on Arabella's door. It seemed an eternity of moments before she heard Arabella call out, "Enter."

Lady Ann was not certain how she expected Arabella to appear, but when she entered, she gazed stupefied at her very normal daughter of yesterday. Arabella calmly rose to greet her, dressed in her black riding habit, her velvet hat set high above smoothly arranged curls, the black ostrich feather curving over the brim, nearly brushing her cheek.

"Good morning, Mother. Whatever has you up and about so very early?"

Underlying the calm voice was an arrogant, almost challenging note that rendered Lady Ann acutely uncomfortable. Had she not seen Justin, not visited the earl's bedchamber, she would have felt the complete fool.

"You ride as usual?" she asked quietly.

"Of course, Mother. Is there any reason why I should not?"

Lady Ann found that she could not rise to the challenge. If Arabella did not wish to confide in her, she could not press the matter. She thought forlornly that Arabella had never taken her into her confidence. Only her father had shared her thoughts, her fancies. "No, my dear, if you wish to ride, it is certainly your affair. I simply could not sleep and thought to bid you good morning. That is all."

An arched black brow shot up in suspicious inquiry. "I fear you will grow overtired if you do not get your rest, Mother. Now, if you will excuse me, no doubt Lucifer is saddled and waiting for me." Arabella drew on her gloves, tipped her hat to a more jaunty angle, and walked to where her mother stood. She kissed her lightly on the cheek, her expression softening almost imperceptibly, and walked quickly out of the room.

Lady Ann stood staring after her daughter, a worried frown spreading over her forehead.

As Arabella guided Lucifer past the old abbey ruins to the country lane that led to Bury St. Edmunds, her gaze was clear and straight, her gloved hands steady on Lucifer's reins.

Poor Mother, she thought, now chiding herself. I treated her despicably. She has not the knack of hiding her feelings. However did she guess that something was wrong?

She flicked Lucifer on the neck, urging him into a gallop. If only she could leave behind her all the ugliness, the pain, the hatred of the night before. But even as the wish flashed through her mind, she saw her father's face—stern and contemptuous. It was weakness, cowardice, to deny any experience that touched one's life. Her shoulders straightened from long habit, and her firm chin thrust forward aggressively. Touch her life! God, Justin had ripped through her life, doing his utmost to destroy her! The nagging soreness between her thighs was bitter proof that he had violated her body. She would not let him ravage her mind and spirit as well.

She tried to reconstruct his words, to give them meaning, not to excuse him for what he had done to her, but to allow her to understand. Absurdly, he believed that the comte was her lover. Though he had not called him by name, she thought with bitter amusement that the only other choices were Dr. Branyon and dear old Crupper! Even in the light of day, Arabella could not fathom how Justin had drawn such a damning conclusion. Someone must have lied to him, convinced him that she had betrayed him. But who? She frowned between Lucifer's ears. It was obvious that he had believed the lie. Then why had he gone through with their marriage? *How very stupid you are, Arabella; he told you why himself.*

*Had he not wedded you, he would have lost the greater portion of the estate.*

Lucifer's breathing was becoming laboured, his silky mane showing flecks of white lather. Absently she looked about her and realized with a start that she had ridden past the Roman ruins without even noticing. She drew up and patted her horse's neck. She suddenly remembered a phrase she had overheard her father say to one of his friends: "I rode the wench until she would have thrown me off, if she could!" She thought ironically that at least the meaning of his crude remark was now clear to her.

Almost unwillingly she turned Lucifer about and headed at a slow trot back to Evesham Abbey. She must have ridden for hours, for the sun was reaching its zenith in the sky.

She could feel her bitter calm begin to crumble the nearer she drew to *his* home. Justin would be there, waiting. She would have to face him, not just today, but tomorrow, a lifetime of tomorrows. For a fleeting moment she considered confronting him, to plead her innocence, to demand to know who had told him such a damning lie. She pictured such a scene in her mind and saw herself as a rejected supplicant. Instinctively, after his rage of last night, she knew that he would still disbelieve her. She pictured renewed fury and savage reprisal. In that instant she hated her womanhood, hated his superior strength and the knowledge that he could dominate her through sheer physical power.

Arabella shivered despite the hot sun that beat down upon her black riding habit. Surely he would not force her to submit to him again. His revenge upon her had been thorough and merciless.

She guided Lucifer into the stableyard, pulled up before her sweating groom, and slid to the ground. She hated the feeling of wariness, of dread that washed over her as she neared the front doors of Evesham Abbey. God, if she did not have her pride, she would have nothing. He must not know how he had hurt her, disillusioned her. She thought again of his words of the night before, spat at her in his fury. She had played his words over and over in her mind, yet there was one word he had spewed at her that she did not understand. Strangely, it seemed vitally important to her that she know the meaning of that word.

She glanced up at the sun, guessed that it neared luncheon,

then let herself quietly into a side entrance. She thought only to avoid seeing Justin before it was absolutely necessary. Softly she trod through her home to the library, slipped through the door, and shut it quietly behind her. Arabella was not a profound scholar, certainly not much addicted to the use of the dictionary. Thus she spent several minutes perusing the book-lined shelves to locate it. She had always assumed that any words her father did not use were not worth knowing about. She was beginning to think that in this instance she was wrong. She pulled the leather-bound tome from the shelf, wet her fingertips on her tongue, and began to rifle through the stiff pages.

Her fingers ran down the columns until she found the word she sought. "Sodomy," she read, "Middle English and Old French 'sodomie'; as in the biblical reference, Sodom and . . ."

Arabella suddenly felt movement behind her and whirled about, nearly dropping the dictionary. She gazed up in consternation at the earl, who stood with negligent ease, his hand resting flat on the desktop. Her mouth went suddenly quite dry. She felt guiltily conspicuous, as if she had been caught in wrongdoing.

"Well, my dear wife, what word could be of such interest to bring you to the dictionary?"

She recoiled at his cold, insolent tone. Her eyes fell upon the word, so very damning by itself, and with a jerky, uncoordinated movement she tried to slam the dictionary closed. He moved with graceful speed and wrested it from her arms. "Surely we could have no secrets?" he mocked. "Come, Arabella, if you wish to know the meaning of a word, you have but to ask me."

She drew up and strove with all her might for a proud, calm countenance. "It is of no importance, I assure you. Now, if you will excuse me, sir . . ."

"Ah, but I do not wish to excuse you, Countess. Stay, I wish to find your word." His eyes stopped in the middle of the page. "How very interesting to be sure—'sodomy.'" His black brow shot up, comprehension spreading over his face. Slowly he closed the dictionary and placed it on the desk. He turned to face her, and despite her resolve, Arabella took a quick step backward. His eyes roved over her, stripping her naked, condemning her. "Poor Arabella, did not your lover give you a term to describe your ... activities? How very remiss of him."

"Get out of my way, sir!" she flared, suddenly rushing forward. "I will not stay and be so crudely insulted!"

He grabbed her arm and wrenched it behind her back. "You will listen to whatever I have to say to you, dear Countess. There, that is much better. Now, my dear, 'sodomy' is defined as any unnatural act of sexual intercourse. Does that definition provide you suitable meaning?"

"Stop it!" she screamed at him. "You are vile and despicable! How could you believe such of me? Dear God, Justin, who told you such a filthy lie?"

His gray eyes narrowed to slits and his jaw worked spasmodically. Suddenly he released her arm and swung away from her. He had sworn that he would not again allow his bitter anger and disillusionment to get the better of him. But she so enraged him with her sham anger and righteous indignation! He managed to say levelly, without turning to face her, "No one told lies of you, Arabella. You have only yourself to blame for my knowing the truth."

"In God's name, Justin, what are you talking about?"

He turned back to her, his voice a curious blend of sarcasm and bitterness. "In the event you do not understand what an unnatural act of sexual intercourse involves, dear Countess, you have but to think of your lovely rounded hips. Ah, yes, now I see enlightenment shine in your eyes. Did you enjoy it, Arabella?"

"You make me sick, you filthy whore's son!" She raced from the library. She heard him call after her in a taunting voice, "You begin to repeat your vile oaths, wife. Strive, I beg you, for more original and accurate epithets."

"Another macaroon, I think, my dear." Dr. Branyon smiled at Lady Ann as he slipped another cookie onto his plate.

"Elsbeth, more tea?"

"No, thank you, Lady Ann," Elsbeth replied, turning her wandering attention to her stepmother.

"I suppose it is not so very odd that the earl and Arabella do not join us." The comte spread his hands expressively, a knowing gleam flashing in his dark eyes.

As such a remark was not to Lady Ann's liking, indeed

quite inappropriate for Elsbeth's innocent ears, she did not deign to favor him with a reply. She turned to Dr. Branyon. "Paul, I trust you will join us for dinner this evening. It is Thursday, you know, and Cook will prepare Arabella's roast pork."

"Delighted, my dear." Dr. Branyon glanced at the clock on the mantelpiece and hurriedly rose. "If I am not to miss Arabella's pork, I must go now and see to my patients. Six o'clock?"

Lady Ann nodded and walked from the parlour to the front door with him. He turned before he descended the front steps and took her hand. "Ann, something bothers you. Come, my dear," he continued, misjudging her silence, "you know that you must become used to the fact that Arabella is a married lady."

"Oh, Paul," she said miserably, "I assure you it is not that. Something is amiss between them, I am certain of it. I feel so wretchedly helpless."

Dr. Branyon frowned into her clouded blue eyes. It was on the tip of his tongue to make light of her concern, but he had found over the years that her perceptions about people were usually appallingly accurate. He said carefully, "Since I have not seen them today, I can offer no comment. This evening . . . well, let us see what passes between them."

How he hated to see her upset! Without thought he lifted her hand to his lips. As his mouth brushed her palm, he felt a slight tremor in her hand that made her fingers close convulsively over his. He forgot everything except his need for her. He gazed hungrily at her lips, then into her eyes. She returned his look steadily, slight colour suffusing her cheeks.

"Ann, my dearest love . . ." he whispered with such longing that Lady Ann did not notice the groom approaching with his horse. He smiled ruefully. "The front steps are hardly a private place. I would speak with you further, Ann."

"When?" she inquired without preamble. She quickly lowered her eyes to the snowy white folds of his cravat, uncertain about her forwardness.

He chuckled and released her hand. "I was right. You have been sapping Arabella's strength. Look, you have already learned her directness."

"Oh . . . I did not mean . . . that is, Paul, I would not

wish you to think me unbecomingly forward, or . . . or *brassy*." She bit her tongue between her teeth.

"My little goose," he whispered, his voice caressing, "it is one of Arabella's most endearing qualities." He paused a moment, weighed his chances, and took the plunge.

"You know, Ann, the fish pond is lovely this time of year. Do you think you would enjoy a stroll around its perimeter tomorrow afternoon, say at one o'clock?"

She replied without hesitation, "I think I should like it above all things."

Dr. Branyon forgot the years he had spent without her, thinking now to the future. "Life is good," he said aloud, shaking his head in a bemused fashion. He rested his hand lightly on her cheek and smiled at her tenderly. "Tomorrow at one o'clock, dearest Ann." He turned and strode down the front steps to his waiting horse, his step light and confident. He waved to her before he wheeled his horse about and cantered down the graveled drive.

"Yes, Paul," she whispered to herself, "life is incredibly good." She felt so full of happiness that, absurdly, she wanted to run after the retreating groom and fling her arms around him. She hugged herself instead.

By the time she returned to the parlour, she had dimmed the outrageous sparkle in her eyes. She thought wryly that only Justin would notice a change in her. But then, in all likelihood, Justin would not be there.

She was surprised upon crossing the threshold to find only the comte awaiting her return. She smiled at him inquiringly.

"My *petite cousine* wished to retire to her room to compose herself for dinner," he explained with his lilting accent.

"I see," she replied, forcing a smile. How she wished now that she had gone directly to her room, or perhaps to the parterre. She wanted terribly to be alone, to turn over each of Paul's words in her mind, to savor the implications of his caressing tone.

"Lady Ann, I am delighted that at last I can speak with you alone," the comte said suddenly, sitting forward in his chair, his voice intense. "You see, *chère madame,* only you can tell me about my aunt Magdalaine."

"But, my dear Gervaise," she protested, a trifle disconcerted, "I hardly know anything about her! Surely Magdalaine's brother, your father—"

"Bah! He could only tell me of her girlhood in France! He knew nothing of her life in England. Please, tell me what you know of her," he pleaded, his black eyes at their most beguiling.

"Very well, but let me think a moment." Lady Ann jostled her memory, piecing together bits of information about her husband's first wife. "I believe the earl met your aunt while on a visit to the French court in 1788. I do not know the sequence of events, only that they were wed quite soon at the Trécassis château and returned to England shortly thereafter. Elsbeth, as you know, was born in 1789, but a year after their marriage." She paused and smiled at the eager young man. "But of course, Gervaise, you cannot be much older than Elsbeth yourself. I imagine that you were born near to the same time."

The comte shrugged in vague agreement and waved his elegant hands for her to continue.

"Now I come to the point where I am not certain of my facts. I believe Magdalaine returned to France shortly after the revolution broke out. I do not know her reason for traveling at such a dangerous time." She shook her head. "You, I am certain, know the rest. Unfortunately, she became ill soon after her return to Evesham Abbey and died here in 1790."

"You know nothing more, *madame?*"

"No, I am afraid I do not, Gervaise."

The young man sat back in his chair and drummed his tapered fingertips together. He said slowly, his eyes intent on Lady Ann's face, "It would seem that I can add to your store of knowledge. I do not wish to wound you, Lady Ann, but it seems that when your late husband came to France in 1787, his fortune was sadly in need of repairs. My father, Magdalaine's elder brother, told me that the Comte de Trécassis offered the earl a huge sum of money upon the marriage. There was an . . . additional portion of her *dot* that was to be paid later, upon fulfilling certain conditions."

Lady Ann was silent for a moment, her thoughts drawn back to her own huge dowry and the earl's none-too-subtle haste in wishing to marry her. She remembered her bitter disillusion as a shy, self-conscious girl who had inadvertently overheard her betrothed blithely tell one of his friends that her dowry was well worth the "smell of the shop." Though her father had been raised to a modest baronetcy, her grandfather had borne the unforgivable stigma of being a city merchant. It occurred to her now to wonder why the Comte de Trécassis would offer such a huge dowry for Magdalaine's hand. After all, Magdalaine's lineage was impeccable, the Trécassis being mixed in bloodline to the Capets. It was almost as if her dowry were some sort of bribe.

The comte rose and straightened his yellow-patterned waistcoat. "Do forgive me, *chère madame,* for taking so much of your time."

Lady Ann shook away eighteen-year-old memories and smiled. "I am sorry, Gervaise, that I could not tell you more. But, you see"—she splayed her white hands apologetically—"Magdalaine and your family were hardly ever mentioned in my presence."

"Understandably so. Oh, Lady Ann, I neglected to tell you that I find the pearls you are wearing most elegant. As the Countess of Strafford, your jewel box must be under guard," the comte said gaily, the lilting accent heavy in his voice.

"I thank you, Gervaise, for your charming compliment," Lady Ann said absently, her thoughts flown to the evening, when she would see Paul, and to the morrow.

She continued in a dry tone as she rose, "As to the Strafford jewels, my dear boy, I assure you the prince regent would not even deign to bestow them upon Princess Caroline, whom, I understand, he holds in great dislike!"

"Most curious, that," the comte murmured.

"Yes, indeed. One wonders how such an alliance could be formed with the mutual distaste apparent in both parties."

"Eh? Oh, yes, certainly. It is the royal way, *chère madame.*" He bowed over her hand and strolled from the parlor.

Lady Ann shook out her skirts and walked to the door. Perhaps she would wear the pink silk gown tomorrow, with its rows of tiny satin rosebuds. Surely it was not so very bad to break the monotony of her black mourning just one time. As she mounted the stairs to her room, she thought of the rather daring expanse of white bosom revealed by the gown, and smiled confidently.

Dinner that evening was set back because the smithy had been clumsy in his shoeing of a horse and badly cut his hand. "Poor fellow," Dr. Branyon said with a sympathetic shake of his head, "furious at himself, he was. Evidently it was the first accident he's ever had that was ' 'is own buggerin' fault.' "

Certainly his story was not all that amusing, Dr. Branyon thought as he led Lady Ann in to dinner, but nevertheless it deserved better than the strained smiles it received from the earl and Arabella. The comte had laughed delightedly, though the doctor suspected he had not quite understood the lapse into the smithy's vernacular. Elsbeth smiled demurely, as one would have expected her to, but not quite in her usual way. Dr. Branyon found his eyes drawn to Elsbeth again as they entered the dining room. He had carelessly described her to Lady Ann once as a "fluttering little mouse, afraid at any moment of falling into a baited trap." Now he was not quite so sure. There seemed to be a new self-assurance about her, her quietness born of a kind of confidence rather than her fear of putting herself forward in an unbecoming manner.

"Come, Arabella," Lady Ann said gaily, "you are now the Countess of Strafford, and I must perforce relinquish my chair to you!"

Arabella gazed blankly at her mother for a moment, ready to take her usual place at the table. Realization brought with it a vehement shake of her head. "Oh, no, Mother, I have no wish to supplant you! It is altogether ridiculous. I will keep my usual seat, I thank you!"

Arabella's knuckles showed white on the back of her chair as the earl interposed with calm authority, "Lady Ann is quite correct, Arabella. As the Countess of Strafford, it is only proper that you take your place at the foot of the table."

"Father always called it the 'bottom' of the table," Arabella flashed acidly. "Come, let us cease this nonsense, my roast pork grows more leathery by the moment!"

"You will sit yourself where appropriate, madam. Giles, will you kindly assist her ladyship into her place."

The second footman, never having rubbed Miss Arabella against her grain in all her eighteen years, turned beseeching eyes to Lady Ann.

"Come, my dear," Lady Ann persuaded gently, "do allow Giles to seat you." She silently chided herself for having ever raised the matter in the first place. Decidedly there was a great deal amiss between the newly wedded couple, and she had inadvertently added fuel to an already smouldering fire.

She waited with held breath to see if Arabella would turn the dining room into a battleground.

Arabella drew her lips into a tight line, as if angry words would pop out if she did not keep her mouth locked closed. To persist, she knew, would serve only to call further attention to the unhappy situation that existed between her and the earl. She could not, however, resist a pettish shrug of her shoulders as she sank into the tall-backed chair that Giles nervously held for her.

Following a very silent first course of turtle soup, Dr. Branyon inquired of the earl, "Have you made the acquaintance of old Hamsworth, Justin?"

A slight smile indented the corners of the earl's mouth. "A crotchety old reprobate and, I think, a tenant who has well served the land. He provided me with quite a long list of the improvements he wished to see made on the estate."

"He was forever doing the same with Father," Arabella added without thinking.

"And what was the outcome?" the earl asked, his eyes meeting hers down the long expanse of table.

"Father never listened to him, so he was forever trying to bribe me."

Justin thought of the leering old man and his vulgar observations on one of the milkmaids, and felt his hand tighten about his fork. "What were his bribes?" His tone was so very harsh that Elsbeth's almond eyes flew from her sautéed mushrooms to his face in frowning confusion.

Arabella felt an uncontrollable demon burgeon inside her. She allowed a knowing smile to flit over her face and raised her brows coquettishly. "How very odd that you should ask, my lord. When I was five years old, his bribes took the form of apples from his orchard. Of course," she continued smoothly, "as I grew older, old Hamsworth became more . . . creative. Then, however, he was certainly not to be considered precisely *old*."

Her reward for so outlandish a tale was a dull flush of anger that spread over her husband's bronzed features. She returned to her dinner, finding that if her pork was not actually leather, it tasted so in her mouth. She was only dimly aware throughout the remainder of the meal that her mother and Dr. Branyon conversed almost solely with Elsbeth and the comte.

"Arabella."

She raised her head at the sound of her name. Lady Ann continued softly, "Whenever you would like the ladies to withdraw, you have but to rise."

What an awesome power, to be sure, and she had not even thought of it! Swiftly she pushed back her chair, leaving poor Giles in the lurch, and rose. "If you gentlemen will excuse us, we will leave you to your port." How very simple it was! She looked the earl straight in the face, then turned on her heel and strode so quickly from the dining room that Lady Ann and Elsbeth were taking double steps to keep pace with her.

"Whatever is wrong with Arabella?" Elsbeth whispered to Lady Ann as they trailed after her into the Velvet Room. "And his lordship. He spoke to her so very coldly." Elsbeth looked at her stepmother, her eyes alight with curiosity.

"Sometimes, my dear," Lady Ann said finally, "married people, when they are first wed, do not always agree. 'Tis a lovers' quarrel, nothing more." If only I could believe that, she thought hollowly. Dear Elsbeth, she thought, how very innocent she is. It seemed that Elsbeth had accepted her simple explanation, her attention already flitting elsewhere, perhaps to her future season in London. Yet, Lady Ann was puzzled, for it had been days since Elsbeth had made any reference either to her ten thousand pounds or to their projected trip.

Lady Ann eyed Arabella, who was restlessly pacing in front of the long French windows. She turned to her stepdaughter. "Do play for us, Elsbeth. Perhaps some of your French ballads."

Elsbeth complied willingly, sat herself gracefully at the pianoforte, and soon melodious chords filled the room. Lady Ann walked to her daughter and laid her hand on her sleeve. "Why ever did you tell such a whisker about poor old Hamsworth? You know perfectly well that your father never allowed you within a mile of his cottage!"

Arabella raised her chin warily. " 'Twas but a joke, Mother."

"One that made Justin very angry. What you implied, my love, was not at all the thing, you know."

"It was what the earl expected, nay, *wished* to hear," Arabella replied harshly.

"Arabella, whatever are you talking about?" Lady Ann cried, appalled. "How can you say that such a story as you concocted is what he wished to hear? Why, it is absurd! He is your husband, not some jealous lover for you to taunt!"

Arabella raised her fine gray eyes to her mother's agitated countenance. Her dinner began to churn uncomfortably in her stomach. She had very nearly given herself away. If only she were gazing into her father's world-wise eyes rather than her mother's so very innocent blue ones! She took a tight hold on her disillusionment, shrugged her shoulders, and said with the light tone of affectionate dismissal, "Pray, Mother, do not take what I say seriously. The earl and I had a slight misunderstanding, that is all."

Before Lady Ann's look of incredulity translated itself into words, there was a swirl of black satin and Arabella called over her shoulder, "I shall set up the table for lottery tickets."

To Arabella's relief, the earl and Dr. Branyon did not join in the game of lottery tickets. She found, though, that the excitement of winning and losing her fish did nothing to enliven her spirits. Because the earl believed the comte to be her lover, her most innocently spoken phrases took on a guiltily wanton meaning to her. She tried vainly to ignore the comte and found to her horror that a dull flush crept over her cheeks when his compelling dark eyes rested upon her. If she were not certain herself of her own innocence, she would have pronounced herself to be guilty. The friendly word and glance of yesterday seemed today fraught with sensuous dual meaning. She was consumed with self-consciousness and fell into a deep and brooding silence.

When Crupper entered with the tea tray, her nerves were taut to the breaking point. She assumed her new duty of dispensing tea without a murmur and luckily without mishap. As soon as she had filled the last cup, she rose hurriedly from her chair. She made a poor attempt at creating a yawn and said with uncharacteristic breathlessness, "It has been such a long day! But see, I am yawning most prodigiously! I wish all of you a good night!"

She nodded to the group in general, avoiding all the eyes that seemed to look through her pretense, and made for the door.

"Do wait a moment, my dear," the earl's voice stopped her. "I myself am also ready to retire."

Arabella wanted to run, but knew she could not. He had adroitly cornered her, and to protest would announce her fear to everyone. She stood in tense silence until the earl, with his customary laconic grace, had made his round of good nights. She thought he lingered purposely.

Dr. Branyon quelled the abiding sense of foreboding he felt when the earl slipped his arm through Arabella's and guided her from the room. He hoped devoutly that Ann would not ask him to speak to the earl, for he had no desire to be the recipient of a freezing set-down. Through the evening, he had sensed that Justin was in the most saturnine of moods and unapproachable to any but the most mundane of inquiries. Even his wry observation that the comte exhibited unending affability had elicited the cold response, "It perhaps serves his best interest to be all things to all people." He had then said more to himself than to Dr. Branyon, and in the most oblique manner: "I shall shortly know if our young French relative has the spirit of a dove, the fangs of a viper, or simply the dishonorable instincts inherent in his French blood."

Arabella maintained a wary silence until they reached the top of the stairs. "I would go to my room now," she managed in a strangled whisper.

Justin placed his fingers about her arm. "Of course, you mean to say *our* room. That, my dear, is our destination."

"No," she hissed, and wrenched away from him. She sped down the corridor to her room and flung the door wide. A sense of unreality seized her. All the furniture was swathed in ghostly holland covers. Her favorite pictures were gone, her personal belongings nowhere to be seen. The room was stripped of her presence. With a gulp of panic she raced to the armoire and pulled at the ivory knobs. All her gowns, cloaks, and bonnets were gone; even her slippers, lined in a colourful row, had vanished. She turned slowly and saw the earl standing in the doorway, his arms crossed negligently across his chest.

"I . . . I do not understand," she stammered, her fingers twitching nervously at the holland cover encasing her favorite wing chair.

The earl straightened and said matter-of-factly, "I decided your room was not big enough for both of us. Thus, during dinner I had your belongings removed to the earl's bedchamber. If Evesham Abbey's ghostly visitors return, we will simply have to accustom ourselves. Now, come, wife, your husband awaits his pleasure."

Arabella slipped her hand into the pocket of her gown, closing her fingers over the smooth ivory handle of her small pistol. When she had espied it next to her jewel box before dinner, she had wondered at herself for not remembering it earlier. Ironically, her father's gift would protect her now from the man he had so carefully chosen for her. She drew up now to her full height and demanded with scathing sarcasm, "Were you intending another rape scene tonight, my lord?"

He shrugged his shoulders indifferently. "It will be as you wish it, madam. If your lover is to enjoy your favours by day, I see no reason why I should not be equally indulged at night."

He speaks to me as though I were a trollop from Soho, she thought. Because she had a small deadly pistol, she allowed her anger full rein. "God, what a mistake my father made in choosing you! However did you manage to conceal from him your vulgar, lowly instincts? To think that *I* must protest my innocence to one such as you. I will tell you but once again, my lord, for I fear you are deaf to all truth: I have no lover!"

"It is true that your father made a mistake, but not, I assure you, in my character. It is fortunate that he is not here to witness the perfidy of his own daughter. Come, Arabella, I grow tired of this nonsense." That she continued to lie to him fueled his smoldering anger, his raging sense of injustice. He had not intended to rape her tonight, in spite of her taunting remarks at dinner about the lecherous old Hamsworth, but rather to force her to experience pleasure at his hands. He wanted to force her to passion, to make her surrender to him. Though he would not admit it to himself, he wanted to win her, to make her forget the comte.

He crooked his finger at her impatiently. Without another word, Arabella preceded him from the room. Though he did not again take her arm, she sensed a coiled readiness in him and knew that if she attempted to flee, he would capture her in an instant.

When they reached the earl's bedchamber, he stepped back and waited until she entered the room. Even before she turned to face him, she heard the key grate in the lock.

"I will play your lady's maid, Arabella. Come here and let me unfasten all those buttons."

"No," she said with desperate calm. "You will not touch me, Justin."

She saw his nostrils flare in sudden anger at her refusal. But an instant later a smile of lazy confidence played about his mouth and his eyes glittered with the challenge she had flung at him. He said with slow emphasis, "As I said before, it will be as you wish it. Do you want your gown shredded, Arabella? For that is what your refusal will mean. But realize, my dear, after a week or two, you will have no more gowns. Not, of course, that I mind having you naked during the day as well." He strolled confidently toward her.

Arabella flew to the other side of the great bed, knowing that there was nothing she could say to dissuade him. Her eyes measured her distance from him, and her fingers curled about the butt of her pistol.

"Since you wish to be sportive, it is just as well that we excused ourselves early." Still confident, he stalked her with maddening slowness, walking around the side of the bed. She could retreat no farther, her back finally touching the long velvet curtains.

"You will come no closer to me, Justin." As she spoke, she withdrew the pistol from her pocket, held it straight out in front of her, and leveled it at his chest.

He smiled at her grimly and took another step. "Put the pistol down, Arabella, I would not wish you to hurt yourself."

Her father had trained her to exhibit what he called an "admirable sangfroid" when confronted with unpleasantness. She strove to fulfill his teaching. "I am really quite well trained, my lord. And I do not actually wish to kill you, you know. But, Justin, come one step nearer and I shall put a bullet straight through your arm."

He stared at her with a curious mixture of anger, frustration, and admiration on his face. Damm it, he believed her! As a matter of course, he quickly calculated his chances of disarming her. He made no movement toward her. He could well imagine that the late earl had trained her well. At this distance, she could and readily would, he believed, put a bullet through whatever part of his anatomy she chose. He saw that she was regarding him with a kind of cold detachment, her head steady as his own would be before a battle. He turned on his heel and without a backward glance strode into the adjoining dressing room and slammed the door.

Arabella shifted the pistol to her other hand and wiped her sweaty palm on her skirt. She felt her bravado begin to crumble as she envisioned a succession of endless nights in similar conflict. She felt awash with bitter disillusionment. God, was she to hold her husband off at gunpoint for the remainder of her days? She shook her head despairingly, too drained to think rationally about what she should do.

She gazed tiredly at the bed, but passed it by. She sank down into a larged stuffed chair beside the fireplace, curled her legs beneath her gown, and wearily laid her face against her arm. Somehow, she wished she could cry, but she knew she would not. Crying solved naught. She kept her fingers curled about the butt of her pistol.

Arabella awoke with a shivering start early the next morning, her legs cramped from their long hours in one position. To her confusion, she saw that a blanket was covering her and that the small pistol lay on a tabletop near her chair. Her heart seemed to lurch into her throat as she realized that Justin had entered the room while she slept. He could have done as he wished with her. Yet he had merely covered her and removed the pistol from her fingers. She rose slowly and stretched her aching muscles. She did not understand him.

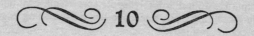 **10**

"The lilies grow in great profusion."

"The laws of nature make it so. There must be a lily pad for each frog."

"But see, the reeds are so very thick! It is difficult to walk through them."

"Indeed, and so very green." Dr. Branyon gazed fondly down at Lady Ann, his amusement at her diversionary comments barely held in check. Delicate colour suffused her creamy cheeks. He asked with gentle humour, "Are there other fascinating observations about this delightful sport that you wish to point out to me, my dear?"

"I . . . I do not think so," she replied in a small voice. Why ever am I so very nervous, she thought, torn between amusement and vexation at herself. I must cease behaving in such a ridiculous manner.

"Excellent! Now we may get on with the business at hand. Come, my dear, I shall volunteer my coat so you can settle yourself among the so very thick green reeds."

For the first time since she had met him here at the fish pond, she managed to bring her eyes to his face. How she loved his face, so smooth and lean; and the deep lines on either side of his mouth—his doctor's-smile creases, she had once teased him.

He clasped her hand in his and led her to the other side of the pond. He found a likely spot, spread his coat upon the springy moss and grass, and gave her a flourishing bow. "For your pleasure, my lady."

"I should have brought a picnic lunch," Lady Ann murmured as she sank down gracefully onto his coat and smoothed the flounce of her pink gown daintily over her ankles.

"After eighteen and some odd years, my love, I want no piece of chicken to come between us," Dr. Branyon replied in a caressing tone.

He sat down close to her, his nearness rendering her somehow deliciously nervous. She felt suddenly warm, and with unsteady fingers untied the bow below her left ear and lifted off her bonnet.

Dr. Branyon picked up the bonnet and gently tossed it off to one side. Slowly he lifted his hand to her face, letting his fingers trace over her smooth cheek, her straight nose, and come to rest lightly against her pink lips. "You are so very lovely," he said with a husky quality in his voice that made her heart hammer with unwonted force against her ribs.

He gently slipped his hand behind her neck, over the thick coil of heavy blond hair, and drew her to him. He thought she looked like a young girl readying for her first kiss. He had the good sense and patience to realize that her gesture was a tentative one. He kissed her gently, barely touching his lips to hers, savouring the silky smoothness of her soft mouth. He felt a fluttering response in her and tenderly placed his hands on her shoulders and pushed her down on her back. Her eyes flew open and he read uncertainty, perhaps fear in their depths. Immediately he released her and balanced himself on his elbow beside her. He had been certain for years that the earl had not treated her well. Yet, there was an air of fragile innocence about her that even her husband had failed to extinguish. Perhaps when they were married, she would speak of him.

"You will marry me, will you not, Ann?" he asked aloud, finishing his silent thought.

She smiled up at him, a lazy impish smile, now devoid of uncertainty, and replied saucily, "Indeed, I fear that I must,

Paul. I would be a terribly loose woman were I to kiss a man I did not intend to wed."

"Then I must kiss you again to doubly ensure your compliance!"

She was laughing when he kissed her, and his tongue entered her mouth. She could not help the shock of fear that made her grit her teeth suddenly against him. In that instant it was the earl, and not Paul, whose mouth was grinding against hers, bruising her, forcing her lips open. How she had hated the vulgar wetness of his tongue. Even when he had kissed her, she had felt it a kind of vile rape.

Dr. Branyon instantly drew back and gazed at her with such understanding that she unleased her terrible memories. "Paul, do forgive me. It is just that *he* would hurt me . . . that is," she stumbled on, "he was not terribly kind when he would . . ." She fell into strained silence and averted her face.

He had a savage gnawing to know what the earl had done to her, yet he sensed it was too soon for her. He asked softly, "Do you trust me, Ann?"

She turned to face him, lifted her hand, and touched her fingers to his firm mouth. "I trust you more than I feared him," she said simply, realizing with some surprise that she truly believed her words.

He gathered her into his arms and pulled her gently to him. He pressed his hand against the small of her back and felt her snuggle close against him, her full breasts molded tantalizingly against his chest, her belly and thighs pressing gently against his. She slid her arms about his neck and buried her face against his neck. Just having him close to her, feeling his warm breath on her neck, made her replete with happiness.

He wondered with a certain wry embarrassment if she could feel his hard, throbbing manhood pressing against her. For one of the few times in his life he was thankful for the many layers of clothing women wore. He wanted to caress her rounded hips, but forced his hands to remain on her back.

They lay silently in each other's arms until the sun began its rapid downward descent. "Wake up, my little sluggard," he whispered in her ear, soft tendrils of hair tickling his chin.

"You know very well that I am not asleep, sir," she said with languid drowsiness. She raised her head from his neck and sighed as other concerns edged into her mind. "Paul, whatever shall we do about Arabella and Justin?"

He did not answer her until he had kissed her lightly on the tip of her nose and helped her to rise. As he dusted off his coat, he looked down at her upturned face and said thoughtfully, "You may think that I have rust in my upper works, but I cannot help but believe that their . . . difficulties in some way involve the comte."

Lady Ann looked startled. "The comte! But in what way? I do not understand how Gervaise could have anything to do with it!"

"Nor do I, my love—at least, not precisely."

She paused a moment to tuck errant wisps of hair back into the smooth coil of hair at her neck. "I think . . . nay, I know that Justin was unkind to her on their wedding night."

"Surely, Ann, that cannot be so! You must be mistaken." Dr. Braynon looked at her incredulously. "I would think that our confident little Bella would have most charmingly seduced her bridegroom without a by-your-leave! As to Justin, I cannot believe that he would be so green as to frighten her."

Lady Ann coloured. She could not bring herself to tell him what she knew.

He smiled tenderly, wondering a moment at her silence. "I cannot tell you not to fret, my dear, for I know that you will do so anyway. If the opportunity arises, I will speak to Arabella. The comte, I fear, is another matter entirely. I own I cannot like him any more than does Justin."

"I believe him to be a harmless enough young man, but you know," she admitted with a slight frown, "now that I think about it, it was rather odd of him to speak to me at such length about Magdalaine."

"Magdalaine?" he repeated carefully.

She nodded. "He wished to know about her life in England. Of course, I know very little of her. He, mind you, then proceeded to tell me about her family's rather unusual dowry settlement with the earl. It seemed that not all of her dowry was given to the earl upon their marriage. I really do not know why he told me all that, for Magdalaine died so very quickly after her return from France, indeed two years after her marriage to the earl." She paused for a moment and then looked up with a sudden smile. "How very stupid of me, to be sure! Paul, you were attending her when she died, were you not? Gervaise should speak to you if he wishes to know more about his aunt."

Dr. Branyon looked away from her and said grimly, "Yes, I was with Magdalaine when she died." He added with brusque finality, "As to Magdalaine's dowry, I know nothing of her family's arrangements with the earl. Further, I would give that young puppy a piece of my mind were he to come to me with such questions!"

Lady Ann looked searchingly at him, bewildered by the vehemence of his reaction.

As they wended their way through the geometric patterns of the parterre, he asked her in a voice of casual interest, "Did the comte wish to know anything else from you, Ann?"

She considered the matter, then replied with some amusement, "No, nothing of importance, save that he wondered about the Strafford jewels. He thought that as the countess, I must have a jewel box worth a king's ransom! I told him straightaway how very ridiculous that was."

"Hmmm," was all that Dr. Branyon replied until they reached the front steps of Evesham Abbey. He took Lady Ann's hand to his and squeezed it reassuringly. "I must not stay, Ann. Pray, do not worry overly about Arabella. I shall try to speak to her soon." He raised her hand to his lips. "Select a wedding date, my love. If you feel you could brave society's strictures, I would as lief not wait for eight more months."

"Yes, Paul, I shall give it much thought," she replied.

*Why can I not feel anything? Please, God, let me feel something? Is it your punishment for my sin? Oh, please, let me feel my love for him!*

His lips roamed hungrily over her small uptilted breasts, and she wound her fingers in his short black curling hair to press him harder against her. He thought her gesture born of a desire that matched his own and tugged vigorously at her smooth, taut nipples.

She gritted her teeth at the pain, willing herself not to cry out. She brought her hands up to cup his smooth chin and eased his mouth away from her breast to her lips. His flashing black eyes were smoky with desire, and she saw a gleam of impatience in their coal-dark depths.

She knew sudden fear. She must not let him guess that his passionate embraces did not bring her pleasure, indeed, froze all feeling inside her. Instinctively she moaned softly into his mouth and arched her back up against him. She felt a quickening in him, and for an instant knew an overwhelming desire to push him off her, to beg him not to drive his hard manhood into her. She held her breath, ashamed at such unnatural thoughts, and suffered his grinding mouth and probing tongue. She must remember that he loved her, that, above all things, she did not want to lose him, to give him a disgust of her.

She tried to relax, to inhale the sweet smell of hay. *It is you who are the lucky one, the chosen one. He does not want Arabella or any other woman. To give him your body is proof of your love for him.*

Suddenly he reared back on his knees, clutched her knees, and pulled them apart. She closed her eyes as his fingers fumbled to part her. She heard him growl with frustration, and a red veil of shame clouded her mind. She felt his fingers, wet with spittle, rubbing at her, probing her. She winced even as his fingers delved inside her, and in a haze of misery wondered yet again how she would bear that thick shaft of pulsing flesh pushing inside her.

He poised himself over her, unable to contain his desire, and shoved inside her, feeling as he did so the eruption of all his senses, a moment's supension of thought and time. His seed flooded the small taut passage, easing his way, and he hurtled into the depths of her. He felt an ecstatic instant of animal victory, felt an affirmation of his maleness. Her small hands clutched at his shoulders, and he believed yet again that he had conquered her as a man must a woman, and by his own passion given her a woman's fulfillment.

He eased his weight off her, kissed her moist lips lightly, and rolled on his side next to her. She felt leaden, her body sticky and prickly as the cool air settled upon the thin sheen of sweat left by his body.

"I adore you, *ma petite cousine*," he murmured sensuously, knowing it his duty as her conqueror, as her lover, to reassure her with binding words that cost him so very little. Certainly it had heightened his vanity to seduce his shy cousin, yet, too, he had guessed that to ensure her absolute compliance, he had also to possess her body. Her furtive virginity had pleased him.

"And I you, Gervaise," she whispered adoringly, her body already stilled to its outrage. She thought how very blessed among women she was, to be loved by one so very handsome as he, with his dark eyes, almond-shaped as were hers, and his flashing white teeth. He was more handsome than the earl, whose very size terrified her, particularly now that she knew what men demanded of women's bodies. Her soaring spirit dimmed. If only she could feel her own pleasure, glory in but a moment's passion. She tried to turn her mind away from such selfish, ignoble desires. She must believe that to have him, to let him delight in her body, was enough for her.

"You know, Elsbeth," he said after a moment, "I spoke to Lady Ann about your mother, Magdalaine. She knew far less than I do about her . . . circumstances."

Elsbeth pulled the edge of his cloak over her and turned on her side to face him. "What do you mean, her circumstances?" She was vaguely disconcerted that he was not speaking about her, about their future together.

He quickly patted her cheek and let his fingers rove over her breast. He had moved maladroitly, caught her unawares. He shrugged indifferently and yawned. She smiled, lulled, again satisfied that his attention was focused upon her.

"Perhaps I should say 'circumstances,'" he continued with careless interest. "My father merely told me some rather unusual stories about your mother. Are you not interested in your mother, Elsbeth?" he asked with gentle reproach in his voice.

"But of course," she quickly protested. "It is just that she died so very long ago, when I was but a baby. As to any stories about her, I should be delighted to hear them."

"Perhaps then sometime soon," he said carelessly. How very easily he could divert her thoughts, to call forth the insecure lonely child, striving so desperately to please. Though he was certain that he had bound her to him, he wondered if her loyalties to Lady Ann and to Arabella might render her incapable of doing what he wished.

He appeared to grow bored with the subject. It was enough for the moment that he had planted seeds of curiosity in her mind. He let his gaze wander up and down her body with silent intensity. He could not know that she was frantically searching her mind for something of interest to distract him. With sudden inspiration she exclaimed, "Gervaise, I do think it commendable that you care to know more about my mother. Did you know that my maid, Josette, was also my mother's nurse? She knew my mother from a baby, and indeed, accompanied her here to Evesham Abbey after her marriage to my father."

His eyes ceased their downward journey, resting now vaguely on her smoothly rounded belly. How very stupid of him! Josette, of course! Now he would not need to count upon Elsbeth. Would not Josette feel loyalty to the de Trécassis family, to him? He felt a surge of supreme confidence. Thinking to reward Elsbeth for providing him the answer to his problem, he spurred the cold embers of desire and swept his hand between her thighs, glorying in the dampness of his own seed that still clung to her. He jerked away his cloak and pulled her possessively against him. For an instant he thought she pushed feebly against his chest, but then she moaned softly against his neck and wrapped her arms about his shoulders.

Elsbeth glanced at the small gilt clock on the table beside the copper bathtub, sighed contentedly, and lowered herself deeper into the warm, scented water. She felt supremely happy, even as she had scrubbed herself until the soft flesh between her thighs smarted from the assault. She basked in the warm water, the violent, embarrassing man's side of love all but forgotten, her mind soaring with unbounded pleasure into a romantic image of Gervaise as her dashing, gallant lover.

"Come, my lamb, it grows late. You would not wish to be late for dinner."

Elsbeth turned toward her rheumy-eyed maid, Josette, vaguely aware that there was an unusual sharpness in her withered voice. "Come, mistress," Josette repeated, waving a large towel toward Elsbeth.

"Ah, very well," Elsbeth replied languidly, and rose, her arms outstretched.

"Really, my lamb!" Josette exclaimed, horrified. "You are a lady, not a *grisette* to flaunt her naked body!" She quickly bundled Elsbeth into the towel, averting her eyes as she did so.

Elsbeth eyed her faithful old maidservant with a secret woman's smile. How very old-fashioned she was, she thought, forgetting that but a short time before, she would never have emerged from her bath until Josette had positioned her towel. "Oh, do not scold me," she cried gaily. "I am much too happy!"

Josette grunted, pulled Elsbeth's chemise over her head, and forced her arthritic fingers to tie the dainty ribbons. The twitching pain in her fingers made her snap crossly, "Just because you are now a rich young lady, with ten thousand pounds, 'tis no reason for you to go bounding about screeching like a scullery maid!"

"Oh, Josette, it is not *that*," Elsbeth confided in a rush. "I may as well tell you, you sharp-eyed old eagle, for you will know soon enough." She whirled about and clasped Josette's gnarled hands, pulling her wispy gray head close to hers. "I am in love," she whispered happily.

Josette felt a bizarre moment of muddled confusion. No, it was not Magdalaine who was in love. Elsbeth! She grasped at the vague realities that filed in lopsided order through her mind and drew back with a gasp of shock. "Oh, no, my little pet! You cannot love the earl! He has wedded with Arabella!" She groped to remember. "He has wedded with Arabella, has he not?" she asked, not terribly certain.

Elsbeth gave a trill of laughter and hugged the familiar stoop-shouldered old woman. "Yes, indeed, the earl has married Arabella. 'Tis not the *earl* I am speaking of!"

"But who, then?" she demanded with awkward slowness. She wished that the dainty, smiling girl in front of her were not so very like Magdalaine. Such transports, such gaiety, when Magdalaine was in love!

"My cousin, of course. The comte."

"The comte," Josette repeated, her voice incredulous.

"Dear Josette, is it not marvelous? Am I not the luckiest of women? He loves me, and now that I am independent, I may wed him without the shame of being penniless!"

The old woman became suddenly rigid in Elsbeth's arms. She shoved the girl away and dashed her stiffened fingers across her forehead.

"Josette, whatever is the matter?" Elsbeth cried as the old woman backed slowly away from her. Her beloved wrinkled features seemed to crumble, as if some great unknown force were collapsing her forward. She whipped back her head and shrieked, "No!"

Elsbeth recoiled and gazed dumbfounded at the old woman. Her mind has finally snapped, she thought with simple compassion. "Now, Josette—" she began.

The old woman's anguished cry sent Elsbeth staggering back. "No! You cannot wed him! Magdalaine, no!"

"I am not Magdalaine, Josette. Come, look at me. See, I am Elsbeth, her daughter."

Josette stared at her young mistress and began to shake her head back and forth, wisps of gray hair escaping from her mobcap and whipping across her thin mouth. "It is God in his final retribution," she muttered in a singsong voice. She could no longer bear to see the eager, concerned young face, and turned away, shuffling wearily from the room.

"Josette, wait!" Elsbeth called, gooseflesh rising on her arms and an inexplicable knot of fear growing in her breast. The door closed and she jound herself alone. Clumsily she dressed herself and coiled her black hair into a thick roll at the back of her neck. She shook her head sadly. Josette was quite mad, her mind slipped irrevocably back into the past. *But why, Josette, your muttering about God and his retribution? Of course, you thought I was Magdalaine, but still, why would you say such a thing about my mother?*

Elsbeth forgot her questions when she was told by Lady Ann that Lady Talgarth and Miss Suzanne Talgarth were expected momentarily for dinner. She silently bemoaned Josette's strange mood that had left her to clumsily knot her own hair. Upon the arrival of Lady Talgarth and Suzanne in a flurry of sparkling jewels and clinging satin and lavender gauze, she patted her own black gown, aware that a small lump of jealousy had risen in her throat. She felt awkward and tongue-tied, as she usually did in the presence of the voluptuous and laughing Suzanne. She gazed at Lady Ann and Arabella and decided that all the Deverill women faded into insignificance in their black silks—like dull-feathered magpies framing an exotic bird in exquisite plumage.

She was insensibly cheered when, as they filed into the dining room, Gervaise whispered meaningfully in her ear, "How very fragile and delicate you are, *ma petite*, not like that pink-and-white English cow."

"Gervaise, really," she chided, quite pleased. She heard the earl chuckle, and looked up to see his dark head bent close to Miss Talgarth's golden curls. Her eyes flew to Arabella, and she saw with confusion that her half-sister was smiling openly at the couple.

*Excellent, Suzanne,* Arabella was thinking. *I could not have planned for a more effective diversion. Father was really quite wrong about you, Suzanne. Witless, missish little fool indeed! If he could but see you now, I would wager that he would be vying with Justin for your favors.*

"I declare, I do not know what I shall do with the girl," Lady Talgarth was saying, the weary shake of her crimped sandy curls belied by the ringing pride in her strident voice. "Two offers of marriage in her first Season, Ann, and the chit keeps both gentlemen languishing on tenterhooks!" She bent her penetrating stare down the table. "Arabella, surely you met young Viscount Graybourn? Such an eligible young man, to be sure!"

Arabella arched her brows in startled speculation. "Dear me, ma'am, of course you cannot be referring to that clumsy young man with spots on his face!"

Suzanne gave a trill of laughter. "You see, Mama, Arabella quite agrees with me. You forgot to add, Bella, that at but twenty-and-five, he is already paunchy. I had it on the best of sources that the only reason Lord Graybourn rises before noon is that he is afraid that he will miss his breakfast!"

"Really, Suzanne, such an appraisal is hardly kind," Lady Talgarth protested, her sharp eyes resting disapprovingly upon Arabella as she spoke.

Arabella shrugged and lowered her eyes to her plate. As the footman, Giles, served the rich consommé, Suzanne raised coquettish wide eyes to the earl, pursed her pink lips, and said playfully, "I think that I would prefer a gentleman with more worldly experience. Perhaps a gentleman with military training . . . like you, my lord. How very protected and secure you must feel, Bella."

Arabella felt her fingers tighten about the stem of her wineglass. She noted with a passing glance that the earl's eyes had narrowed ever so slightly and that he tugged at his cravat as if it were too tight. She smiled at Suzanne and replied in a level voice, "Perhaps it is wisest, Suzanne, to look to oneself first for such things as protection. It is many times difficult, I think, to determine beforehand the actions of another."

"You see"—Suzanne flashed even white teeth—"Bella has again defended my opinion! Though," she added, wrinkling her nose, "I understood not a word she said!"

"Dear Miss Talgarth," the comte interposed, his accent pronounced, "surely it cannot be so very important, these years of worldly experience you speak of. My dear mademoiselle, a French gentleman comes into the world with such gifts."

"In my opinion, it is all one and the same," Lady Talgarth announced obscurely, unaware of the sudden tense undercurrent of emotion in several members of the table. Tenaciously she harked back to her grievance. "I am certain that neither Arabella nor you, Suzanne, can accuse Lord Hartland of being paunchy or of having spots."

Arabella saw that Suzanne faltered, and observed with innocent candor to Lady Talgarth, "Indeed, you are quite correct, ma'am. And as to *experience*, why, at fifty years old, having already buried two wives, not to mention his several quite expensive aspiring offspring, he would appear quite unexceptionable."

Justin barely repressed a "bravo." Lord, Arabella had routed the old harridan with the smoothness of vintage wine!

"Did the prince remove to Brighton for the summer?" Lady Ann asked with desperate gaiety, wishing she was close enough to Arabella to soundly kick her shin.

Suzanne turned to Lady Ann and replied artlessly, "Oh, yes, and although Papa is complaining sorely from his gout, Mama has persuaded him that I, at least, should pay a long-overdue visit to my aunt Seraphina. Her house faces Marine Parade, you know, and one can observe simply *everyone* going to and from the Pump Room."

"Will Lord Hartland and Viscount Graybourn set up in Brighton, Suzanne?" Arabella teased.

"To be sure, Bella, but I am not so stupid as to allot them all of my attention!"

"I shall, of course, accompany Suzanne to my sister's," Lady Talgarth said pointedly to Lady Ann.

Justin tapped the stem of his wineglass with his fork to gain everyone's attention. "Let us drink to your visit to Brighton, Miss Talgarth, and to the gentleman who will be so lucky as to pluck such a lovely rose."

As Arabella drained her wine, she thought with wry

amusement how very adept Suzanne had become in her handling of gentlemen. She was certain that the lovely rose could show her thorns most effectively, if crossed the wrong way. Lady Ann cleared her throat and shot Arabella a meaningful glance.

Arabella rose and nodded to the earl and the comte. "If you gentlemen will excuse us, we will repair to the Velvet Room."

Justin rose also and said pleasantly, "I do not think we need to linger over our port this evening, my dear. If you ladies do not mind, we would join you now."

Lady Talgarth observed to Lady Ann in a whisper calculated to penetrate the ear of Crupper, who stood at the far end of the dining room, "How very odd it seems for Arabella to be in *your* place, my dear Ann."

Arabella pretended not to hear and looked back only when Suzanne tugged on her sleeve. "Goodness, you walk so very quickly! Come, Bella, don't mind Mama. You must know that she is jealous as a cat because you have contracted such an eligible alliance before me."

"You do not mind, do you, Suz?" Arabella asked affectionately.

Blond curls fluttered and bobbed over small shapely ears. "Oh, fie, Bella! Just imagine, if *you* caught an earl, no doubt I shall become a duchess!"

Arabella looked down at the dimpled laughing face and found herself smiling. "You will make a perfect duchess, Suz."

"You know, it would serve Mama right were I to marry our spotty viscount. All the money that has been lavished on fripperies and gowns for my Season—why, Papa was livid when the only result he saw was the visit of a gentleman who could not even play at whist!" She paused a moment and sat daintly beside Arabella, arranging her lavender skirt in becoming folds about her. "Oh, my, Elsbeth is going to play. I do hope Mama will not insist that I follow such a performance!"

After a third Bach prelude, Suzanne began to fidget. She put her blond head next to Arabella's ear and whispered behind her lavender-gloved hand, "How very lucky you are, Bella. The earl is so very handsome and . . . and masculine!

If I were not a properly brought-up young lady, I should long to be wicked and ask you all about your wedding night!"

The stark memory of pain and bitter humiliation tied a knot about Arabella's tongue. It was some moments before she was able to answer evenly, "Well, you would not be so wicked as to ask, Suz. You must discover all about wedding nights when your own comes."

"Such a spoilsport you are," Suzanne chided, her eyes dancing with mischief.

After Elsbeth's performance had received its usual accolades, and Suzanne had complained most convincingly to her mama of a sore finger, Arabella found herself paired with the comte against the earl and Suzanne in a game of whist.

She soon discovered that the comte's skill was not to be despised, and began to play with the daring and skill that her father had taught her. Without intending it to be so, she found herself engaging in silent battle against her husband, the comte and Suzanne fading out of her thoughts. When Lady Ann halted their game for tea, Arabella and the comte had soundly thrashed their opponents. Suzanne, an adorable widgeon at cards, merely laughed gaily and fanned the deck of cards in colourful profusion about the tabletop.

"You were just like Jeanne d'Arc, strewing her enemy in her path," the comte said admiringly, and to Arabella's mortification, clasped her hand and brought it to his lips.

"You . . . you refine too much upon a simple game, Gervaise," she replied stiffly, knowing the earl's eyes had suddenly narrowed dangerously.

"No, the comte is quite right, Bella," Suzanne added. "A veritable dragon! Do you not recall, as a child, you were always trying to drum the strategy of the game into my head?"

"You have far too lovely a head for nonsensical games, Miss Talgarth," the earl murmured provocatively, and drew his arm through hers.

"You tell monstrous untruths, my lord," she cried. "Come, admit it, you could most willingly have wrung my neck when I trumped your winning spade!"

"His lordship finds the lovely Miss Talgarth most amusing, is it not so, cousin?"

Arabella raised black eyes to the comte's mocking face and said repressively, "I daresay, monsieur, but then again, I myself find Suzanne most amusing."

When, amid wraps and dashing bonnets, Lady Talgarth and Miss Talgarth took their leave, Arabella quickly excused herself, not meeting the earl's eyes, and hurried up the stairs. She locked the door to the earl's bedchamber, and heaved a sigh of relief, only to gasp with surprise as the door to the adjoining dressing room slowly opened. She stood frozen in the middle of the room, as the earl strode toward her.

He saw her eyes fly to the small nightstand, guessed her pistol lay in the drawer, and drew to a halt. He watched her closely as her hands balled into fists and her face paled in the dim candlelight. A picture of Arabella, dancing toward him in her nightgown, smiling confidently and unafraid, darted through his mind. Their wedding night seemed an eternity ago. He said to her in an even voice, "You will not need your gun tonight, Arabella. I merely came to wish you a good night."

She nodded her head jerkily and watched him turn about and stride into the adjoining room and close the door behind him.

Heavy pellets of rain slammed against the windows and cascaded in thick sheets onto the rows of rosebushes, flattening them against the outside wall of the library. Arabella sighed in frustration at her enforced inactivity and hurriedly scanned the dark-paneled shelves for a suitable book to while away the afternoon hours. How very strange it was that she, the Earl of Strafford's daughter, should be roaming furtively about the abbey, purposely avoiding nearly all of its occupants. Even Dr. Branyon, who was expected later in the afternoon for tea, had joined the ranks of those whose penetrating stares made her feel like a guilty intruder in her own home.

"Oh, damn, how absurd it is!" she muttered, and grabbed the first colorfully bound book that caught her eye. Once in the earl's bedchamber she realized with a wry grin that she had selected a book of plays by the French writer Mirabeau. As her French was as deplorable as her efforts at the pianoforte, deciphering the lines word by word brought her no pleasure. After a while she looked up from her shadowed corner and rubbed her eyes. She was struck again by her desire to be alone, be hidden away from everyone. Had she not unconsciously selected the darkest corner of the room to pass the afternoon?

By the time she had forced herself to translate the supposedly witty lines in the first act, the book lay open on her lap and her head languished drowsily against her arm.

Arabella was not certain what awakened her, perhaps her fear that the earl had come into the room to find her, but in an instant she was alert, her muscles tensed for action.

She gazed across to the more lighted portion of the room and saw with some confusion the stooped figure of Josette, Elsbeth's maid. The old woman moved to *The Dance of Death* panel, looked quickly about her, and began to run her gnarled hands over the carved, uneven figures on the surface.

Arabella rose from her chair and walked from her shadowed corner, a question already framed on her lips. "Josette, whatever are you doing here?"

The old woman jumped back from the panel, her arms flopping to her sides. She gazed in consternation at the young countess, her throat so dry with fear that only jumbled incoherent sounds erupted from her mouth.

"Come, Josette, whatever is so very interesting about *The Dance of Death* panel? If you wanted to examine it, you had but to ask me. Surely it is no excuse for you to be sneaking about!" Arabella frowned at Josette, her mind suddenly alert to the trapped, confused look on her face.

"Forgive me, my lady," Josette finally managed to utter in a strangled whisper, "it is just that I . . . that I . . ."

"You what?" Arabella demanded relentlessly, determined to get to the root of the matter. Why, the old woman looked as if she expected the grim laughing skeleton to reach out from the panel and grab her by the throat!

The old woman wrung her hands, clasping them over her sunken breasts. "Oh, my lady, I had no choice, I . . . I was forced to . . ." she broke off suddenly, her eyes rolling upward. Before Arabella could question her further, she broke into a frenzied, loping gait and fled from the room.

Arabella made no move to stop her. She stared at the closed door, wondering what the devil the old woman had meant. After a few moments she walked to *The Dance of Death* and stood for a long while gazing at the bizarre panorama of grotesque carved figures. She let her fingers move over the surface. The skeleton screamed his soundless commands to his demonic hosts. The panel was as it always was. Arabella stood a moment longer, then turned with a shrug and returned to her darkened corner.

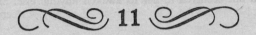

## 11

Arabella quietly slipped through the door of the adjoining dressing room, her wrapper knotted loosely about her waist and her black hair streaming down her back. She glided noiselessly to the earl's bed. "Justin, Justin, wake up!" She leaned over him, her voice an intense whisper.

His eyes flew open and he struggled up to a sitting position. "What? Arabella?" he asked, at once startled and alert. He could barely make out her pale features in the dim early light of dawn.

Arabella drew a deep breath. "It is Josette, Elsbeth's maid. She is dead, Justin. I found her but a moment ago at the foot of the main staircase. I . . . I think her neck is broken."

"Good God!" he said, threw back the bedcovers, insensible to the fact that he was quite naked, and added impatiently, "Come, Bella, hand me my dressing gown."

As she handed him the rich brocade dressing gown, she tried to avert her eyes, but found that her gaze nonetheless swept down his powerful muscular body. She stepped back nervously, sudden colour flooding her cheeks.

The earl appeared quite oblivious of her discomfiture, and said brusquely over his shoulder as he strode toward the door,

"Well, don't just stand there! Come on, Bella. You did come to me first, did you not?"

"Yes," she replied simply, now wondering briefly why it had not occurred to her to awaken anyone else. She took a double step to catch up with him. "I could not sleep, you see, and thought to fetch a glass of milk."

He waved away her explanation and said grimly, "Thank the lord the servants are not up and about yet."

She stood back as he leaned over the twisted form of the old woman and made brief examination. He rose after a moment and nodded. "You are quite right. Her neck is broken." He was silent, his gaze drawn up the stairs, then back to the shapeless body. A slow frown spread over his smooth brow, drawing his black brows together.

"What are you thinking, Justin?" Arabella asked, her eyes following his up the winding staircase.

"I am really not certain at this moment what I am thinking," he replied slowly. Suddenly efficient, he added briskly, "We must do first things first. Fetch a blanket to cover her while I carry her to the back parlour. I will send for Dr. Branyon."

Dr. Branyon arrived but an hour later, his face drawn with concern. He had imagined any number of frightful accidents, for the stableboy could tell him nothing.

As he gratefully accepted a cup of steaming coffee from Arabella later in the Velvet Room, he said, "There are several broken bones, but she died, as both of you supposed, from a broken neck in the fall down the stairs. 'Tis a pity." He sighed. "Lord, it is hard to believe that she has been in England for more than twenty years. She was Magdalaine's maid, you know. Elsbeth will be quite upset over her death." He turned to Arabella. "You have waked your mother? I suggest that Ann inform your sister. I will remain and give her a drought to calm her, if necessary."

"Yes, I have told Mother," Arabella replied. "She will be down presently."

Lady Ann remained with Elsbeth for most of the day, emerging only briefly for luncheon.

"I had no idea that my cousin would be so concerned over a servant's death," the comte observed, a hint of incredulity in his voice.

"Josette was like another mother to Elsbeth," Lady Ann

said quietly. "That Elsbeth feels her death sorely is not to be wondered at."

Arabella found that she was staring at the comte with open disapproval. As if he felt the restrained indignation of those present, the comte spread his hands before him in rueful apology and hastened to say, "Do forgive such an impertinent observation, Lady Ann. It must be that the English take such matters to heart more than we French do. Of course, you are correct. I applaud my cousin's feelings. An unfortunate accident, to be sure."

The earl rose abruptly and tossed his napkin over his plate. "Paul, if you would care to join me in the library to make final preparations . . . The coffin maker will be here shortly." He nodded to Lady Ann and Arabella and strode from the dining room.

It was late in the afternoon when the coffin maker left bearing his grim cargo. Though Arabella could not explain it, she felt compelled to observe his departure. The earl emerged from the great front doors to stand quietly beside her on the steps.

"God, how I hate death," she said hoarsely, more to herself than to him. "But look"—she pointed after the lumbering black coach that carried Josette's body—"it is like the very harbinger of death, with those black plumes on the horses' bridles and the ghastly black looped curtains in the windows." She added bitterly, "But look at me, swathed in all the trappings of death. I am a daily reminder that death's power is supreme! Oh, God, why do those we love have to disappear from our lives?"

The earl brought his eyes to rest upon her pale strained face and said gently, "Your question is the plaything of our philosophers. Even they can postulate only absurdities. Unfortunately, it must always be the living who suffer, for those we loved are beyond pain." He paused a moment to gaze out at the immaculate perfection of nature's making. "It is a depressing thought that we are set in the midst of this enduring nature for but a moment in time." He shook his head ruefully. "Now it is I who am talking nonsense! Bella, why don't you donate all your black gowns to the curate? Your love and memories of your father are within you, after all. Why submit yourself to the ridiculous restrictions of society?"

A thoughtful expression rested in her gray eyes. "Father always hated black," she admitted slowly. As she turned to go, she remembered Josette's strange visit to the earl's bedchamber the day before. "Justin, perhaps it is nonsense and means nothing at all, but Josette was sneaking about *The Dance of Death* panel yesterday afternoon. She did not see me, for I was dozing in that large chair in the corner of the room. She seemed frightfully upset when I took her to task for being in the earl's bedchamber. She scampered out as if the devil himself were on her heels."

The earl looked keenly down at her. "Do you recall, Bella, did she give you an excuse for being there?"

"Only some vague phrases about her being *forced* to be in the room. She really made no sense at all. Her behavior has become quite strange, you know. Perhaps her wits were so addled, she believed Magdalaine still to be alive and in the earl's bedchamber." She paused and shook her head.

"There is something else, Bella?" the earl asked, regarding her intently.

"You're going to think that I have rust in my bandbox, but what the devil! Justin, why ever was Josette wandering about in the middle of the night without a candle to guide her?"

For an incredible moment Justin felt himself drawn to a long-ago sweltering night in Portugal. He and several other soldiers were scouting the perimeter of a scrubby wooded area on the outskirts of a small village in search of the elusive guerrillas. There was an almost discernible odor of danger that reached his nostrils. He jerked his companions to their bellies against the rocky ground just as shots rang out above their heads. Now, as then, he scented danger—certainly not in the form of cutthroats lurking about the grounds of this stately mansion, but danger nonetheless. He felt he could say nothing of his vague feelings to Arabella, and thus turned to her and said lightly, without thought, "Perhaps old Josette was off to meet a secret lover. A candle would surely find her out!"

She withdrew from him as if she had suddenly been whisked to another county. She felt guilt and shame fill her eyes. His suspicions of her reduced her to flushed, bitter silence.

"Arabella, wait, I did not mean . . ." He stopped, angry with himself, but she was gone.

"Would you believe it, Bella? Our spotty viscount just happened, mind you, to be in the neighborhood on his way to Brighton! Mama cooed and made a great fuss over him! Bless Papa, for he treated him most vilely. Of course, it was his gout that made him so cross, but it sent Mama into a dither! How she scolded him about ruining my prospects!" Suzanne Talgarth drew up her mare and patted her neck. "Papa guffawed until he was positively purple in the face when I told him that if Arabella Deverill could catch an earl, then I was assured of a duke!"

Arabella reined in Lucifer and looked thoughtfully at her friend. "You know, Suz, it is a great joke, but I do not think it wise that—"

"Lord, Bella, whatever is the matter with you? What is not *wise*?" Suzanne demanded as Arabella's silence grew overlong.

Arabella shook her head. "You will think me a nodcock, undoubtedly, but when I think that girls are raised and encouraged to romantically idolize the vision of some ridiculous man who will be their husband—well, it makes me want to scream!"

"You must take care, Bella, for that sounds like a woman disappointed," Suzanne chided. "Come, I do not think you a nodcock precisely, I just think it unnecessary of you to be giving me advice. You know, sometimes I think it is you who are the great romantic, Bella, not me. Do you really believe me so naive as to think that I will find a *grand amour*?" She laughed and gently flicked the reins on Bluebell's glossy brown neck. "Come," she called over her shoulder, "we are almost at Bury St. Edmunds. It's such a lovely day, let's explore the ruins."

As neither young lady was much in the mood to explore the remnants of the long-ago days, Suzanne, being of a tenacious mind, soon dropped gracefully to a grassy mound in the shade of a large elm tree, patted the spot beside her, and continued her thoughts of many minutes before. "No, I would never believe in a *grand amour*. Indeed, such a notion is ridiculous, particularly after observing Mama and Papa all these years! In fact," she said with a tiny frown, "such a thing as love must indeed be for the common people."

"I had no idea you were such a snob, Suz," Arabella said wryly, smoothing the folds of her blue riding habit about her ankles. How marvelous it was to box away all those dismal black gowns!

"No, not a snob, Bella, merely a realist. Undoubtedly my duke will be well over forty, running to fat, and a gamester in the Carlton House set. But, do you not see, I will be 'your grace,' have countless servants to carry out my every whim, and enjoy what one is supposed to enjoy."

"You really do not believe in . . . loving the man you are to wed?" Arabella asked slowly, a knot of unhappiness twisting in her stomach.

"Fie, what a child you are, Bella!" She cocked her piquant oval face to one side and observed slyly, "Oh, I forget the handsome earl! He is a terribly dashing figure of a man, Bella. How lucky you are to wed such a *nonpareil* in a marriage of convenience! It was in your father's will, to be sure, but still, you could have done far worse for yourself!"

"Yes, it was my father's idea," Arabella said noncommittally, unable to prevent a tinge of bitterness from creeping into her voice.

"How strange it is," Suzanne mused after a few moments, "when we were children, I never quite imagined you as a married lady. You were always so very certain of yourself, so very forthright and strong. If you were not so pretty, you could probably pass quite well as a gentleman."

"You are being quite nonsensical, Suz. How indeed could you ever question that I would not marry? I would certainly not relish following in the footsteps of that ridiculous Stanhope woman, or, for that matter, my aunt Grenhilde! As to my being certain of myself and strong"—Arabella paused, carefully choosing her words—"perhaps it would be better for me now were I more bending . . . more submissive."

"I begin to think that you and the earl are in a tug of wills, Bella," Suzanne said severely. "And it is obvious to me that despite all the bravado and wild exploits of our youth, you are simply not wise in the ways of women."

"Whatever do you mean by that?" Arabella demanded, somewhat annoyed.

The twinkling laughter dropped from Suzanne's eyes and her voice dropped to a serious tone. "I will tell you, Bella. You have a strong character, but it is simply not a *woman's* strong character. No, now don't interrupt me, for I believe that I am getting to the kernel of the corn! I have never known you to dissemble, Bella. You are always forthright and honest to a fault. You see, that is exactly your problem. Gentlemen think that we dissemble even when we are honest. And when we dissemble, as we are forced many times to do, they do not know the difference anyway! Therefore, my dear friend, why disappoint them?"

"Such a sage you have become! My dear Suzanne, I invited you to ride with me to cheer me up. You must know that Elsbeth has sunk into total gloom since her maid, Josette, fell to her death. Here I find that all you wish to do is to dissect my character! It is too bad of you!"

Suzanne sighed and pursed her pink lips together. She stretched out her legs and wiggled her toes inside her soft calf riding boots. "I see that all my wisdom goes unheeded. I will tell you, Bella, I think you almost as much a romantic ninny as dear Elsbeth."

Arabella turned startled eyes to her friend. "Come, Suz, stop twitching your toes and tell me what you mean! Elsbeth a romantic? Why, the thought is absurd. She is such an innocent child despite her twenty one years!"

"Poor Arabella! Even Elsbeth knows how to dissemble. Have you not observed how she hangs on to the comte's every word? I swear she is much taken with the young Frenchman. He is her cousin?"

"Yes, of course he is her cousin. Her mother was his aunt. But really, Suz—"

"Oh, Bella, how can you be so blind? Your dear half-sister is not such an innocent child! I vow she has quite set her sights on her young cousin."

*Elsbeth and Gervaise? It cannot be possible! But wait, Arabella, think back. Have there not been many times when Elsbeth and Gervaise have both been absent during the day? Has Elsbeth not seemed to become more confident, more sure of herself? And she seems to talk so freely with Gervaise!*

The implications of such an admission to herself brought her surging to her feet. *Justin believes the comte to be my lover! I did not understand. I had no answers save my avowals of my innocence. Can it really be that Elsbeth, my shy, uncertain Elsbeth, is the comte's lover?*

Suzanne untangled her shapely legs and rose to stand beside Arabella. There was a blind glazed look in her friend's eyes that quite unnerved her. "Bella, what has upset you so? I daresay that I could be in the wrong about Elsbeth and the comte . . ."

Arabella turned to gaze down at her friend. "No," she said slowly, "you are really quite right. I have been blind to what is going on about me." She added urgently, her riding crop tightening in her hand, "I must return to Evesham Abbey now, Suzanne. I have much to think about."

Arabella swung upon Lucifer's back and dug in her heels before Suzanne could put two thoughts together.

The earl stared thoughtfully down at the single sheet of paper from his friend Lord Morton, of the ministry. Jack certainly conducted an efficient operation despite French control on the continent. He read the few lines once again, then shredded the letter and watched the fragments settle atop the logs in the grate. He lit a match and watched the remnants grow black about the edges and then crackle into orange flame.

He was on the point of leaving the library when the door opened and Lady Ann appeared. "My dear Justin, I am so glad that you have not yet gone out, for I wished particularly to speak with you."

The earl's thoughts flew to Arabella, and he grew instantly wary. "It is true that I was on the point of riding to Talgarth Hall, Ann, but of course I have still a few minutes. Would you care to sit down?"

Lady Ann disposed herself neatly on the sofa and patted the place beside her. She said quietly, "I have no intention of bringing up uncomfortable topics, Justin, so you may be at your ease. It is Elsbeth I wished to discuss."

"Elsbeth? Surely all decisions relating to her are in your domain, Ann." He crossed a booted leg over the other and waited none too patiently for her to speak.

"I . . . I know that you do not think . . . highly of Gervaise de Trécassis," she began slowly, aware that his eyes hardened at the mention of the young gentleman's name.

"You are quite right, Ann," he interrupted. "In fact, I intend to ask Elsbeth's young cousin to, shall we say, curtail his visit to Evesham Abbey."

Lady Ann shifted her position, cast a despairing glance at the earl's set face, and persevered. "I would that you would not, Justin, for it is to her cousin that Elsbeth has turned since Josette's death. He is all the family she has left, you know. I had guessed that you wished to send him away. Oh, Justin, can you not give Elsbeth more time to forget her sorrow? Just a week longer?"

*I could tell you much about our young Frenchman. What would you believe, my innocent Ann, were I to tell you that it is not Elsbeth who desires his company, but rather your own daughter?*

Before he could reply, the library door burst open and Arabella rushed into the room. She drew up short on the threshold, dismay flooding her face. "Oh, I thought you were alone, my lord! How . . . how are you, Mother?"

"I am quite well, Arabella. You make it sound as though I were a visitor in my own home, my dear. Do not rush away, for I was just on the point of leaving. Justin," she said as she rose, "please consider what I have said. Perhaps we can speak of it later." *This is something indeed,* she thought, patting her daughter's hand as she passed her, *Arabella seeking to be alone with her husband.*

Suddenly Arabella grasped her mother's hand and held it fast. The look on the earl's face was forbidding. It struck her forcibly that Suzanne's observation about Elsbeth and the comte might only serve to make her appear the more guilty in his eyes. If she had not been aware of the closeness between her half-sister and the comte, then most assuredly Justin would not have noticed. She wanted to strike out in her vexation. Even now she read mistrust and condemnation in his eyes. She drew back, positioning herself closer to the door, behind her mother.

" 'Tis not important," she managed to say. "I am sorry for having disturbed you, my lord . . . Mother. I think I shall go to my room now."

"Wait, Arabella," the earl said sharply as she turned to flee. Lady Ann was aware that Arabella was using her as a physical shield between her and her husband. She saw her daughter tense as the earl drew near to her. He pulled a key from his waistcoat pocket. "If you wish to go to the earl's bedchamber, you will need this key."

Lady Ann had held her peace long enough. "My dear child, first of all, I was just leaving. You did not interrupt us! Secondly, why ever, Justin, have you locked the earl's bedchamber?"

The earl replied smoothly, "I discovered loose floorboards about the room. I did not wish any of the servants to come to harm. Thus, until I have seen to repairs, I wish to keep the room locked. Here you are, Arabella."

"Thank you, my lord." Arabella clutched the key from the earl's outstretched hand, turned, and rushed from the room.

Lady Ann looked sadly after her daughter. "Oh, Justin, will you not tell me what is amiss between the two of you?"

"No, Ann," he replied firmly. "Now, if you will excuse me, I really must pay my visit to Lord Talgarth. I shall consider what you have said about the comte, Ann."

"You are both behaving idiotishly!" she cried, her frustration turning suddenly to anger.

The earl's black brows snapped together. "Do not press me, Ann," he said tersely.

"I shall press you, Justin," she flared, planting herself firmly in front of the door. "Arabella has never in her life been of a timorous nature. Yet I have seen her change since her marriage to you into a silent, withdrawn, even frightened girl. I demand to know just what the devil has happened! What have you done to my daughter?"

He stepped back, the angry set of his face turning to a look of intense bitterness. He spoke rapidly, and so very low that Lady Ann had to lean closer to him to make out his words. "Do not ask again, Ann, what I have done to your daughter! Timorous nature, indeed! If Arabella has learned to tread warily since our marriage, when in my company, she has only herself to blame! That I have retaliated in kind does me no honour; yet, I will tell you, any action I choose to pursue with your daughter is justifiable!"

"I . . . I do not understand you," Lady Ann cried. "You speak as though Arabella has done you a great wrong!"

"Such an observation you may pursue with your daughter, Ann, not me. I believe that I shall dine at Talgarth Hall. Your servant, ma'am!" He strode from the room without a backward glance.

## 12

Elsbeth inhaled deeply the sweet smell of fresh strewn hay. Her destination was a small stall in the far darkened corner of the barn. It had been at least a week since she had slipped away from Evesham Abbey to meet him here; indeed, now that she thought about it, Gervaise had not spoken to her of his masculine need for her since Josette's death. She honoured him for such noble sentiments. His sensitivity to her grief after her old servant's tragic fall made him all the more noble in her eyes.

Yet as she spread her cloak upon the straw, smoothing the edges with loving hands, she frowned. She had sensed that during the past several days there was much on his mind. She even imagined now, chiding herself even as she did so, that he had hesitated perceptibly at her blushingly offered suggestion that he meet her here this afternoon. His slight pause before agreeing brought jealous visions of Suzanne Talgarth to her mind.

The week that she had not lain with the comte had served to nurture her romantic notions that their physical union was an exquisite proof of their love for each other. She had even prayed that she would feel delight at the touch of his hands, swoon when his lips touched her.

She began to grow nervous as she waited in the dim-lighted stall. Surely he must have been detained by a very pressing matter! She was on the point of rising to stealthily gaze out the front door of the barn when she heard a rustle of movement and Gervaise slipped silently into the stall.

"Oh, my love," she breathed happily, "I was growing worried at your tardiness. Nothing serious occurred to detain you?"

The comte dropped gracefully onto the cloak beside her, taking in her flushed eager countenance. "No, dear Elsbeth. I was merely in conversation with Lady Ann. It would have been unseemly to excuse myself abruptly."

She leaned forward and clasped her arms about his neck. She felt so terribly guilty at any doubts she had had of him. She felt a light kiss touch her hair and waited for him to take her passionately into his arms. She drew back, a look of puzzled inquiry accentuating the almond shape of her dark eyes as he made no movement toward her. Surely after a week he should ardently desire her. "What troubles you, my love?" she asked softly, unwilling to acknowledge the instant of relief she had felt when he did not instantly gratify his desire.

"You are perceptive, my little cousin," he said gently. He considered his next words carefully. "You must know that the earl and I do not deal well together. His antipathy toward me grows daily. At times I have noted him observing me with narrowed eyes. He is scarcely civil."

"Oh, it is too bad of him!" Elsbeth cried, suddenly fearful. "He is jealous of you, Gervaise, I know it! He sees that you are the more refined gentleman, the more noble of character." She paused, her small features crumbling in dismay. "Whatever shall we do?"

Satisfied with her reaction, the comte smiled a tender, slightly bitter smile, and said softly, "You are always so sensitive to the actions of those about us, dear Elsbeth. Perhaps you are correct about the earl." He sighed forlornly, clasping her small hand as he did so. "In any case, just a while ago he more or less ordered me to leave Evesham Abbey by the end of the week. Our time together grows short, my love."

Elsbeth started forward. "Oh, no! It cannot be so! Gervaise, I cannot let you go away from me!" Tears gathered at the corners of her dark eyes and readied to streak down her pale cheeks.

The comte gently flicked away the tears and said bracingly, "We must be brave, dear Elsbeth. This is, after all, the earl's domain. His decisions, whatever his motives may be, must govern the actions of those about him. In short, I have no choice in the matter."

Elsbeth sagged to her knees, misery flooding her. She had lost Josette, and now she could lose Gervaise as well. "I will speak to the earl," she babbled. "Perhaps he will listen to me! No, I shall plead with Lady Ann, for she has a fondness for me. I will tell her of our love, that we wish to wed, that I shall die of unhappiness if you are torn from me!"

He knew momentary panic at the thought of her speaking either to the earl or to Lady Ann. "Ah, my little one," he interrupted urgently, stemming her frantic flow, "you must not—nay, I forbid you to—demean yourself in such a fashion!" He grasped her slender arms. "No, that is not the way. Listen to me, Elsbeth, we will make other plans. You will accompany Lady Ann to London when her period of mourning is over. I will meet you there and we will flee together. I will take you to Bruxelles."

The abject look of misery fell from her face at his words, and her eyes shone with excitement. "Oh, my dearest love, it is a fine plan! With my ten thousand pounds, we shall not have to worry about anything. You are so very clever, Gervaise, you will wisely invest it and make us terribly rich!"

Relief flooded through him. Now, at least, he need have no further worries about Elsbeth.

Suddenly the light in her shining eyes dimmed. "But, Gervaise, Lady Ann will not wish to go to London for another six months! Must we be parted for such a long time?"

The comte snapped his fingers. "We have spent years without knowing each other, what is a mere six months? You will see, little cousin, that the time will fly."

"I suppose you are right," Elsbeth said quickly, sensing that he was growing impatient with her protests. "But I shall miss you terribly."

"And I you." He scanned her gentle features, now finally certain that she was responding as he wished her to. He prepared to rise. She took him off his guard when she grabbed his hand and cried passionately, "Please stay with me now!"

He was stunned into momentary silence. The thought of making love to her brought a tightening to his chest that threatened to choke him. He tried to moderate his voice, to cloak the bitterness that gnawed deep within him. "Elsbeth, I do not think it wise that we meet like this again. You know that sharing each other gives me great pleasure, but 'twould be fatal to our plans were we to be discovered or even suspected. Surely you must realize that. We must think of the future."

Elsbeth was so caught up in the tragic vision of her and Gervaise being torn from each other that the gift of her body now seemed to be her ultimate pledge of her faith and love. Passion flowed through her. "Just one last time, then, Gervaise. Hold me and love me just this last time!"

The urgency in her voice, the passion shining from her dark eyes stirred revulsion in him, not at her, but at himself. Yet he could not let her doubt him. He forced himself not to pull away from her. He clasped her slender shoulders, leaned forward and pressed his lips against hers.

In her frantic desire to secure their final moments together, to lock them forever in her mind, Elsbeth forgot her fear and felt an exquisite tremor of desire sweep through her at his touch.

He felt cold, benumbed, and when her lips parted against his, he could bear it no longer. He jerked away from her and rose shakily to his feet. "Elsbeth, oh God, I cannot," he whispered. Her dark eyes grew almost black in her confusion and hurt. He tried to calm his voice, to reassure her. "I cannot, my little cousin. I—I have promised to ride with Arabella. Surely, you can see that if I am late, she might suspect. We must be brave, Elsbeth. The end to all this will come soon, I promise you."

"But Gervaise—" she began, then seeing the set cast to his features, silently nodded.

Before he crept stealthily from her, he kissed her lightly, passionlessly, on the cheek. She read intense sadness in his gentle gesture. She withheld her tears until he was gone from her.

Lady Ann lifted her booted foot and allowed the groom to

toss her into the saddle. "Thank you, Tim," she said as she adjusted the folds of her riding skirt becomingly about her legs. "I do not need you to accompany me, I am riding to Dr. Branyon's."

Tim tugged respectfully at the shock of chestnut hair at his forehead and stepped back as Lady Ann flicked the reins on her mare's neck. Tulip broke into a comfortable canter down the front drive.

The frown that Lady Ann had momentarily banished in the presence of the groom now returned to crease her forehead. She drew a deep breath of fresh country air and pulled Tulip in to a more sedate pace. The mare snorted her gratitude. "You are like me, you old lazy cob," she said half-aloud, "you stay comfortably in your pleasant stall and regard with a jaundiced eye anyone who disturbs your pleasure."

Lady Ann had not ridden in months, and she knew that her legs would protest their unnatural position in the morning. But even aching muscles did not seem important at the moment. She felt so very helpless and frustrated, her anger at Justin from the day before turned to deep melancholy. Evesham Abbey was a cold, immense empty tomb, and she found she could not bear it another moment. Justin was gone off somewhere, Arabella was very probably riding *ventre à terre* in any direction that would not bring her into contact with her husband, and as for Elsbeth and the comte, Lady Ann had not seen either of them since lunch.

It occurred to her as she wheeled Tulip toward Paul's tidy Georgian home that stood at the edge of the small village of Strafford on Baird (Baird being the serpentine river that flowed through the very center of the green), that Paul might not be at home. After all, unlike herself and the rest of the gentry, his time was occupied with concerns that were not always in his control.

They had not had much time together since Josette's death. Today she felt that she must see him, observe the ready twinkle in his brown eyes, let her frustration flow away at his words of solid good sense.

"Now, dear old Tulip, you can rest your tired bones," she said, turning her mare into the small yew-tree-lined drive.

"Afternoon, milady," she was hailed by a sturdy sandy-haired boy, tall and gangly-framed, nearly of an age as Arabella.

"It is good to see you again, Will," she replied as the boy limped forward to take the reins of her horse. "You are looking quite fit."

"Aye, milady, 'tis nearly well I am."

"Is Dr. Branyon at home, Will?" Lady Ann felt her breath catch in suspense.

"Aye, milady. Just returned from Dalworthy's. Crotchety old man broke his arm, you know."

"Excellent," she said, not hearing about the broken arm. "Please give poor Tulip some hay, Will." She slid gracefully to the ground and tripped happily up the three narrow steps. She grasped the old brass knocker and gave it a resounding thump. To her surprise, Mrs. Muldoon, Dr. Branyon's fiery, fiercely loyal Irish housekeeper, did not answer her summons.

"Ann! Good heavens, my girl, whatever are you doing here?" Dr. Branyon stood in the open doorway, his frilled white shirt loose about his neck, his face alight with astonished pleasure.

Lady Ann found herself flicking her riding crop nervously against her black boot. "I . . . I wanted to surprise you, Paul."

He smiled at her gently. "How rude of me, Ann. Do come in. I fear that we will have to fend for ourselves for our tea. Mrs. Muldoon left me in the greatest panic this morning for Leeds. It seems her sister and all three children have contracted the mumps!"

"Oh, how very distressing," Lady Ann said, not at all distressed. She followed Paul into the front parlour, a cozy, light-filled room that had always put her at her ease the several times she had visited his home.

"A charming confection," he said, eyeing her dashing riding hat with a grimace. "Do remove it."

"As you will, Paul." The bow under her left ear did not succumb to her fingers, and her fumbling brought a laugh from Dr. Branyon.

"Here, my dear, allow me." The bow magically unfurled at the touch of his hand. He lifted the bonnet from her blond curls with a grin and tossed it on a nearby table. "Now, come sit down and tell me what new calamity brings you here. 'Twas not just to surprise me, I know."

"You are right, Paul. 'Twas a calamity indeed! Justin and I finally came to verbal battle over Arabella. I could not bear to see the poor child in such a panic at even being near to him. It was not a particularly pleasant exchange."

"Come, my dear, slow down a bit. Tell me exactly what happened." Dr. Branyon lifted her white hand and squeezed it reassuringly.

Lady Ann embarked upon the scene with Justin and Arabella the day before in the library. "Before Justin hurled from Evesham Abbey to ride ostensibly to Talgarth Hall," she concluded, "he more than intimated that Arabella had done him a great wrong, and that if I wished to know the truth, I must pursue it with her. Of course, Bella avoids me, indeed all of the household, as if we were carriers of the plague!"

"What of the comte?" Dr. Branyon asked somewhat obliquely.

"Gervaise? Come, Paul, surely you can no longer suspect him of creating any haggling between Justin and Arabella. Why, he has been more with Elsbeth than with Arabella."

"Very well, Ann, I shall accept your word on that."

Lady Ann suddenly sat forward. "Oh, Paul, do forgive me. Here I am cutting up your peace with my stupid affairs! A cup of tea would be just the thing. But show me Mrs. Muldoon's hoard of canisters and I shall endeavor to brew something hot, that will, I trust, at least resemble tea."

Dr. Branyon looked for an instant as if he would say more. But he rose, held out his hand, and smiled tenderly down at her. "Come, my love, we will contrive together."

Lady Ann felt her cares slide from her shoulders as he grasped her hand in his. At his touch, she realized that a cup of tea was the last thing she wanted. She clutched at his hand and slid her other arm to his neck. She felt the strength and tautness of his body, felt herself being drawn willingly into the depths of his brown eyes. She wanted desperately to merge with him, to become one with him, to let him take her out of herself. He stood rigidly before her, unmoving. Vaguely she realized what she was doing, that he was trying not to encourage her in this folly, but she did not care. In a husky voice that she scarce recognized as her own, she whispered, "Oh, Paul, I do love you so. Please, my love, do not send me away."

He grasped her arm convulsively, as if to pull her away. She bent her energies on willing away his scruples. Always he wanted to protect me, she thought, and with a wistful beguiling smile she stood on her tiptoes and touched her lips to his. She felt a shock of awakening in him. She slipped her hand into the loose opening of his shirt and touched his smooth chest. As he still held stiffly away from her, she leaned forward and pressed her cheek against his bare chest.

Dr. Branyon felt suddenly like a drowning man who had no wish to be saved. He groaned into the lovely soft curls atop Lady Ann's head, and in a last token effort to save them from what he thought to be folly, said unsteadily, "Ann, my love, I do not wish to give rise to any gossip. You must realize that . . ." But as he felt her pursed lips close over his mouth, all his pent-up desire burst forth, and he pulled her fiercely to him.

Her smallness and fragility delighted him. The feel of her woman's rounded body, curving to meet his, its fullness and hollows merging against him, made him ache with desire. Earth-bound concerns wielded a last appeal, and before he swept her into his arms he asked with passion so thick upon his tongue that neither of them really heard, "Ann, you are certain . . . it is what you want?"

Her answer was mute. Her lips opened upon his mouth, tentatively searching, yet bold and venturesome. Scruples, reason, all fragments of his rational world dissolved at her silent gesture of acquiescence.

He took the worn carpet stairs two at a time, reminded fleetingly of the interminable years of nights he had wearily and alone trod to his bedchamber. He clutched her to his chest, as if to reassure himself that she was not some fantastic creation of his imagination.

He laid her in the middle of his large four-poster bed, as tenderly as he would a small helpless infant, and eased himself down beside her. He thought of her fear, born he knew of her husband's harsh, jaded appetites, and remembered how she had drawn away from him that day at the fish pond. He read no fear or hesitation today. Her blue eyes were bright with excitement and her cheeks flushed a delicate pink.

She moved her hands up about his neck and pulled insistently. "My dearest Ann," he whispered, and covered her mouth with his. Her lips parted as naturally as rose petals basking in the warmth of the spring sun.

He left her soft mouth to kiss her eyes, her delicate ears, her throat. He felt her fingers draw apart the loose string on his shirt. As her hands swept over his shoulders and down his bare chest, an urgency rushed through his body, leaving him trembling with desire. "God, Ann," he moaned into the hollow of her throat, "you are driving me to the brink of madness."

"Take me with you, Paul," she whispered. She pulled away from him and began to tug ruthlessly at the buttons on her riding jacket. As she rose to stand beside the bed, she felt a heady exhilaration, a sense of purpose and design. Swiftly she shrugged out of her riding jacket and unfastened the myriad small buttons on her white blouse. She loosed her skirt and with a gentle sway of her hips let it drop to her ankles. She stood a moment in her shift and riding boots, and was suddenly amused at the odd picture she must present. "I fear I must ask your assistance now, Paul." She laughed and raised a booted foot toward him.

He rose with alacrity, and she felt small and protected by his largeness. He whisked her up and tossed her on her back on the bed. " 'Tis against all common sense to pull off one's boots while standing." In a trice her boots had joined the pile of clothing on the floor. "Your shift, Ann," he said gently.

"Yes, my shift," she repeated in a whisper, and slowly drew the lace straps from her shoulders. It was the first time in her life that she felt no embarrassment about undressing in front of a man. Her stockings and shift slid down her legs together. Any uncertainty vanished in her at his sharp intake of breath.

"Come, Paul, I refuse to be alone in my natural state. 'Tis most unfair and grossly inefficient." He had really not thought to stand in front of her and strip to his natural state, for the evidence of his desire for her was painfully apparent.

He swept his eyes over her body and forgot himself. Naked, he eased down beside her, gently cupped her chin in his hand, and flooded her face with kisses. Slowly he let his hands move to her full white breasts. "God, but you are beautiful," he murmured. His fingers traced the faint white lines, stretch lines from her pregnancy with Arabella. He let his hand rove downward to her rounded belly. There were no marks of childbearing, the soft whiteness ending with delicate perfection in the blond wedge of curling hair. He let his fingers rest there, and brought his lips down to gently caress her breast.

She gasped aloud.

"Ann?" His eyes searched her face, alert to any sign of fear. Her eyes had taken on a kind of smoky sheen and she grasped his face between her hands with such passion that his doubts were dissolved a final time. His fingers grew more purposeful and rhythmic in their movement. She clasped her arms about his back, shudders of pleasure rippling through her.

"Paul, please," she cried.

He reared over her and with an immense effort at control slowly guided his manhood into her. He strove to govern his body, mentally reviewing every trivial event of the morning, even to the making of the cast for Dalworthy's broken arm.

Suddenly she tensed beneath him, and then quivering spasms racked her body, spinning her up and beyond herself. He felt her reach her ultimate pleasure, clasped her tightly to him, and gave his body its release.

Lady Ann whispered presently with languid humour, "Will you still marry me, Paul, now that I am a fallen, loose woman?" She lifted her face from the hollow of his neck.

He grinned at her wolfishly. "I will carefully consider the matter, beloved, when you have told me the sum of your competence. I would not wish folk hereabouts to believe that I have married beneath myself."

She gave a chuckle deep in her throat, replete with sated pleasure. "Beneath yourself? Oh, dear, whatever can we do, then, for I am most assuredly beneath you."

He tightened his grip about her back and buried his face into her loose blond curls. "I have a remedy for such a complaint," he said with a grin, sweeping his hands down to knead her rounded hips.

"One of your vile potions, I suppose," she complained breathlessly. She felt his flaccid manhood grow turgid against her belly and craved for the first time in her life to touch a man. She slipped her small hand down over his firm abdomen and grasped him.

He groaned and pressed her hips hard against him. "You

are a temptress, Ann." He clasped his hand over hers, and together they guided him inside her.

"Oh," she whispered, wondrous at how easily she was taking him into her.

He grinned, and grasping her hips, rolled her on top of him. "Now it is I who am quite beneath your touch."

Delicate colour suffused her face. As he pushed her up to sit astride him, her full breasts brushed his face, and masses of blond hair swung across his lips and chest. It did not matter that she did not reply, for her lithe, sensuous movements against him were ample response. He let his fingers tangle in the curls that swirled loose about her shoulders, then lowered his hands to knead her soft hips. He pushed her farther and farther in her pursuit of pleasure, until finally she flung back her head, grasped his shoulders, and cried aloud her release into the silent room. When she fell exhausted forward on his chest, he rolled her to her side and took his own pleasure.

Lady Ann awoke with languorous slowness and stretched her arms and legs with feline grace.

"Well, my little sluggard, 'tis about time you rejoined the rest of your fellow humans."

Lady Ann forced her lids to retract, and gazed into Dr. Branyon's twinkling brown eyes. He was seated beside her on the bed, and for a fleeting instant she thought she must be ill, with her beloved Paul in attendance.

"Oh, dear," she said obscurely, memory of her passion flooding through her. She felt a light coverlet over her, soft against her naked body. Reason with all its troublesome details brought her struggling to her elbows. "Good heavens! Paul, what time is it? How long have I slept?"

The coverlet fluttered downward, and unable to resist, Dr. Branyon leaned over and gently tugged the lacy edges from their resting place atop her breasts. He cupped her breast in his hand.

"Paul!" she cried, momentarily embarrassed, for her body responded to his gentle assault and her nipple grew taut with pleasure. She flushed scarlet and hastily pulled the coverlet up about her neck.

He laughed softly, lightly kissed her lips, and drew back. "I have brought my lady tea of my own making. I vow that Mrs. Muldoon would be quite proud of my prowess. As to the lateness of the hour, my dear, it is only teatime. You will not have to steal into Evesham Abbey fearful of your reputation!"

The strong dark tea curled pleasantly in her stomach and she sighed with pleasure. A shadow darkened the blue of her eyes. "How I wish I did not have to return." She sighed.

"It will not have to be for very much longer," he said carefully, setting his cup upon the tray. "I have been thinking, my love, while you slept. I see no reason why we should not announce this very evening that you will become my wife."

An impish grin curved up her lips. "I will succumb to your request, Paul, for I would be unable to keep myself from shouting my happiness to the world."

"You are prepared for the malicious gossip of our neighbors?"

"Fie on our neighbors! I have been so terribly decorous for all of my life. To possibly forgo the pleasure of Aurelia Talgarth's or Eliza Eldridge's company would not overly trouble me."

"And Arabella?"

"Oh, Paul, surely she must have guessed. Justin did, you know. I daresay it will come as no great shock to her. And, of course, she is very fond of you."

"If you are certain, Ann," he temporized.

She looked at him archly. "I begin to think that you protest too much! Can it be that now you have sampled the wares, you do not wish to—"

"If you ever say such a thing again, Ann, I shall throttle you!" His uncharacteristic forcefulness made her blink. He leaned over and ruffled her messed curls. "Come, little one, you must dress." He added with mock severity, "I do hope that you manage to suppress that complacent, quite smug smile, else everyone will most assuredly guess that you have been pleasurably occupied this afternoon."

She tried to bring down the corners of her mouth and failed. She said with adorable frankness, "Paul, I had no idea that love . . . physical love could be so . . . well, *enjoyable.*"

The twinkle in his brown eyes warmed her. "I would fill your days and nights with such pleasure, Ann. We must hope that the folk hereabout will come to no serious harm, at least in the next year, for the doctor intends to be very busy at home."

"Only for a year, Paul?" she murmured provocatively.

He rose and gave a shout of delight. "Perhaps a year and a half, then." He whisked the coverlet back and grasped her about the waist. He was intoxicated at the sight of her. Regretfully he withdrew his hands. "If I help you to dress, you just might end up having to steal into Evesham Abbey!"

Lady Ann arrived at Evesham Abbey in barely enough time to dress for dinner. "I shall join you shortly, Paul," she whispered. Turning to the butler, she said, "Crupper, do tell Cook that Dr. Branyon will be with us for dinner this evening."

"Yes, my lady." Crupper nodded, dourly observing the unusual sparkling countenance of his mistress. "If you will accompany me to the Velvet Room, Dr. Branyon. You would prefer a glass of sherry, sir?"

"That would be fine, Crupper." Dr. Branyon winked at Lady Ann and dutifully followed the dignified Crupper down the corridor.

Crupper eyed Dr. Branyon as he presented him with a glass of sherry. He had not lived in this world for sixty-two years without becoming adept at scenting romance. Though the doctor was not a lord, he was nonetheless a fine gentleman. 'Twas the first time, he thought, ruminating on the situation as he descended the flagstone steps into the kitchen, that he had ever seen the Lady Ann so very . . . He fell back on "sparkling," unable to find precisely the apt word for her glowing person. True, it was but a short time since his lordship's demise, but what matter? Miss Arabella was settled with the new earl, and life was too short anyway to worry overly about such things. He smoothed his sparse gray hair, wondering if Lady Ann would cease to be a "ladyship" when she wedded Dr. Branyon.

Had Lady Ann not felt so unbearably happy, she would have felt the undercurrent of tension at the dinner table. She saw the participants at the large table through a pleasant blur, their words and tones softened by the time they penetrated through her haze of contentment. She felt a slight blush steal over her cheeks when Dr. Branyon, upon folding his napkin and clearing his throat, rose at his place.

"Justin . . . monsieur," he said in a clear voice, "before the ladies adjourn to the Velvet Room and leave us to our port, I should like to make an announcement."

Only the earl's clear gray eyes held comprehension at the doctor's preface. Arabella looked up with detached interest.

Dr. Branyon, having noted the knowing gleam in the earl's eyes and the supportive nod of his head, proceeded with aplomb. "Lady Ann has done me the honour of accepting my hand in marriage. We shall marry as soon as possible and, of course, live very quietly until her nominal year of mourning has passed."

The earl rose with alacrity and raised his glass. "My congratulations, Paul, Ann. It is no great surprise, to be sure, but still a welcome occasion. I propose a toast—to Dr. Branyon and Lady Ann!"

Arabella's fingers froze about the stem of her wineglass. *No great surprise! My mother and Dr. Branyon? Oh, Father! Your body is rotting in some forgotten ruin of a village in Portugal and your wife is calmly planning to wed another man!*

Bitter, angry words rose like bile in her throat. She gazed across the table at her mother and saw with barely contained fury the delicate pink of her cheeks, the new brilliance of her eyes.

"Arabella. The toast, my dear." She turned her head and stared stupidly at the earl. She heard the hint of sternness in his voice. He approved the match! She turned her eyes to Elsbeth and Gervaise. With her newly acquired insight, she saw them almost as one being, Elsbeth's dark eyes and hair blending, as if with the same artist's brush, into a blurred mold of Gervaise. It was as if one pair of almond-shaped eyes regarded her, their focus as one, their thoughts as one . . . their bodies as one. She thought they showed mild surprise, nothing more. Was she the only one who had not guessed?

"Arabella, child, are you all right?" Her mother's gentle voice, so vibrant with concern. Was there a pleading note in her tone? Was she seeking approval from her daughter, seeking forgiveness for her betrayal?

*My blindness has known no bounds. I have been but a wooden puppet, unseeing, my very mind and thoughts frozen inside myself. How very surprised Dr. Branyon appears at my silence. Does he believe that I will condone his deception? God, has my mother been his mistress all those years?*

"Arabella!"

*My husband's voice, harsh now, condemning. Does he not see, does he not understand?*

Arabella rose unsteadily from her chair, her fingers clutching white on the edges of the table. She felt crushed with the weight of her own unawareness. Her voice sounded out as a fallen autumn leaf, its spine snapped and broken underfoot. "Yes, Mother, I am quite all right. Did you call for a toast, my lord? Very well, you shall have your toast!" She clutched the frail wineglass in her hand, raised it slowly, and with the precision of despair hurled it at the marble fireplace. The crystal shattered into a myriad of tiny slivers, tinkling as they fell upon the cold hearth. She felt as if each tiny piece of glass were piercing at her very being. She heard a shocked, sharp intake of breath—from whom, she did not know. Only vaguely did she see the earl move angrily from his chair. She whirled about and raced from the dining room.

Justin threw his napkin down upon the tabletop. "Paul, Ann, do not attend to her! Please, all of you"—his voice embraced Elsbeth and the comte—"take your coffee in the Velvet Room. If you will excuse me now, I would speak to my wife."

Lady Ann's face was perfectly white, her lips drawn in a thin line, for she did not wish to cry. She saw the smoldering anger in the earl's gray eyes and sought frantically for some way to protect Arabella from his wrath. "Justin," she cried, half-rising. He did not attend to her, and strode without a backward glance from the dining room.

Dr. Branyon walked to her side and clasped her hand. "Come, my dear," he said gently, "let us go into the Velvet Room as Justin said. Elsbeth . . . monsieur?"

Lady Ann said sadly, "How very stupid of me not to have realized, even foretold Arabella's reaction! She worshiped her father, you know."

The comte was so startled by Arabella's outburst that he acquiesced with a mere nod. He slid Elsbeth's arm through his. As they followed Lady Ann and Dr. Branyon past the wooden-faced footman, Elsbeth suddenly tugged at his arm, holding him back.

"Oh, Gervaise, whatever shall we do now?" Her lower lip trembled and her features crumbled in consternation.

As he was thinking about Arabella, he did not immediately grasp the significance of her despairing tone. "London," she whispered urgently. "Lady Ann was to take me to London! Now she will not go. Whatever shall we do?"

He dropped his voice to a consoling caress. "Do not worry, little cousin. I shall simply devise another plan. Do not, I pray you, make your stepmother think you do not approve her choice. Such a display as Arabella gave was, I thought, most distasteful." He sensed that Lady Ann was a supporter, and he had no intention of appearing backward in his felicitations.

"Yes, Gervaise," she replied, brightening. "I also think that Arabella's behavior was most shocking. You will think of something, I know you will."

Justin strode into the main hall and made directly for the staircase. He took the steps two and three at a time and was midway to the first landing before Crupper realized his destination. He waved his hand at the earl's back, shook his head when there was no response, and turned back to his post by the front doors. He simply refused to shout after his lordship. Such an ill-bred action! Certainly not done in a nobleman's establishment!

The earl's anger was evident even to Grace, Arabella's maid, who scurried from his path the moment she saw his forbidding countenance. His nostrils flared and angry cords stood out taut on his neck. How dared she serve her mother such a devastating blow? he thought angrily. Had she not eyes in her head to see where Lady Ann's affections were so obviously placed?

Justin jerked at the handle on the bedroom door. It was locked, as of course he had expected it to be, but his futile fumbling at his own bedroom door only added to his anger. He flung into the adjoining room and sent his valet, Grubbs, staggering back in surprise.

"My lord!"

Justin paid no heed, and but an instant later stood in the middle of the earl's bedchamber. He wanted to bellow out her name, but saw that the room was quite empty. "Be damned," he swore, turned on his heel, and strode back downstairs.

"Crupper, have you seen her ladyship?" he demanded, crossing the flagstone of the entrance hail.

"Why, yes, my lord," Crupper replied with prim composure. He sniffed with overt disapproval.

"Well?"

"Her ladyship left the house, my lord. Very quickly, I might add, if you will forgive my saying so."

"Damnation, man," the earl exploded. "Why the devil did you not tell me before?"

Crupper drew to his full height. "If you will pardon my liberty, my lord, your lordship was near to the top of the stairs before I was aware of your presence."

"I am beset with witless fools," the earl muttered, and swept past the offended butler into the warm night.

It did not occur to the earl to simply let her return whenever she wished to. He mentally reviewed her favorite haunts—the old abbey ruins, the fish pond, perhaps even the Deverill cemetery. For some reason he could not define, he knew that she would not be bound for any of her usual places. No, he thought with decision, she would seek escape, away from Evesham Abbey, away from her mother, away from him. Lucifer!

Without a further check on his reasoning, he ran full tilt to the stables. He was just in time to see Arabella, her skirts billowing out about her, astride Lucifer, galloping away into the dark night.

"James," he yelled.

His spindly-legged head groom emerged in the lighted doorway, his protuberant eyes widening at the sight of his master's face. He waited miserably for a raking-down from the earl, but none was forthcoming. The earl knew that Arabella's word was indisputable law with all the servants.

"Fetch my stallion, James, and be quick about it, man!"

"Aye, my lord." James scurried away, the urgency in the earl's voice lending speed to his every movement.

As the seconds crept by, the earl was mentally calculating the distance that Arabella would have on him. His bay stallion was Marmaluke-trained and of Arab stock. But Lucifer! Damn, the beast was strong as ten horses and fast as the wind.

The moon hung as a slim crescent, barely lighting the vague outlines of the country road. The earl rode, head down, nearly touching his horse's glossy neck, his body molding into the form of the animal. His intense demanding pace brought back memories of another ride in the night, so long ago in faraway Portugal, the critical dispatch folded carefully in the lining of his boot. He felt the same sense of purpose and urgency. He had been elated with the success of his mission when horse and man had very nearly dropped from fatigue at the end of the eight endless hours.

Rickety turnstiles, unpainted wooden fences, small rutted paths—all flew past in a blur of semidarkness. The earl knew of a certainty that Arabella would stay to the main road. She would want nothing to impede her headlong flight.

As he rode, he pictured again her reaction. Even though he was forced to admit to himself that he did indeed understand why she had behaved as she did, his anger still did not diminish. He wanted to run her down and wrest her from her horse's back. His eyes glittered at the prospect of her pounding at his chest, ranting at him.

At first he could not believe his eyes. Were he not so very angry with her, he would have been sorely tempted to laugh aloud at the very undramatic scene before him. In the middle of the road walked Arabella, in full evening dress, leading a limping Lucifer.

She halted as he reined in beside her. "Well, madam, I see that you have ended your own merry chase!" He swung from the saddle and faced her, legs apart, his hands on his hips.

She seemed oblivious of his anger, to the ferocious irony of his words. "Yes," she said wearily, "Lucifer threw a shoe. I shall have to speak to James. It is quite ridiculous that he should throw a shoe."

The earl frowned. This was not at all what he had expected. He fanned his anger. "Of course, such a very tame ending to your thoughtless ride must be a letdown! Did it not occur to you, you corkbrained little fool, that you could have been beset by robbers? Ended up in a ditch with your neck broken?"

"No, but now that you have pointed it out, I shall regret that neither occurrence befell me." Her gray eyes were wintry, cold ice crystals gleaming in her pale face, her voice leaden and flat. It seemed to him as if she was disagreeing with him over some inconsequential, quite paltry matter.

He ground his teeth and advanced a measured step toward her. She stood her ground and regarded him with at best casual interest. "Do you plan another rape scene, my lord, or perhaps a beating? If you will allow me a choice, I would far prefer the beating."

He had expected anger on her part, indeed rather looked forward to her unbridled she-devil behavior. But yet, he thought, there seemed to be no passion left in her. Her voice and very stance seemed uncaring, remote.

He found that he wanted to push her to anger. He said contemptuously, "Despite what you may think, raping you would bring me no pleasure. As to beating you, I would as soon waste my energies flailing a spiritless old horse!"

She turned away from him indifferently. "If you have done with me, then, my lord, it is a long walk back to Evesham Abbey." She tugged at Lucifer's reins.

"No, madam, I am by no means done with you!" he said harshly. "What I have to say to you is best done far away from the ears of your family."

She dropped Lucifer's reins, walked to the side of the road, and sat down on the grassy bank. "Very well, then, be done with it."

He strode over to her and stood facing her. He seemed almost like a black silhouetted giant of a man, blocking the moonlight from her eyes. She turned and fastened her gaze on the bank beside her, and waited.

"Damn you, Arabella, look at me!" he exploded.

She made no move to obey him. He dropped to his knees in front of her and grasped her shoulders, shaking her until she raised her eyes to his. "Now, you will listen to me, you rag-mannered termagant! How dared you serve your mother such a turn? Even the meanest intelligence could have easily deduced that she cares mightily for Dr. Branyon. I admit that I expected their announcement to come a bit later, but it is of no importance. Your mother deserves happiness. God knows, a good deal of the nineteen years she spent with your father could not be termed pleasant. Why, Arabella, why were you so unthinkingly cruel to her?"

He saw flames of anger kindle slowly in her icy wintry eyes. "Why, Arabella?" he demanded, pushing her further.

"How dare you approve such a match!" she hissed between clenched teeth. "Even publicly proclaim your approval! You had no right, my lord, just as she has no right to so crassly betray my father's memory! No, I had no idea that she had formed a *tendre* for Dr. Branyon. I think her actions, as well as his, to be despicable and dishonourable!"

She was panting now, bitter venom erupting from her

throat. "Should I perhaps congratulate my dear mother for at least waiting for my father's death? Just how long, my lord, do you think they have been lovers? Poor Father! Cuckolded by a faithless wife and a man he trusted!"

He looked into her distraught face and found that he could not question the anguish of her words. He groped frantically to understand her. She had spoken openly, bitterly of her mother cuckolding her father, and her rage at the belief that her mother had been unfaithful to her father could leave no doubt at the sincerity of her condemnation of such an act. Yet had she not herself taken a lover before they had married? Had not she cuckolded him? Had she some sort of strange morality that had allowed her to take a lover before she married? And, for that matter, had she willingly given up the comte after her marriage to him? He wanted to throw her own act in her face, demand that she explain to him. Yet he found that his anger was melting away at the misery of the woman behind the facade of destructive words. He had to deal with her bitter despair over her mother first. He silenced his questions. He masked his voice with calm authority, for he knew that she would despise any gentling emotion coming from him.

"You must stop your ranting now, Bella, and attend to me. I find it extraordinary that I, who have known Lady Ann only passingly during the past several years, would swear upon my honour that she was never unfaithful to your father. Whereas you condemn her with a snap of your fingers! No, Arabella, do not turn away from me. Do you honestly believe that she would be capable of such an act?"

She gazed at him stonily, unspeaking.

"Very well. Though you do not wish to answer me, I will assume that you are pondering my words. Now, to your father." The earl paused a moment, weighing even now whether or not to speak forthrightly, without distorting the truth. He decided that only if she knew the truth about her father could she be brought to find forgiveness for Lady Ann. He said quietly, "Do you remember when we first met—by the fish pond the day your father's will was read? You cannot deny that you thought me your father's bastard—you openly spoke your beliefs."

"Stop it!" she cried angrily. "That is quite different, as you well know!"

"Different? Are there different rules of conduct for a husband? I will tell you, Arabella, your father's marriage to Lady Ann was a sham. He wed her only for the huge dowry she brought to him. He spoke openly of his 'bargain' and of his derision of her merchant family. He thought nothing of openly flaunting his mistresses."

She tried to clap her hands over her ears, to shut out his hated words.

"No cowardice from you, now!" he said harshly, pulling her hands to her sides.

"I will not listen to you! You are making this up to protect her!" Yet she felt the coldness of doubt sweep through her.

"No, Arabella, I have no need to invent stories. In fact, several times when I met with your father in London and in Lisbon, even once in Brussels, I was entertained most charmingly by his mistresses. I remember him joking about his little milksop of a wife, about her coldness, her bourgeois fear of him. He said to me once, admittedly when he was in his cups, 'You know, my boy, I have at least forced the little fool to see to my pleasure. She does not do it well, but I am a tolerant man. One should be, of course, to one's wife.'"

"No!" she gasped, quite white. "He could not . . . Please, Justin, he did not say those things!"

"Yes, Bella, he did. He was a man of demanding, extreme passions. That Lady Ann suffered from his nature is to be regretted. But do you not see, his very nature also made him a great leader. His men trusted him implicitly, for he never felt fear or uncertainty. He launched offensives that would have left lesser men trembling in their boots." The earl softened his voice. "His character also gave you a father to admire, respect, and adore. He loved you above all things, Arabella. I do not wish you to condemn him or blindly exalt him, for he deserves neither. I remember he told me once, not above a year ago: 'Be damned, Justin! It is just as well that my Bella had no brothers. After her, they would perforce have been disappointments to me.'"

She did not reply, yet he knew she was listening intently to him now.

"I would that you now consider your mother. She was unflaggingly loyal to your father, and you cannot question that she loves you dearly. She deserves your understanding, Bella

. . . your approval . . . else you have dimmed her chance for happiness."

Arabella rose slowly to her feet and shook loose blades of grass from her skirt. He stood beside her. His eyes searched her face for a clue to what she was thinking. He sensed a change in her, yet he could not be certain. He wondered if perhaps she was thinking of her own sham of a marriage, a marriage of convenience that she dreaded enough to seek comfort in the arms of another man. He remained silent, waiting for her to speak.

"It grows late, my lord," she said finally. "If you would not mind, I would ride pillion. Would you send James to fetch Lucifer?"

He responded to her matter-of-factness calmly. "Of course." He tethered Lucifer, then cupped his hand and tossed her onto his horse's back. He mounted behind, waited for her to arrange her skirts about her comfortably, rested his arms lightly about her waist, and click-clicked his horse forward.

It occurred to him that he had not even asked her just where she had intended to ride. Most probably, he thought, she had had no idea herself. Arabella was so wrapped up in settling her own thoughts about her father and mother that it was not until they had nearly reached Evesham Abbey that she realized how strange her bitter denunciation of her mother must have seemed to him. She felt his hands lightly about her, but she did not turn her gaze from the road ahead. Whatever her mother had or had not done, there was to be forgiveness for her, yes, and understanding. But not for her.

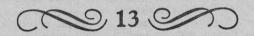

# 13

The earl did not see his wife from the time she had slipped quietly away from him the night before until well after breakfast the following morning. He stood at the breakfast-parlour window sipping his second cup of coffee, gazing out onto the colorful parterre. He saw Arabella there, walking beside Lady Ann, her longer stride shortened to match her mother's step. Though he could not, of course, hear their words, he fancied he saw Arabella smile. He turned from the window, he saw Arabella take her mother's hand into her own. A smile softened his features and remained there, even as he bid Crupper a resounding good day.

"A good morning to you, my lord," Crupper said, sensing that order had finally been restored.

"I shall be in the library, Crupper," the earl said in passing.

"Yes, my lord."

The earl's smile became rueful. "Ah, Crupper, I shall also be eminently disturbable." He had not gotten beyond a second column of numbers for spring market prices when Crupper most obligingly entered the library and pulled him from the task.

" 'Tis Lady Talgarth and Miss Suzanne, my lord. There is also a gentleman accompanying them—a Lord Graybourn."

"The spotty viscount," the earl said half to himself. "They are in the Velvet Room, Crupper?" He rose and shook out the fine lawn ruffles at his sleeves.

"Yes, my lord. The family are there, of course." He sniffed. "I might add, my lord, that the young French comte is still here."

The earl, aware of Crupper's distaste for the French in general and Gervaise in particular, merely smiled as he fell into step behind his black-clad butler.

The earl heard Lady Ann say without guile to the turbaned dowager, "Dear Aurelia, how very kind of you to pay us a visit this morning!" Lady Ann tried to keep her eyes from straying to Lady Talgarth's bosom, which strained against a style of gown much too young for her years and bulk.

"Ah, here you are, my lord," Lady Talgarth said, turning to welcome the earl. "We were showing our dear Lord Graybourn about the countryside. A visit to Evesham Abbey cannot be excluded from such a jaunt!"

"Certainly a pleasure, ma'am," the earl murmured. He lifted her beringed hand and kissed her plump fingers.

A merry smile played about Suzanne Talgarth's pink lips as she observed the earl's gallant display. She said softly to Arabella, who stood at her side, "If only poor Lord Graybourn had thought to kiss Mama's hand! I vow had he done so, Mama would have forced me to wed the little toad!"

"Here, I forget my manners, my lord!" Lady Talgarth reluctantly withdrew her hand from the earl's and turned to Lord Graybourn. "My dear Edmund, allow me to present you the Earl of Strafford."

The earl turned to take in the viscount's physical appearance. Lord Graybourn had not been particularly favoured by nature, only by fortune and birth. He was not above medium height, and the extra weight he bore made him look shorter than his actual inches. In five years, he would be fat as a flawn! He was endowed with rather protuberant eyes of an indeterminate colour. He affected dandyism, a most unfortunate circumstance, for the heavy jewel-encrusted fobs and rings, the high starched shirt points, and the fawn breeches that stretched over his ample stomach were simply not suited to his person.

Surprisingly, Lord Graybourn had a quite firm, pleasant voice. "A pleasure, my lord. I trust we do not inconvenience you with our visit this morning."

"Not at all. It is always a pleasure to see our nearest neighbors." The earl took the offered hand and pumped it. He drew the viscount forward for introductions to Arabella, Lady Ann, Elsbeth, and finally Gervaise. He was pleased that no quelling frown was necessary for Arabella. Indeed, she greeted the viscount warmly, politely inquiring after his journey from London.

Gervaise appeared to undergo a pronounced foreign transformation. He lisped his greeting to the discomfited viscount, who did not understand a word he said, and proffered a deep, flourishing bow reminiscent of the French court of Louis XVI. The viscount, believing such a formal greeting was in deference to his own noble lineage, and not wanting to seem discourteous, endeavored courageously to return a bow of similar style. His cumberland corset creaked in protest at such an unnatural demand.

Gervaise flashed a dazzling, knowing smile and gazed around complacently.

Even though he had succeded in making the poor viscount look the fool, he was not to be rewarded. He saw an angry gleam in Arabella's eyes. To his further chagrin, Elsbeth, who had stood quietly at Lady Ann's elbow, stepped forward and said in a clear, sweet voice, "I am Elsbeth Deverill, Lord Graybourn. I am most delighted to meet you, sir." She extended her small hand, and the viscount, in a flight of confident gallantry, brought her fingers to his lips. She blushed charmingly and dipped a curtsy.

"The pleasure must belong to me, Miss Deverill," he replied. For some reason quite unknown to him, he felt loath to release the hand in his grasp.

"But look, Bella," Suzanne whispered, "your French cousin has had his nose much put out of joint! And to think that I dreaded this visit!"

Lady Ann interposed. "Come, let us all be seated. I shall ring for tea and morning cakes."

Once they had taken their places, Arabella turned to Lord Graybourn. "What news can you give us of the fighting in the Peninsula, sir?"

Lord Graybourn sought frantically to piece together bits of

news that came from time to time to his unwilling ears. While always ready to denounce Napoleon with patriotic fervor, he found the details of battles and the precarious fates of the European countries to be tedious in the extreme. He cleared his throat, dusted cake crumbs from his fingers, and replied with what he hoped to be the voice of informed authority, "Most proper that your ladyship should inquire," he said, remembering that the former Earl of Strafford was a famous military man. " 'Twould appear that in the Peninsula the issue remains undecided. Of course, all of England still suffers from Napoleon's blockade. I understand," he continued carefully, not wishing to disappoint the daughter of the famous Lord Deverill, "that Percival is under continuous pressure from both at home and abroad."

"Shocking!" Lady Talgarth exclaimed with vague disapproval.

"Yes, but what precise news of the Peninsula?" Arabella persevered, not realizing that the poor viscount had given her every scrap of news he could remember. He floundered.

The earl interposed smoothly. "Did I not tell you, my dear? Massena is now in Portugal with sixty thousand men under his command. From my information, I understand that Wellington will launch an offensive against him in the fall. With the experience and pluck of Wellington's men, I believe we will taste victory."

Lady Ann added, "Let us also hope that Wellington will not have to turn his eyes elsewhere. Do not forget that with Napoleon's marriage to Marie Louise only four months ago, Austria now owes no loyalty to England. The French emperor is very carefully scattering England's friends to the four winds."

"French emperor indeed! I have heard it said that the Corsican has deplorable manners," Lady Talgarth proclaimed to no one in particular.

Arabella said with a twinkle in her eyes, "But, my dear ma'am, judging from the continuous cortege of mistresses, right under the nose of Josephine, it would seem that not everything about the man is deplorable."

"Humph!" Lady Talgarth huffed.

"Bella, surely now he has mended his ways," Suzanne said with a saucy smile. "After all, he has a new bride to cherish."

Elsbeth said with great conviction, "How I grieve for the

poor Austrian princess! Torn from her family as a political bribe to that horrid man!"

"Do not forget, Miss Deverill, that Napoleon ardently desires an heir," Lord Graybourn said, much struck by the young Miss Deverill's sensibilities.

"We poor women!" Suzanne sighed soulfully. "Bartered and traded about so that we can be the carriers of your precious men's names!"

The earl laughed. "Come, Miss Talgarth, you paint us as uncaring fellows. 'Tis most unjust of you."

Arabella said quietly, "You do not agree, then, my lord, that most gentlemen prefer their wives to remain quietly in the background, bearing their offspring and unobtrusively spinning away at their looms?"

"You do speak metaphorically, do you not, my dear? I cannot imagine you spinning, or, for that matter, occupied quietly in any pursuit for more than five minutes."

Suzanne lifted her saucer in mock toast to the earl. "Quite true. Admit, Bella, his lordship has scored a point! Just yesterday during our ride, I could not hold you in conversation for much longer than five minutes!" Suzanne wrinkled her nose at Arabella, who promptly fell into uncomfortable silence. She could hardly defend herself in front of the earl, Elsbeth, and Gervaise.

"Even as a child, Arabella," Lady Talgarth admonished, "you were always bounding about! How very unsettling for your dear mama."

Lady Ann said with a smile, "I have always admired Arabella's energy, dear Aurelia. Though perhaps it was unsettling upon occasion, I never knew boredom. That, I think, is most important."

Lord Graybourn followed this exchange with difficulty. The Countess of Strafford seemed a most pleasant young lady with a ready wit, certainly not at the moment at all bounding about. He was not certain that he quite approved the rather sour note added by Lady Talgarth. He turned to Elsbeth to change the topic. "Have you ever visited London, Miss Deverill?" he asked kindly.

"Not as yet, sir. I had thought to . . ." Elsbeth lapsed into silent embarrassment, her almond eyes flying to Lady Ann.

Lady Ann said with composure, "Our plans are at present rather uncertain, Lord Graybourn. But I do not doubt that

Elsbeth will accompany us for an extended stay during the winter."

"Oh, Bella, you are going up to London?" Suzanne asked excitedly. 'Tis famous! What fun we shall have!"

There was a hint of defiance in Lady Ann's calm voice. "No, Suzanne, I do not speak of Arabella. Elsbeth will accompany me and my husband to London."

Lady Talgarth rocked back in her chair. "My dear Ann! Whatever do you mean?"

The earl interposed gracefully. "Allow me, Ann, to give our happy news to Lady Talgarth. We will shortly welcome Dr. Branyon into the family, ma'am."

"My congratulations, Lady Ann," Lord Graybourn said heartily, unaware that he had slipped into dangerous waters.

"I thank you, Lord Graybourn," Lady Ann replied with quiet dignity. "Dr. Branyon has been a dear and loyal friend of the Deverill family for countless years."

Lady Talgarth drew up her formidable bosom. "My *dear* Ann! You cannot mean it! Why, how very *odd* of you, indeed!"

Mother and daughter drew together. Arabella turned to the incredulous Lady Talgarth and raised her black brows with arrogant hauteur. "I daresay *some* might consider it *odd*, ma'am. I myself think that my mother is far too young and beautiful to remain a widow." Her eyes flitted with silent emphasis over the matronly figure of Lady Talgarth, who was enviously aware that she was not many years older than Lady Ann. Arabella added, her voice softening as she turned to her mother, "Dr. Branyon is a man of the highest character and respectability. I will welcome him as my stepfather."

Bravo, Arabella, the earl silently applauded. He nodded with a smile to his wife.

Lady Talgarth suddenly harked to the fact that Lady Ann was not, after all, of the gentry born. She had even heard it mouthed that Lady Ann was of merchant stock. She drew her lips into a tight line of disapprobation. Breeding will tell, she decided with a superior shrug. She wanted to box her daughter's ears when Suzanne said exuberantly, "I think it is marvelous, Lady Ann! Dr. Branyon is a trump! I did not like the idea of you living in that cold old dowager house, anyway."

Suzanne beamed, unaware that her mother's eyes had become narrow slits. Lady Ann cast an anxious glance at Lady

Talgarth. She managed to say with tolerable calm, "That is surely enough about my affairs. Lord Graybourn, how long do you make your stay? I understand your destination is Brighton."

Lord Graybourn hastened to reply. "I had intended to stay only a day or two, my lady. But the kindness of my hostess"—he looked hearteningly at Lady Talgarth—"as well as the hospitality you have extended to me, makes me hopeful that I shall be asked to remain for a few days longer." The viscount's eyes rested momentarily upon Elsbeth.

This inadvertent gesture was not calculated to find favour in Lady Talgarth's eye. She pushed herself up from her chair amid yards of rustling lavender silk and tapped her fan against her hand until the gentlemen had also risen. She drew an audible breath and glared balefully, not at Lady Ann or Arabella, but at Elsbeth. She then cast a meaningful glance at Suzanne, one that promised full reckoning.

Suzanne, well used to her mother's flights of injured dignity, tossed her blond curls, rose, and gave Lady Ann a quick hug. "I see that our visit is ended, Lady Ann. Please accept my congratulations."

"Of course, my dear." Lady Ann rose and smiled graciously at Lady Talgarth. "We most enjoyed making the acquaintance of Lord Graybourn, Aurelia. You are, needless to say, most welcome at Evesham Abbey at any time."

"Indeed, a most *enlightening* morning, my dear Ann." She gazed repressively at her daughter. "I daresay we will, however, be far too occupied to bring Lord Graybourn to visit again. You will cetainly understand."

Lady Ann merely nodded.

"Come, dear Edmund," Lady Talgarth said with unnecessary force.

He managed to move with moderate speed to her side. He smiled at everyone, a rather nice smile, Elsbeth thought, and bid his good-byes.

No sooner had Crupper bowed their visitors from the Velvet Room than Arabella collapsed on the sofa and burst into laughter. "I was certain that Lady Talgarth would burst her seams!"

Lady Ann sighed. "I suppose that she had to be told, sooner or later. The poor viscount, really a quite unexceptionable young man, 'twas a pity he had to be here when she was told."

The earl remarked from his post by the fireplace, "I fear the remainder of the viscount's visit will not be a happy one. The poor fellow is quite unsuited, in any case, for the dashing Miss Talgarth." His gaze rested for a moment on Elsbeth. Not wishing to put her to the blush, he straightened and turned to his wife. "If you are over your fit of mirth, I propose that we adjourn to the dining room for luncheon."

The earl's speculative look had plummeted Elsbeth into a spate of guilt. How very fickle of her to think Lord Graybourn a charming man, to believe that his sensibilities were quite in tune with her own. She found that she tended to avoid her cousin's eyes at the dining table. She thought his unkindness to the viscount most uncivil and not at all the way a proper gentleman should behave. Her displeasure at his behavior made her uneasy. The cold slices of ham did not sit well in her stomach.

As for Gervaise, he was of the cynical opinion that the damned English were all the same. He had merely joined in what he had thought to be an English game of showing up the fat viscount for the fool that he was, and just look at what they had done—drawn their ranks together against him, the French outsider! Even Elsbeth, half French that she was, had sided against him. He managed to hide his displeasure, for there was much he had to accomplish today. At the close of luncheon, he managed to place himself next to Arabella.

"My dear Countess," he addressed her with great charm, "I have been most remiss in my attentions to you."

"Why, not at all, Gervaise," Arabella replied uneasily, her eyes flying to her husband's face. To her confusion, she saw no displeasure or anger written there.

Gervaise spread his hands in flourishing denial. "Ah, but yes, Arabella." He sighed, his voice a caress. "As you know, I must take my leave in but two days' time. If you have no other plans for the afternoon, I should like for you to conduct me on more explorations of your fair countryside."

Arabella felt in an agony of indecision. An unexceptionable enough request, under normal circumstances. Her eyes darted again to her husband's face. To her further surprise and confusion, he smiled slightly and nodded. She wanted desperately to speak to him, but he rose and walked with Elsbeth and Lady Ann from the dining room.

She felt an almost physical stab of pain in her chest. She turned to Gervaise and masked her pain with a bright smile. "I shall be delighted to explore with you, monsieur. Where do you wish to go?"

He paused before replying, as if uncertain. "A most difficult decision, Arabella, but I think I should like to visit your old abbey ruins once again. The few minutes I have spent there was not enough. Such a romantic place, full of ghosts of your English ancestors! I wish to be drawn back into the past, to forget the cares of the present!"

Arabella thought his flight of fancy a bit overdone, but forbore to comment. They agreed to a time, and Arabella excused herself to don more serviceable clothing.

When she emerged into the entrance hall not long thereafter, dressed in an old blue muslin gown and stout walking shoes, she found that she hoped for a glimpse of her husband. She even went so far as to ask Crupper, "Have you seen his lordship?"

"Yes, my lady. Told me, his lordship did, that he did not wish to be disturbed for the rest of the afternoon."

"I see." She chewed her lower lip in vexation, wondering what Justin was doing. "Very well, Crupper, I shall be spending the afternoon with the comte at the old abbey ruins."

"As you please, my lady."

She looked up at him curiously. Why the devil should Crupper sound so disapproving? Did everyone believe her to be a fallen woman? She hunched her shoulder at him and went out to stand on the front steps. Gervaise appeared not many minutes later, nattily dressed, as was his habit, a smile of anticipation on his handsome face.

As he did not realize that his attentions to her were a source of great discomfiture, he did not hesitate in his flattery. "How very lovely you are, Arabella. An afternoon in your company will fill my memories for many a lonely day to come."

"Indeed," she replied repressively, disliking artifice. If only Gervaise had never come to Evesham Abbey, she thought, how very different my life with Justin would be.

She fell into step beside the comte, silently pursuing her thoughts. She wondered bitterly whether Justin, if he did not believe her to be unfaithful with the comte, would have simply thought it someone else. Perhaps poor Lord Graybourn, she thought with fatalistic humour.

"A lovely day, Arabella. Finely suited for our explorations."

She drew herself away from her grim thoughts and said lightly, "Yes, Gervaise."

The old abbey ruins were bathed in the rich golden lights of the afternoon sun, the rays striking the three stone arches that still stood, casting circular shadows over the large area of fallen rubble. Arabella tried her best to capture a mood of adventure. "Well, Gervaise, here we are. The time we visited here before, I neglected to tell you of the abbey's history. As you can see, the original abbey was a huge structure, covering most of this hill. On this level, only the three arches remain. Now, of course, it is very neatly tumbled about itself. Its history is not a very happy one. My father told me that it was a noble sanctuary of learning for nearly two hundred years before it was pillaged and burned in the twelfth century in a battle between King John and one of his barons." Gervaise appeared fascinated with her recital, and she warmed to her subject. "When I was a child, I explored some of the old chambers that still exist under this level. See"—she pointed to the far perimeter of the ruins—"where the fallen rocks have been cleared away? Just below are the chambers—monks' cells, I believe they are. I fancied that if I was very quiet I could hear the monks still intoning their services."

The comte looked up with innocent interest. "Elsbeth was telling me of a subterranean passageway. There are chambers still intact down there?"

"At least four or five chambers stand as they did seven hundred years ago. They are in a row off the only passage that remains uncollapsed."

His interest seemed to kindle, his eyes shining with the fervor of an ardent archaeologist. "We must not waste a moment! I must see these chambers!"

Arabella hesitated. "I fear it cannot be safe, Gervaise. I have seen some of the stone crumble just in the past ten years."

"I would not dare to ask you to submit your person to any hazard, dear Arabella. I insist that you remain here in safety.

I shall explore the old rooms." Masculine authority rang in his voice.

Her common sense submerged itself in pride. "It is ridiculous that you go alone, Gervaise. I suppose that no harm can befall us just this one last time."

"As you will, Arabella, as you will." He gave her a flourishing bow and stepped back.

"Follow me and stay close," she said over her shoulder.

Arabella skirted the massive stones to the far side of the ruins. Here all larger stones had been rolled away to preserve for as long as possible the passage below. In some places the ceiling was so thin that tiny shafts of light could be seen filtering down into the darkness below. She turned to where crooked slabs of stone still framed the stairway leading downward to the lower chambers. She peered inside.

"Oh, dear, you see how very dark it is! I have forgotten to bring candles."

She was surprised when the comte drew two candles and matches from his waistcoat pockets. "*Voilà*, dear Arabella! As you see, I have come prepared to explore!"

She took a candle from his outstretched hand. She smiled. "I daresay that you are quite prepared, Gervaise. We must light them now, for at the bottom of the steps 'tis like night itself."

They made their way carefully down the jagged rock steps into the subterranean passage. But for the flickering of their candles, the darkness was complete. Arabella stepped gingerly over fallen stones. "Be careful where you step, Gervaise," she whispered, her voice echoing eerily. She paused a moment and lifted her candle above her head. "But look"—she pointed—"the walls are clammy with moisture. Is it not strange when the sun shines so brightly above us?"

Gervaise obediently stepped nearer to the wall and ran his fingers over the rough wet surface. "It is fascinating. Where are the monks' cells, Arabella?"

"The passage forks to the left just ahead. The passage to the right crumbled many years ago. It is too bad that the chambers are empty. There is really not much to see."

"It matters not," he said behind her.

The passage ended abruptly, and Arabella raised her candle. "You see, but this one corridor remains. The rooms are in a straight row along the left."

She slipped through the narrow doorway into the first cell. "Do not put your weight against the doorframe," she warned. "You can see that the stones are already working themselves loose from the oak beams."

They stood side by side in the small stone room, their candles casting bizarre images on the damp walls. The air was musty and close. "I suppose it must have been more pleasant . . . seven hundred years ago, I mean." Arabella stooped and ran her fingers through the soft sand that covered the floor.

"I wish to see the other cells," Gervaise said, moving away from her as he spoke. "Do not disturb yourself, Arabella, I shall be back soon."

She nodded, quite content to stay where she was. It was so very peaceful here, and she wanted to be alone. She saw his candle flicker its slender light outside the cell, then disappear.

She looked about the chamber, thinking wistfully how large it had appeared to her as a small child. She pictured a rude wooden cot along one wall and perhaps a small table along the other. Certainly the room was too tiny for anything else.

She was jerked suddenly from her reverie at the sound of a loud thumping noise overhead, just above the oak-beamed doorway. She clutched her candle close to her and stepped forward, only to hurl herself back when, an instant later, stones above the doorway worked themselves loose and spurted to the floor in front of her.

"Gervaise!" she yelled, his name ending on a near-scream.

The only reply was the deafening sound of falling stone. She watched in horror as larger and larger stones worked themselves free of their ancient molding and crashed to the floor, blocking the open doorway. She screamed and fell back choking, her nostrils clogged and her eyes burning from gritty dust and sand that swirled about her. Her candle flickered in protest, and she whipped about, cupping her hand about its precious flame. A rock struck her shoulder, and she cried out more in surprise than in pain. She scurried to the corner and huddled down against the wall, her legs drawn up to her chest.

As if in a final spate of fury, the walls began to tremble around her. She tensed her body for the inevitable pain. She sobbed aloud, a cry of undefined regret, of sheer hopelessness torn from her throat. In the dim candlelight she saw the far wall of the cell gently collpase forward, strewing more stone and rubble toward her. She closed her eyes tightly and buried her face against the wall.

The oak beams overhead gave a final groan and fell silent. She raised her head and knew a moment of surprise that she was still alive. She raised her candle and peered about her. She swallowed another sob. Alive, yes, but buried amid a tomb of rubble. She surged to her feet and screamed, "Gervaise! Gervaise, are you all right? Where are you?" She waited many long agonizing moments before she heard his voice on the other side of the crumbled doorway.

His voice was muffled by the thick stone between them. "Arabella? Is that you? Thank God you are alive! Are you safe?"

She felt insensibly cheered at the relief in his voice. "Yes," she called back, her voice catching on a sob. "I . . . I think I am all right. There is much fallen stone and dust, but I am as yet unharmed."

His voice came clearer now, confident and sure. "Do not worry, Arabella. The passage still seems safe. I am going to fetch help. I swear that I will not be long. You must be brave. I shall return soon!"

She drew a shaky breath. Thank God the passage had not caved in! She tried to calm herself. After all, Gervaise was unharmed, and he would bring Justin to save her. She must be patient. She wiped her hands across her forehead and saw in the flickering candlelight traces of smeared blood. How odd, she thought, I really feel no pain at all. She investigated further and found that a falling stone had cut into her scalp, matting her hair with blood.

The silence grew eerie, and the minutes stretched out endlessly. Slowly she crawled to the center of the small cell. The sand floor was strewn with jagged pieces of stone, each positioned, it seemed, to poke and cut her palms and knees. She gritted her teeth against the sharp, painful jabs. Carefully she cleared a small space and sat up, lifting the candle to look about her. The doorway looked as if it had vomited stone, leaving only a small space at the very top. She remembered the sound of collapse from the wall beside her, and swerved the candle about.

The breath caught in her throat, then spurted free. She

screamed, a piercing, horrified sound that echoed back to her. Amid the fallen stone, stretched out toward her like death beckoning from hell, was a skeleton's hand! The bony fingers nearly touched her skirt. She scrambled back on her heels and closed her eyes, fighting down another scream. The image of a cowled monk, his head and face covered in a rough woolen robe, filled her mind.

She forced her eyes open and gazed again at the grotesque curling fingers. Slowly she raised the candle and forced herself to look into the hollow created by the collapsing wall. The skeleton's outstretched arm was attached to only part of a body. It lay on its side, facing away from her, yet the head was twisted nearly backward, its fathomless hollowed-out eye sockets staring at her, unseeing. Broken teeth hung loosely in the gaping mouth. A white peruke was askew atop its ghastly fleshless head.

Arabella shuddered, gooseflesh rising on her arms. The remains of a long-dead monk would have been less terrifying. She felt a ghastly chill, the formless cold sweep of death.

For several moments she fought silently to force her courage to the forefront. As if to prove to herself that she had conquered her unreasoning fear, she reached out her fingers and tentatively touched the filthy worm-eaten velvet sleeve that covered the skeleton's arm. How strange, she thought, it was still soft to the touch. She looked more closely. It was the skeleton of a man, dressed in a dark green coat and velvet breeches that fitted below the knees. She remembered as a child that her father had worn such a style. The man could not have been buried more than twenty years in his lonely tomb. She leaned closer and saw a gaping hole over the man's chest. It gave witness to his manner of death.

It required a great effort of will for Arabella to slip her fingers into the coat pockets. Surely the man must have had some paper, some document to reveal his identity. The pockets were empty. She drew a deep breath and plunged her hand into his breeches pocket. Her fingers closed around a small square of folded paper. Slowly she drew it out and sat back on her heels.

She unfolded the paper and saw that it was a letter. The ink was so faded with age that she had to hold the candle dangerously close to its yellowed edges.

She managed to make out the date—1789. The month had

become illegible over the years. She looked down at the body of the letter and wanted to cry out in vexation, for it was written in French. With frustrating slowness she translated the letter word by word. "My beloved Charles," she read. "Even though he knows of the growing unrest, the now violent revolts of the rabble against us, he forces me to come. He keeps my baby here to ensure my return. You know he is furious over what he believes to be my family's treachery. He wants the remainder of my promised dowry. Listen, my love, do not repine, for I have a plan that will free us forever from his hated presence. Once in France, I shall travel to the château . . ."

Try as she might, Arabella could not make out the next few lines. They were blurred into indistinct blotches. Who was this Charles, anyway? And this woman? She shook her head and skipped the smudged lines. "Though our little Gervaise cannot escape with us, I have learned to bear the pain of separation. At least he will know safety with my brother. Josette will ensure the safe posting of this, my last letter to you. Shortly, my love, we will be together again. I know that we can escape from him and rescue Elsbeth from his clutches. We shall be rich, my darling, rich from his greed! A new life. Freedom. I trust in God and in you. Magdalaine."

Arabella sat quietly with the letter lying loosely in her fingers. She felt as if Magdalaine had come to her and unraveled the tangled, mysterious threads of her short life. This man, Charles, was Magdalaine's lover. Gervaise was their child. He was not the Comte de Trécassis, but a bastard. She reeled back. Dear God, Elsbeth was his half-sister! She felt unspeakable revulsion. Of course, she was aware of the likeness of their features. But now she no longer saw it as the mere resemblance of cousins, but the deep inherited traits of brother and sister.

Poor Elsbeth! How will she feel when she finds out that her lover is her half-brother?

Arabella felt a sudden wave of anger. Her father's first wife had been unfaithful to him. Indeed, she had borne a child before her marriage to him! Had the Trécassis family bribed her father with some fantastic sum to marry Magdalaine to save themselves from scandal? She looked down again at the letter. If only she could make out the blurred lines. She read once again, "We shall be rich, my darling, rich from his greed!"

She sat silently for a long while, sorting through what she knew and what she could only guess at. She looked back at the skeleton, her eyes fastening on the bullet hole in his chest. She thought of the times her father had expressly forbidden her to explore the ruins. Was it simply because he had feared for her safety? She was forced to admit that her father must have killed this man, Charles. A duel of honour—yes, it must have been a duel of honour!

She suddenly remembered that Magdalaine had died suddenly after her return from France. She felt her blood freeze in her veins. A hoarse sob broke from her throat. "No, please God," she cried aloud. "He did not kill her, too. No, my father could not have murdered her!"

Yet the faded, passionate letter in her hand was so very damning. Hate, pain, and suffering clutched at her from every word. Her only thought now was to protect her father's name, to destroy this wretched letter. She jerked it up and with quivering fingers drew it near to the slender candle flame. She was not certain what stopped her, but she pulled the paper back, folded it again into a small square, and slipped it into the sole of her shoe.

The candle was burning low. It could not be much longer now. Gervaise said he would fetch help. Gervaise! An impostor, a liar. She remembered the strange thudding sound just before the stones over the doorway collapsed. Had he trapped her in here on purpose? Had he tried to kill her?

The candle sputtered and died. Her voice caught on a sob as she was plunged into darkness.

As Gervaise jerked open the great front doors of Evesham Abbey and burst into the entrance hall, he yelled out in frantic concern, "Crupper! Quickly, fetch his lordship! Her ladyship is trapped by fallen rock in the old abbey ruins! Be quick, man!" He panted convincingly, sucking in deep breaths from his exertion.

Crupper was a man bewildered. "Her ladyship? Trapped?" he repeated helplessly, his eyes on the young Frenchman.

"Damm it, man! We must be quick!" Gervaise urged, his impatience with the butler making his voice crack.

Crupper was rescued from his confused distress by the appearance of the earl at the top of the stairs. "What the devil is all this racket? What has happened?" he demanded, hurrying down the stairs.

"It is Arabella, my lord," Gervaise gasped for breath. "We were exploring the subterranean chambers in the old abbey ruins. One of the chambers caved in and she is trapped! We must hurry, my lord!"

"Is she still alive?" the earl asked, his voice hard and cold as granite.

"Yes, yes, I called to her. She is unharmed, but I fear there will be more falling stone." Gervaise gesticulated wildly.

The earl was silent for but an instant. He glanced at the still-confused Crupper, threw back his head, and bellowed, "Giles!"

The second footman came dashing into the entrance hall. "My lord?" He blinked.

"Go quickly, Giles, and fetch James and all the stable hands. Tell them to gather shovels and picks. Her ladyship is trapped beneath the ruins of the old abbey. Go, man, I shall meet you there!"

The earl turned to Crupper. "Inform Lady Ann and Elsbeth. I shall be at the ruins." He turned to follow Giles, then halted abruptly and looked back to see Gervaise quickly mounting the staircase.

"Monsieur!" His voice cut through the air with the sharpness of a rapier.

Gervaise spun on his heel and turned to face the cold set features of the earl.

"You do not wish to assist us?" the earl inquired softly.

"I . . . But of a certainty, my lord! I merely intended to go to my room for but an instant." He felt the earl's gray eyes, like slivers of ice, boring into his mind. He rallied. "Please, my lord, you must hurry! I shall join you in but a moment."

A smile that held no mirth spread over the earl's face. He said gently, "No, monsieur. You will not join me in a moment. I require your presence at once."

Gervaise wavered. He cursed with silent fluency. "As you will, my lord," he tried to say indifferently. It was with an effort that he kept the angry frustration from his face.

The earl turned to the now astonished Crupper and said in a loud, clear voice, "I require that you remain here, Crupper, and, if you will, guard Evesham Abbey. No one—I repeat, no one—is allowed beyond the entrance hall until my return. Do you understand?"

The old man felt mired in confusion. He heard the earl's words and, of course, understood them, though their intent was quite lost on him. "Yes, my lord," he managed to reply. "I will remain here and do your bidding."

"Excellent, Crupper. Monsieur? Let us go." The earl stepped back and waited for Gervaise to precede him through the front doors.

Arabella drew her legs up close to her chest and hugged herself for warmth. She tried not to think of the grosteque skeleton but an arm's reach away, and of the terrible truth that she had discovered. Surely Justin must come to her soon, if, she thought grimly, Gervaise wanted her to be rescued. But what had he to gain by leaving her here? What of Justin? Of course he would come for her. That, she could not doubt. But would he really prefer to be rid of her, freed from a marriage of her father's making?

She felt tears sting her eyes. The wet of her tears mixed with the grime about her eyes and burned painfully. She lifted a corner of her skirt and daubed it against her cheeks.

Suddenly she thought she heard movement from the other side of the wall. She raised her head and peered into the blackness.

"Bella! Can you hear me?"

"Justin!" She surged to her feet, bruises and cuts forgotten. "Justin, it is you! I am trapped in the chamber. Please, oh, please, get me out of here!"

Again she heard his voice, calm and clear. "Listen to me, Bella. I want you to move to the far corner of the chamber and protect your head with your arms. 'Tis a tricky business. The beams are unstable about the door. I want you far away from them in case there is more collapsing."

"But, Justin," she protested, "I can start pulling away stones from inside."

She thought she heard a low chuckle. The voice that reached her but a moment later was irate. "Damm it! Come, Bella, do as I tell you. I am glad that you are quite unharmed, and I wish you to remain that way."

"I will do as you say," she called back. She groped her way

back to the corner and slipped down to her knees and covered her head.

It seemed to Arabella that with each stone dislodged from its place, the walls and ceiling groaned. She shuddered with their every movement. She felt it the most joyous sight imaginable when Justin pulled away enough rubble to ease his body through the opening.

Someone handed him a candle. The small cell was flooded with light. Light and life, she thought thankfully.

The earl called over his shoulder, "James, stay back. I shall bring her ladyship out."

Arabella rose slowly to her feet. Without thought, she walked straight into her husband's arms and nuzzled her face against his shoulder.

"I am glad you are come, my lord," she said simply, raising her eyes to his face.

"Did you ever doubt that I would, Bella?" he asked, unwilling as yet to release her.

She buried her face again in his shoulder. "Perhaps, for just a moment," she admitted gruffly. "I thought perhaps you would be glad to be . . . free of me."

"Foolish Arabella," he chided gently. He rubbed his chin against her hair. He drew back. "Come, wife, let us leave this place. I have no great desire to further test your charmed existence."

"A moment, Justin. I was not alone here." She took the candle from his fingers and carefully moved its light to shine upon the skeleton.

"Good God!" He looked at her and marveled at her steadiness. He dropped to his knees and briefly examined her grisly find. After a moment he rose and dusted off his breeches. "First let us remove you from this place, and then I shall see that this poor fellow receives a proper burial."

He held the light for her as she slipped from her prison into freedom. She thought of the letter now rubbing against the sole of her foot. She felt weighted down with unsought, damning knowledge. There was much to consider—her father's name, and of course, Elsbeth. She determined at that moment to hold her tongue; no one must know what she had discovered, even Justin, until she had time to think, to sort through all that she now knew.

When she emerged into the bright sunlight, she looked

about her, realizing for the first time in her eighteen years how very precious life was. She savoured the hot sun beating down upon her face.

Like a small child awakening from a nightmare, she walked to her mother and threw her arms about her shoulders.

"My poor child," Lady Ann crooned, stroking her daughter's filthy hair. " 'Tis all right now, my love, you are safe."

"Oh, Mama," Arabella gasped. She broke into rasping sobs against her mother's shoulder.

## 14

"Lord, but you are a mess!" The earl laughed.

"Well, you are certainly no stylish Corinthian yourself, my lord," Arabella flashed back.

"Touché, little vixen. We are both in need of a good scrubbing. Grace is fetching your tub. I had best demand the same of poor Grubbs." He turned to leave the earl's bedchamber.

"Justin . . ."

"Yes, Bella?"

"I . . . I do thank you." She felt suddenly tongue-tied, and her eyes traced the pattern of the carpet at her feet.

He said gruffly, "You would do the same for me, would you not?" He hated the thought that she was embarrassed because she felt gratitude to him. Damn, he did not wish her to feel beholden to him.

Arabella still could not force her eyes to his face. She merely nodded.

"I will see you at dinner, my dear," he said levelly, and walked from the room.

Save for the few small scratches about her face, none of the assembled company would have deduced that the Countess of Strafford had undergone a terrifying experience. She looked hale and hearty and sparkling clean. The dinner conversation soon turned to the mysterious skeleton uncovered in the wall of the chamber.

"There was no clue at all to the man's identity?" Lady Ann asked the earl.

"Unfortunately, none whatsoever. From his manner of dress, I would estimate that he met his violent end some twenty years ago. As to how or why, or, for that matter, by whose hand, we can only conjecture."

Arabella chewed harder on the tasty sirloin, so vigourously, in fact, that she bit her cheek. She held all the answers to their questions on a small square of faded paper. She could imagine the shock and horror on their faces were she to tell them that it was her father who had killed the man, Magdalaine's lover. And Gervaise—how would he react, were he to know the truth? Or, perhaps, did Gervaise already know? She lowered her head and toyed with the few errant green beans in the middle of her plate. She wanted more than anything to be alone, away from everyone, to think.

"Dear Arabella, how very awful for you to be shut in with that man's skeleton." Elsbeth shuddered. "I would have died of fright!"

"I very nearly did," Arabella admitted ruefully. "It was most horrible when my candle died out."

Dr. Branyon eyed his future stepdaughter with concern. "I realize, Bella, that you have the constitution of a horse, but I would prefer that you allow me to examine you more fully."

"What? And be victim to one of your vile potions? No, I thank you, sir!"

Dr. Branyon turned to the earl. "Justin, cannot you persuade your wife to reason?"

Justin merely smiled and shook his head. "Let her bear her bumps and bruises in peace, Paul. I am persuaded that she has come to no ill."

"It is I who must ask your apology, dear Arabella," the comte said fervently. "To place you unwittingly into such danger. It is unforgivable!"

Arabella raised her eyes to Gervaise. She heard a note of falseness in his lilting voice that she had never before noticed. She read no concern for her safety in his dark eyes. Perhaps it was relief she saw, relief that he had not been found out. She forced herself to smile brightly at him. "Your apology does you honour, monsieur. I most readily forgive you, for I also wished to explore the chambers. The fault is both of ours."

Lady Ann said in a thankful voice, "All that matters is that you are safe, child. Just no more exploring those old ruins. I remember your father extracting such a promise from you years ago! Come, promise me again."

Yes, Arabella thought, Father wanted me to stay away from the ruins. She said, " 'Tis the easiest promise I will ever have to keep, Mama."

Dr. Branyon shifted his attention to Gervaise. "I understand, monsieur, that you will leave Evesham Abbey shortly."

Gervaise gazed between half-closed lids at the earl before replying smoothly, "Yes, doctor, there are . . . pressing matters that await my attention. I must return to Bruxelles."

Arabella found herself examining Gervaise's face closely. If only she could unravel why he had come to Evesham Abbey in the first place. Surely he could not be so vile as to purposely set out to seduce his own half-sister! By chance her eyes roved to the head of the table. She caught her breath in surprise at the glint of anger in her husband's eyes. She quickly turned her attention back to the small square of beef on her plate. How very stupid of me, she thought. Justin observed me looking at Gervaise. He still believes me guilty of betraying him. How can he be so very blind and deaf to his own wife?

Elsbeth misread Arabella's sudden forlorn demeanor as a certain sign of fatigue. "My dear sister," she cried, "after dinner I shall play some soothing ballads for you."

Arabella looked up at her sister's innocent, guileless face My dear, so very innocent Elsbeth, she thought, I will and I must find some way to protect you. She said, "I look forward to your playing, Elsbeth. 'Twill ensure me a sound night's sleep."

If Elsbeth's playing did little to soothe Arabella's frayed nerves, it did at least create a diversion that earned Arabella's undying gratitude. It was all she could do to keep her eyes from the earl's disquieting gaze.

At the close of Elsbeth's final French ballad, Arabella turned gratefully to Dr. Branyon as he rose and took her hand in his. In a voice not to be gainsaid, he said sternly, "Strong as a horse you may be, my dear Bella, but I must still insist that you now take yourself off to bed. No arguments!"

She smiled up at him impishly. " 'Twould be most unbecoming of me to come to blows with my new papa. I most readily do your bidding, sir." She rose on her toes and kissed him on the cheek.

He patted her hand fondly, then turned to Lady Ann. "I shall fetch you in the morning for our outing."

"Of course," she replied with a smile.

A few moments later, as Lady Ann and Dr. Branyon stood alone on the front steps of Evesham Abbey, she tried to scold him between giggles. "How ignoble of you, Paul! *Outing*, indeed! I was fearful of losing all decorum."

"Shameless little imp," he chided fondly. "You put me to the blush, Ann."

"Fie on you, sir! Be off with you."

"Until tomorrow, my love." Neither of them was particularly concerned that Crupper observed their tender parting.

Arabella was on the verge of taking herself to bed when she chanced to see Elsbeth gaze with clouded confusion at Gervaise. She thought it odd and indeed obtuse of her that she had not before observed how her sister wore her heart on her sleeve. She determined then and there, despite the fatigue that was making her eyes droop, that she would not leave Elsbeth alone with Gervaise. The least she could do was to keep them separated until Gervaise left. She fidgeted about the room for several moments, racking her brain for a suitable topic of conversation.

The earl watched her silent machinations. He saw her eyes rest upon Elsbeth, and then, more pointedly, on Gervaise, and wondered what she was up to. He drew a sharp breath and said to Arabella in a cool voice, "Surely, my dear, it is time that you retired to your bed. I must concur with Dr. Branyon's instructions."

With sudden inspiration Arabella said, "Yes, I should indeed go to my bed. Oh, Elsbeth, would you not accompany me to my room? I should like it above all things if you would tuck me up."

Elsbeth looked up, startled. She had thought to speak to Gervaise, since he was to leave so shortly, to ask him what he planned now that her stepmother was to marry Dr. Branyon. But she could not think of refusing her sister. She readily concurred and rose with alacrity and walked to Arabella's side.

"We bid you good night, gentlemen," Arabella said. She took Elsbeth's small hand firmly in hers and tugged her unceremoniously to the door.

Arabella endured Elsbeth's tender ministrations, so weary that she scarce heeded her sister's repeated references to her "trial." Once arrayed in her nightgown, her thick raven tresses brushed loose down her back, she smiled lovingly at Elsbeth and kissed her lightly on the cheek.

"Thank you, dear sister, for your kindness. You are looking quite as fagged as I. I trust you will also retire now." She scanned Elsbeth's face, alert to any sign of dissimulation. The thought of Elsbeth joining Gervaise made her blood run cold.

Elsbeth yawned and stretched like an innocent child at peace with the world. "Yes, I shall go to my room now. Thank you, Bella, for lending me Grace. I am so very clumsy without Josette." Her piquant face crumpled at the mention of her old servant's name.

Arabella did not know what to reply. She knew that Elsbeth felt Josette's death sorely. She simply patted her sister's hand and said gently, "I know, Elsbeth. I thank you for coming up with me."

Arabella slipped into her bed and blew out the candle beside her. At last she was alone, alone to think, to sort out the many facts and half-truths she had discovered. It was not long before an endless stream of questions came into her mind.

She knew the contents of Magdalaine's letter almost by heart now. She had read it several times again before going down to dinner. As to the letter itself, she had slipped it into the toe of one of her evening slippers, a hiding place that she knew to be safe—even Grace never went poking about in her shoes.

She sat up suddenly. Lord, what a fool she was! Josette must have known everything. Did she not ensure the dispatching of Magdalaine's letters to her lover, Charles? Of course, Josette must have known that Gervaise was Magdalaine's son. Josette . . . dead. Gooseflesh rose on her arms. A tragic fall down the main staircase in the middle of the night . . . with no candle to guide her!

Her mind leaped back to the afternoon. She was as certain

as she could be that the collapse in the old abbey ruins was no accident. But then, if Gervaise had wished to harm her—or kill her, for that matter—why did he return so quickly with Justin to rescue her? What possible reason could he have had?

She shook her head in vexation. It was like wandering through the maze in Richmond Park without the key to show the way out. The key to this maze was the reason why Gervaise had come to Evesham Abbey in the first place. It seemed obvious that her father must have known of Gervaise's existence as the natural son of his first wife. That must be the reason he had not come until after her father's death. But was there something further her father had known about him, something else that had kept him away?

She realized that more than anything she would like to speak to Justin, show him the letter, tell him all of her suspicions. She sighed and turned her face into the pillow. Justin nurtured so much distrust and anger at Gervaise. If she were to tell him what she knew, she could not be certain how he would react. Would he confront Gervaise? Fetch the magistrate? Would everything be exposed? Would Elsbeth learn that her lover was indeed her own half-brother?

She could hear the endless questions about the skeleton in the abbey. Would Justin tell everyone that her father had killed the man, Magdalaine's lover? Would not then everyone wonder if her father had not also murdered his first wife?

She was now miserably uncertain. Was it not possible that she was wrong about Gervaise? Perhaps, just perhaps, he had not caused the collapse in the old abbey ruins. Perhaps, too, Josette's death had been an accident. If only there were more certainties and fewer doubts!

She remembered words her father had spoken many years before: "Know your enemy, Arabella. Look him straight in the face! Trust no one but yourself. It must be your judgment whether to attack or retreat!"

She found that she had made her decision. Gervaise was leaving Evesham Abbey the day after tomorrow. She would confront him herself as soon as she had the opportunity. She would find out the truth, then decide whom she could trust with such knowledge. At last she was satisfied that she had come to some resolution. She snuggled into the warmth of the covers and soon fell asleep.

She was magically transported to the chamber beneath the old abbey ruins. Rock rumbled and fell about her, striking her head, her face, her shoulders. She tossed forward on her face, frantically trying to avoid the sharp, jagged stones, desperately flailing her arms about for protection. Her fingers clasped about brittle, spiderlike projections. She felt her hand squeezed with such force that she was jerked forward. Though she was struggling in darkness, she saw with terrifying clarity what held her so mercilessly. A skeleton's hand held her fast, its fleshless fingers digging into her wrist. She heard a low cry, a moan of hate and pain, the rattle of imminent death. The skeleton rocked up from its prone position, broken teeth falling from its rotted hollow mouth. Slowly, before her eyes, the bones of its hands began to turn to dust and trickle all about her. The head tottered backward and fell, crashing and crumbling to the ground. She heard hellish screams all about her. She felt death upon her, clogging her throat, enclosing her in a shroud of terror.

Arabella awoke, her hands tearing at the bedcovers, a final cry dying on her own lips. She leaped from the bed and stood shivering in the middle of the room. Clumsily she lit a candle and raised it above her head. She drew back with a gasp as the light fell upon the jeering face of the skeleton on *The Dance of Death*. Dream and reality mixed in her mind. Had the screaming come from the skeleton? Could it have been the wailing of an infant? The hopeless cries of a woman? Had she heard the ghosts of Evesham Abbey?

"Arabella! I heard you cry out, is there anything wrong?" The earl appeared in the adjoining doorway, his dressing gown thrown over his shoulders.

The wretched candle would not stop trembling in her hand. She gazed at him and felt the terror of the nightmare slowly pull away from her. She drew a shaking breath. "Yes, I had a nightmare, about that horrible skeleton in the old abbey ruins. Then I thought I heard from our ghosts, but now I begin to doubt that their cries were not my own."

He looked at her searchingly. "Are you all right now?"

She nodded and started to turn away, when suddenly she knew that more than anything she wanted him to stay with her. She thought how very close to death she had come this afternoon. I would have died without ever having known all of living, she thought. She refused to think of all the unspoken barriers, the bitterness, the distrust that lay between them. Somehow, none of it seemed to matter now. She wanted him to make love to her, to become her husband. She thought to speak, to tell him what she wanted, when he said gently, "Come, Arabella, let me tuck you back into bed. You are shivering."

"Yes . . . yes, of course you are right. I am rather cold," she said slowly, and walked to the side of the bed. Her hand was no longer trembling as she set the candle on the tabletop. She pulled back the covers, her every sense aware that he was standing behind her. She crawled to the middle of the large bed and turned to face him, her hand stretching out toward him. "I would that you would not leave, Justin."

The earl hesitated only a moment. At first he thought that perhaps she was still frightened by her nightmare and sought only comfort from him. He looked deep into her eyes and saw that it was not the case. He shrugged out of his dressing gown, took her outstretched hand firmly in his, and slipped into bed beside her.

She drew up onto her knees beside him, clouds of raven hair spilling over her shoulders and onto his chest. Tentatively she splayed her hands across his bare chest and let her fingers rove through the black curling hair, her eyes drinking in the strength of him, his largeness. "You are so beautiful," she whispered, leaning down to rest her cheek against his chest. She knew that she was offering herself to him, risking his disdain at what he might believe to be an unnatural wantonness in her.

"I am just a man, Arabella," he replied softly, still uncertain about the change in her, yet moved by the gentle wonder in her voice and the soft tenderness of her touch. He pushed her hair gently away from her face and pulled her down to him. At the touch of his mouth against hers, Arabella eagerly parted her lips. She felt an awakening in her as she had when he had first kissed her so long ago.

He sensed her passion, yet wondered at the tentative, almost virginal quality of her kiss. He sat up and gently began to unfasten the small buttons on her nightgown. The memory of their wedding night when he had brutally torn her gown from her seared through his mind, and he fumbled. He felt her hands close over his, and together they pulled and prodded at the tiny buttons. She wriggled the gown up to her waist, and together they lifted it over her head.

He lay back down on his back and gazed up at her, still on her knees above him, her long black hair framing her shoulders, falling in loose waves that lazily curved under her milky white breasts.

"You are the beautiful one," he murmured, and reached out to her. He gently pressed her down upon her back.

As his hands slowly explored her body, she felt no regret, no fear. For the first time in her life she trusted a man other than her father. She gazed up at him with passionate anticipation and complete trust.

When he finally entered her, she groaned aloud with pleasure, pushing her hips upward, as if to engulf him.

As he moved slowly within her, he felt her slender body begin to quiver with spasms of pleasure, her hands clutching at his back, drawing him closer to her.

When at last he could no longer contain his desire, he gazed deeply into her eyes and softly moaned her name. She clasped him tightly to her and buried her face into his shoulder.

"Justin . . ." she cried, at once breathless and awash with the sudden aching pleasure. His mouth covered hers, and she felt him tense within her. With a cry he grasped her hips and drove deep, flooding her with his seed.

For a moment Arabella was aware of a great lassitude. Even though she was pinioned beneath him, she did not feel his weight. Words formed in her throat, words of love, of tenderness, of a deep lingering warmth. Even as she clutched him more closely to her, the words died on her lips. Why had he not spoken one word of love to her? She thought bitterly of her intense passion, the way she had flaunted her body. Did he still believe her a trollop? Had she only confirmed in his mind that he was but another man with whom his insatiable wife sought pleasure?

She waited, and the silence grew long between them. Tears stung at her lids and rolled slowly down her cheeks. She saw the hated tears as a confession of her guilt, perhaps of her regret at having betrayed him.

The earl felt her slender body shiver and tense beneath him. He rolled off her and asked tenderly, "You are cold, Bella?"

She could not trust herself to speak, and, indeed, the words clogged in her throat. She shook her head and tried to avert her face.

She felt his fingers gently touch her wet cheeks. "You are crying," he said, surprised. He was bewildered by the abrupt change in her. Had he hurt her unwittingly?

"No!" she cried, struggling to a sitting position. She dashed her hand across her face, hating herself for her simple child's trust. How could she be so stupid to believe that offering herself to her husband would change anything between them?

He stared at her, a frown creasing his forehead. He was confounded by the anger in her and by her tears. In the quiet aftermath of their lovemaking, he had sought to reconcile the fumbling tentativeness of her actions and her intense passion. Now, in the face of her sudden coldness, he believed that she must have compared him with Gervaise and regretted making love with him. "Arabella . . ." he began, his voice harsh with uncertainty and frustration.

She grabbed her discarded nightgown and bounded from the bed. "No, Justin," she panted, her voice catching on a sob. "Please, just leave me alone!"

She held her gown in front of her to cover her nakedness. She did not want to hear his recriminations, his accusations, his scorn at her passion. He held up his hand in a futile gesture to stop her, but she had already whirled around and run across the bedroom to the adjoining door.

## 15

The earl flung back the heavy curtains that covered the long row of narrow mullioned windows in the family portrait gallery. He brushed a light layer of dust from his hands, mentally noting to bring this neglected room to Mrs. Tucker's attention. He would have liked to open the windows to air the room, but a fine gray drizzle had become an earnest downpour.

He was not certain why he had come to the family portrait gallery, save that he wanted to be alone. He gazed down the length of the long narrow room, scarce wider than the second-floor corridors, his eyes resting briefly on the portrait of his granduncle, haughtily staring at the world beneath the dark flaring Deverill brows, his dark hair covered by a white curling wig. What a proud, lecherous old man you must have been, he thought, his mouth twisting unwillingly into a grin.

He turned from the portrait, and the grin abruptly left his lips. Damn, what a confounded muddle everything was in! He had lain in bed after Arabella had fled from him last night, cursing himself, cursing her, his blind rage at the Frenchman nearly overcoming his good sense. Try as he would, he simply could not fathom why she had willingly offered herself to him, only to withdraw from him after sharing tender, passionate lovemaking. He thought of her desire, what he had read as trust and longing in her fine eyes, of her eagerness for his body.

He had wanted to tell Arabella that he loved her, that he forgave her, that he understood how her father's will that foisted a marriage of convenience upon her had sent her flying into another man's arms. He had thought to win her. For that precious moment the night before, when their physical love had bound them together, he believed he had won.

Gervaise was leaving on the morrow, leaving because Justin was finally forcing him to. Yet, even now, he did not know if Arabella's love would leave with him. He simply had to find a way before Gervaise left to prove to her that the wily Frenchman was not worth her affection, that he was, indeed, a vicious, scheming coward.

He crossed to a recessed window seat, sat down, and leaned his shoulders against the smooth stone wall. He reviewed as dispassionately as he was able all that he had found out about Gervaise. All he could accuse him of was being a bastard, raised by Magdalaine's brother, Thomas. But beyond a doubt he knew that Gervaise was playing a deep game, one that had already cost the old servant, Josette, her life. And, he thought, with more anger than he wished to allow himself at the moment, a game that could easily have cost Arabella her life. His was the fault. When he had benignly approved Arabella's outing to the old abbey ruins with Gervaise the day before, it had simply not occurred to him that she was in any danger from her lover. And there, he thought, shaking his head, was yet another question for which he had no answer. If Arabella was the Frenchman's lover, if she really cared for him, why had he not enlisted her aid?

He rose from the window seat and began pacing the flagstone floor. He knew that the key lay somehow in *The Dance of Death* panel in the earl's bedchamber. He had spent hours meticulously searching the surface of the panel, searching for he knew not what. He had thought it such a simple plan to approve Arabella's spending the afternoon with Gervaise, to keep the Frenchman away from Evesham Abbey, while he slipped into the young man's room to search his belongings. He had found nothing, though his search had been interrupted by Gervaise yelling that Arabella was trapped in the old abbey ruins. How obvious it was to him then that the Frenchman's destination upon his return was the earl's bedchamber and *The Dance of Death* panel! But two days remained before Gervaise would leave Evesham Abbey. The earl was as certain as he could be that the Frenchman would not leave without trying again to gain what he had come for.

He pondered silently, his footsteps echoing back to him from the flagstone floor. He must arrange to search Gervaise's room once again. There had to be some clue to tell him what the Frenchman sought to the extent of blithely committing murder to attain it. He looked up to see the rain had stopped and that the sun was groping its way through the gray clouds.

He heard the sound of carriage wheels in the drive. He turned and peered down, to see the Talgarth carriage draw to a standstill in front of Evesham Abbey. He felt a moment of surprise to see Suzanne Talgarth step lightly down the carriage steps, with Giles in attendance with a large umbrella. Had Lady Talgarth relented in her displeasure with Lady Ann's projected marriage to Dr. Branyon? He rose and strolled from the east wing downstairs to the Velvet Room.

As he entered the room, his eyes fell immediately upon Arabella. She raised her attention from a chattering Suzanne, gazed at him but a moment before looking quickly away. He saw her hands twisting in the folds of her gown. He read pain in her fine eyes, and perhaps, he thought, regret.

His voice was unnaturally harsh as he stepped forward to clasp Suzanne's gloved hand.

"Why, Miss Talgarth, how very brave of you to venture forth in such despondent weather. You bring no ill news, I trust."

Suzanne dimpled, shot an amused glance at Arabella's lowered head, and replied with a conspiratorial grin, "I would have you know, my lord, that I willed away this boring weather. You see"—she swept her hand to the sunlit window—"even the elements could not refuse me! No, I bring no ill tidings. I was just on the point of begging a favor of Arabella."

"A favor, Miss Talgarth? Come, I am certain that neither Arabella nor I would think of disobliging you."

Suzanne said audaciously to Arabella, "I vow, Bella, that

you have already been most disobliging to me! If only *I* had made your acquaintance *first,* my lord!"

"You are a baggage, Miss Talgarth," the earl replied amiably.

"I see that you are quite in the doldrums, Bella." Suzanne laughed. "I have been as outrageous as I have the wit to be, and still you do not growl, spit, or even laugh at me! It is too bad of you!"

The corners of Arabella's mouth lifted. "All right, Suz, you have caught my attention. Now, tell us, what brings you here this morning?"

Suzanne looked triumphant. "Mama and Papa are having a card party tonight, with dancing of course for the young people. I am Mama's emissary, come to invite all of you to Talgarth Hall for this evening!"

The earl made a slight, ironical bow. "I begin to think you dabble in the black arts, Miss Talgarth. Your mama left here yesterday in quite a taking. I feared that we would be denied henceforth your charming company."

"True," Suzanne conceded. "But Mama is not precisely *stupid,* you know. Both Papa and I pointed out that the Deverills are by far our most important neighbors, and for her to cut your acquaintance would result in the most dire of social consequences."

Arabella grinned. "Suz, you really are a minx!"

"No, not really," Suzanne replied seriously. "Papa also reminded her that he and Dr. Branyon had been friends for too many years to allow such silliness to sour their acquaintance. Of course, I slipped in that Dr. Branyon was, after all, *her* doctor. 'Why, Mama,' I said, 'whatever would happen if you caught one of your nasty colds? Why, there would be no one about to prescribe for you!' She quite came around at that point!"

The earl said, "Miss Talgarth, you quite terrify me with your logic."

Arabella looked an appeal to the earl. "I should much enjoy a party, my lord," she said tentatively. She could think of nothing she wanted more than to avoid the intimacy of the family on Gervaise's last evening here. There was Elsbeth too. What better opportunity to keep them separated than in a room filled with their neighbors?

To her relief, the earl did not hesitate. If anything, she thought she saw a sudden glint in his eyes, perhaps of speculation, she was not certain. He turned to Suzanne. "Tell your mama, Miss Talgarth, that everyone will most gladly attend her party this evening."

Arabella frowned thoughtfully at her husband. There seemed to be an air of confident complacency about him that she did not understand.

Suzanne rose and clapped her hands happily together. " 'Tis all set, then. How kind of you, my lord, not to take offense at mama's overbearing ways. I must be off now to see Dr. Branyon. I quite convinced Mama," she confided in a lowered voice, "that not to invite him would most certainly put Lady Ann's nose totally out of joint!"

Suzanne kissed Arabella quickly on the cheek, then turned to the earl. She smiled at him pertly, then held out her hand.

The earl looked taken aback a moment, then faintly amused. He gallantly took her hand and carried it to his lips. He said without thought, "You must take care, Miss Talgarth, that my bride does not challenge you to a duel."

Suzanne tossed her blond curls and smiled impishly at Arabella. "Oh, Bella is far too certain of her own charms to ever be concerned about mine!"

Arabella avoided her husband's eyes and with an effort smiled at her childhood friend and gave her a slight shove toward the door. "Be off with you, Suz, before someone pulls out your blond hair!"

Suzanne gave a trill of laughter and moved with Arabella to the door. She confided in a carrying voice, "Do you know that Mama absolutely refused to allow poor Lord Graybourn to accompany me this morning? I vow she fears he is taken with Elsbeth." A look of rather morbid satisfaction crossed her face. "I daresay 'twould serve her right. First you catch an earl, and now Elsbeth seduces my eligible suitor from right under my nose!"

The earl did not regard this interchange. He was far too busy with his own thoughts. It was somewhat amusing to think that Lady Talgarth was the one to provide him with the perfect solution, a final test of the Frenchman's greed.

He said an absent good-bye to Suzanne, then watched Arabella follow her friend wordlessly from the room.

It was over luncheon that the earl informed the others of the invitation.

"How very nice of Aurelia," Lady Ann said, somewhat surprised that she had come around so quickly. In her guileless modesty she decided that perhaps Aurelia was not so very intolerant after all. Her mood lightened. But an hour before, Dr. Branyon had sent his stableboy, Will, to postpone their rendezvous for this morning. It seemed that Squire Dauntry's young son had inconsiderately cut his finger while escaping from his governess, thus requiring the doctor's skill with needle and thread.

Arabella saw a series of rather mixed emotions flit across Elsbeth's face and wondered what her sister was thinking. While Arabella was looking at Elsbeth, the earl's eyes were upon Gervaise's finely chiseled features. He was certain that he saw a momentary darkening in the young man's flashing eyes, then a slight smile of satisfaction about his mouth. The expression was gone in the next instant, and Gervaise's face was wreathed in smiles of innocent anticipation for a simple evening's pleasure.

After the ladies discussed at some length the appropriate gowns to be worn for the evening, the earl sat back in his chair and said cheerfully, "We are now blessed with the sun. Since it is the comte's last day with us, why do not you ladies take him for a final outing around the countryside?"

Elsbeth felt a tug of surprise. As for Arabella, she was too startled to speak.

The earl smiled warmly at her, then at Lady Ann and Elsbeth. "I only ask that you do not make a visit to the old abbey ruins."

With only the slightest of hesitation Gervaise replied gallantly, "I would be most delighted to be in the company of three such lovely ladies."

Arabella tried as best she could to mask the confusion she felt at the earl's request. She sensed her husband's eyes upon her, and thought she saw a plea in them. She swallowed a refusal, thinking now of Elsbeth, and managed to say evenly, "I should be happy, monsieur, to take you about. Mother, Elsbeth?"

The ladies acquiesced and left the dining room to change their gowns. "Excellent," the earl said as he pushed back his chair. "I pray that you will excuse me, for I must direct the carpenter in his work."

"What work, my lord?" Arabella inquired, totally at sea.

The earl looked mildly surprised. "Why, did I not tell you of the loose boards about in the earl's bedchamber, my dear? This afternoon I shall ensure that they are all nailed down properly so we will have no further need to keep the door locked."

"Oh, I see," Arabella said vaguely.

"It is wise to repair such hazards," Gervaise said smoothly. "I myself am of no use at all with such things as hammers and nails. It is I who will have the enjoyable afternoon, my lord."

"I trust so," the earl replied pleasantly.

The estate carpenter thought it rather odd to spend his afternoon pounding useless nails into the solid floor of the earl's bedchamber, but he raised no demur.

When the earl entered his bedchamber near to teatime, ostensibly to inspect the carpenter's work, he cheerfully praised the now overly secure floorboards.

" 'Twas really very little to be done, my lord," Turppin admitted sheepishly.

The earl smiled at him. "You have done just as I wished, Turppin. Here is a guinea for your fine labour."

The bewildered carpenter readily accepted the undeserved piece of gold, gathered his tools, and lumbered after the earl from the room.

"Crupper," the earl ordered once they reached the entrance hall, "take Turppin to the kitchen and provide him with a mug of ale."

Crupper sniffed disdainfully at the "sawdust man," as he condescendingly referred to the burly carpenter. "Yes, my lord," he replied stiffly, and crooked his finger in the carpenter's direction. "If you will follow me."

When the ladies and Gervaise returned from their ride, the earl saw that only Lady Ann appeared to be in a gay frame of mind. Arabella seemed to be particularly quiet. Even as he eyed her appreciatively, thinking how very lovely she appeared, her cheeks rosy from the fresh air and her thick hair tousled charmingly about her face, she turned to return his gaze, unasked questions mirrored on her face. He saw that everyone stayed together in the Velvet Room for tea until it was time to change for the Talgarth party.

While Grace was fetching her bath, Arabella restlessly paced her room. She was certain that Justin was up to something—something that had to do with Gervaise. It was simply not possible that he possessed the same information as she, yet he knew something! She thought about those loose floorboards he had taken great pains to mention at luncheon today—ridiculous! The floor was as sound as the gables on the abbey. And there was his strange reaction to Suzanne's invitation to Talgarth Hall. What made Arabella turn resolutely to the adjoining door was the memory of that silent pleading on his face when he wanted the ladies to take Gervaise for a ride for the afternoon. Damn, she wanted to know what Justin was up to and just why he had wanted all of them away from Evesham Abbey!

She squared her shoulders and knocked on the door. There was no answer. Frowning, she turned the knob. It was locked. "Justin!" she called loudly. There was no response.

Angrily she turned away from the door. Not only did he not wish to see her, she thought, he was avoiding her at all costs.

When all the ladies stood in the entrance hall decked out in their finery, the only gentleman present to pay them the requisite compliments was Gervaise. It was he who carefully placed their wraps about their shoulders. The earl appeared at the last moment, full of rueful apologies.

As the ladies were ushered into the carriage, Arabella sat forward in confusion. Both the earl and Gervaise were riding horseback. Damn him, she cursed silently, he will do anything to avoid me.

Talgarth Hall was a low, rambling mansion of Georgian style, erected by the father of the present Lord Talgarth. A mere upstart, Arabella's father had once commented derisively. Bright candlelight shone through its myriad sparkling windows, lighting the carriages of the local gentry in attendance. Roaring flambeaux were held by a score of footmen, some undoubtedly hired in for the occasion, Arabella thought wryly, all along the drive leading up to the steps of the mansion.

With a flourishing bow the earl opened their carriage door and solicitously assisted each lady to alight. Arabella was the last, and as Justin took her hand, she could not help her fingers clasping his convulsively.

"Come, Bella," he said softly, "let me see a smile on your lovely face."

"Justin . . ." she said, at once confused by his tone and the tenderness in his eyes.

He shook his head and helped her from the carriage. She fancied that he squeezed her hand before he released her to the tender ministrations of the Talgarth butler.

Lady Talgarth swooped down upon them before the butler could announce them formally, her overly bright, toothy smile embracing them all. "How delightful that you could come! My *dear* Ann, how very exquisite you are this evening! The gray is so much more *undaunting* than the wretched black. Of course, one should show proper respect, but . . ." Her voice trailed off meaningfully.

"How kind of you to say so, Aurelia," Lady Ann replied vaguely, choosing to ignore the barely veiled stricture. Her eyes were already searching about her. "Is Dr. Branyon arrived yet? Unfortunately, I was unable to see him during the day." She smiled sweetly into her hostess's glittering eyes.

"I daresay," the lady replied testily, turned, and bade the remainder of the party a brief good evening. Arabella looked as lovely as ever, she thought sourly. Nor could she disapprove Elsbeth's appearance. If only Suzanne were not so very fickle and flighty, she thought despairingly. Lord, she only hoped that Suzanne had the good sense to be dancing with Edmund now! She was doomed to disappointment, for Suzanne, an entrancing vision in a pink satin gown with a gauze overskirt of a paler shade of pink, gave a most unladylike crow of delight and rushed forward to clasp Lady Ann's hands. "How marvelous you look, Lady Ann! How good that all of you could come. Now, we shall enjoy ourselves!"

"Do control yourself, Suzanne," Lady Talgarth said reprovingly.

"Now, Mama," the young lady twinkled mischievously, "you know very well that our party now has *consequence*! My lord . . ." She curtsied demurely to the earl. "I vow a score of young ladies have been fluttering about the past hour or more waiting to meet you! You do not mind, do you, Bella? Your husband is in great demand!"

"Bear him off to his fate, Suz." Now, she thought, even

Suzanne was unwittingly helping Justin to avoid being alone with her. Arabella turned to Gervaise. "Monsieur? Will you not join us? There are many people you must meet."

There was an instant of hesitation in his dark eyes before he acquiesced. "But of course, Arabella," he murmured. "I am at your command."

"Mama," Arabella whispered, "look over by the fireplace. Poor Dr. Branyon, held in captive conversation with the gouty Lord Talgarth. But see, he already observes that you are about to rescue him."

"Hush, child, you must not put me to the blush." But Lady Ann's words were belied by a radiant smile that transformed her features.

Arabella introduced Gervaise to the quiet Miss Dauntry, the fourth daughter of a fondly doting mother. As he turned to lead the young lady to the dance floor, Arabella saw Lord Graybourn sweep by with Elsbeth on his arm.

Suzanne whirled by with Oliver Rollins firmly in tow. He was a chubby, well-meaning young man whom Arabella had bullied mercilessly from their childhood. Suzanne cried gaily, "Do not fret, Bella! I shall send one of *my* gallants to dance with you! But you must give up the earl, for we have an overabundance of young ladies tonight."

Oliver Rollins managed a stuttering hello before being borne away.

Arabella turned at a tap of a fan on her arm. Lady Crewe, a formidable dowager of indeterminate years and bright red hair, stood at her side, two great purple ostrich plumes swinging precariously about her thin face. "You are looking fit, Arabella. I see that marriage agrees with you. A fine choice your papa made." Her narrow eyes swept across the room to rest a moment on the earl, creditably performing his part in the country dance with the very buxom Miss Eliza Eldridge. "Yes," Lady Crewe said more to herself than to Arabella, "he is a fine figure of a man. How very like your papa he appears."

"Yes, it is true. He resembles father most strikingly," Arabella agreed, trying not to show her discomfiture to the perceptive old lady.

Lady Crewe paused a moment and turned a large ruby ring about her bony finger. "Perhaps your mama will be surprised, Arabella, but I do not fault her for marrying Dr. Paul

Branyon. All that nonsense of Aurelia's about his not being a 'lord' is really quite provoking." Her shrewd eyes bore into Arabella's mind. "I can see that you, my dear Arabella, have given your approval. 'Tis most wise of you, my dear."

"Yes," Arabella said in a low voice.

"Good. I will tell you, young lady, that for the first time in nearly twenty years I have found something admirable about your mother besides her good looks and innocent sweetness. At last she has shown character and spirit."

Arabella looked up, blinking rapidly. "I . . . I am sorry, ma'am, but what did you say?"

"Now, Arabella, you are a married lady. I marvel at the fact that your mother survived these nineteen years and still retained her youthful bloom. Perhaps God, in his infinite wisdom, does reward the innocent."

There was sudden understanding in Arabella's eyes, understanding that she would not have had, had Justin not spoken frankly to her about her father. She looked searchingly at Lady Crewe, noting faint traces of beauty still on her thin face. She thought it very likely that once, a long time ago, Lady Crewe and her father had been lovers. She felt no anger, only a mildly detached acceptance of the fact.

Lady Crewe observed the new maturity on the young countess's face and said kindly, "Do come and call on me, Arabella. I believe that we would have many interesting topics of conversation."

"I shall, ma'am," Arabella promised. She realized that she did indeed wish to further her acquaintance with Lady Crewe. She left the older woman's side to join the dancing with Sir Darien Snow, a longtime crony of her father's. He smelled faintly of musk. She saw somewhat sadly that the years were gaining inexorably upon Sir Darien, deep lines etched about his thin lips, the red veins standing more prominently on the backs of his hands. He was as gentle and unassuming as her father had been loud and boisterous. Undemanding as always, he led her through the steps with the practiced grace of long years in society, not importuning her to speak. It was just as well, for Arabella's thoughts were far away from her companion. She espied Gervaise dancing with Elsbeth. If only there were some way to part them! She tugged on Sir Darien's arm, taking the lead from him, to draw closer to Elsbeth and Gervaise. At least she wanted to hear what they were saying. As they drew near, she heard Gervaise say in his lilting caressing voice, "How lovely you are this evening, *ma petite*. These English parties seem to agree with you." Arabella and Sir Darien were swept away in the crush of other dancers, and she was unable to hear any more.

"Thank you, Gervaise. I do much enjoy dancing and parties. My aunt was rather retiring and did very little entertaining." Elsbeth paused a moment before continuing, a hint of guilt in her voice, "I really should write to my Aunt Caroline. She has shown me only kindness, you know."

"Yes, of course," Gervaise replied absently. He gazed down at his half-sister, her dark eyes bright and almond-shaped, as were his. He knew her simple innocence, her unquestioned trust of those about her. If only that wretched old servant Josette had told him sooner that he was not the natural son of Thomas de Trécassis, indeed, that he and Elsbeth were born of the same mother. That he had made love to her that last time, after he knew she was his half-sister, made him hate himself all the more now. He would be gone soon, gone with what was rightfully his. Yet, somehow, he wanted to lessen the pain Elsbeth would feel upon his leaving. He missed a step in the dance and trod upon her foot. He was instantly contrite. "How very clumsy of me, Elsbeth, do forgive me. You see, there are many things I do not do well."

She smiled up at him, and sensing a sadness in him, replied quickly, "It is nothing, Gervaise. Do not speak like that, I beg you. You do yourself an injustice."

"No, Elsbeth," he said softly, "it is true. I . . . I am really quite unworthy of you, you know. I have done much thinking, little cousin. Our plan to go away together, it is impossible. You must see that, Elsbeth. I would be the most dishonourable of men to take you from your family, to expose you to a life full of uncertainties."

He saw confusion darken her eyes. Words tumbled from her mouth. "Gervaise, no, you cannot mean it! There will be no uncertainties. Have you forgotten my ten thousand pounds? As my husband, the money would belong to you!"

"Husband!" he cried harshly. "*Your* husband? Come, Elsbeth, it is time that you learned more of the realities of

life. It is time you became a woman! You can no longer behave as a child!"

"I . . . I don't know what you mean, Gervaise," she stammered with deepening confusion. "You tell me to become a
woman. Did you not teach me what it was to be a woman
grown?" She tensed in his arms, hardly aware that her feet
still moved to the music.

"You are such a romantic child!" His lips curled, and he
forced his voice to mockery. "All I did, Elsbeth, was take
your virginity and provide you with a romantic summer idyll,
nothing more."

"But you said that you loved me," she whispered, her
words a plea for understanding.

He replied with a flippancy that made her shiver, "Of
course I told you I loved you. Were you a woman and not a
child, you would have known that passionate words of love
make an *affaire* all the more exciting and pleasurable."

She asked in a voice scarce above a whisper, "Then you do
not love me, Gervaise?"

"Of a certainty I love you," he said coldly, "as my . . . my
cousin. It would be unnatural were I not to care for you in
that way."

"Then why did you tell me we would elope together? Do
you not recall your promises to me?"

He laughed unpleasantly. "I said only those things *you*
wished to be told, Elsbeth. A wife will never be a part of *my*
plans! That you chose to believe otherwise must show you
that you are naught but a romantic child. Come, my dear, it
is time for you to emerge from your innocence. Thank me
for telling you the truth now. I vow it kinder than leaving
you to uncertainty. You would never have heard from me
again, you know."

"Was I really such a child to give myself freely to you?"
she asked, tears now swimming in her eyes.

"Yes, you were," he replied after but a moment's hesitation. "You desired substance and reality when there was
naught but dreams and phantoms. You must learn to face
life, Elsbeth, not cower and weep like a helpless child. You
will thank me one day, I think. Hearts do not break—another
piece of foolish nonsense. You will forget me, Elsbeth. Forget
me, and grow strong, become a woman. Do you begin to understand?" His eyes softened, yet she did not notice, for her

head was bowed. Gervaise looked up to see Lord Graybourn walking purposefully toward them. As the dance ended, he said softly, "You are English, Elsbeth. Your future belongs in England, wedded to an English gentleman. You have tasted a brief *affaire de coeur*. It is over now."

"Yes, it is over," she repeated vaguely. She sniffed back her tears and looked up into his face. "I would that you take me to Lady Ann, Gervaise."

After Gervaise left Elsbeth, he gazed about the crowded room, his eyes resting finally upon the earl. Soon now Gervaise could test his wits against the earl's. He watched him meditatively for a moment, then turned to take the hand of Miss Rutherford. He saw Elsbeth being led onto the dance floor by Lord Graybourn, and his eyes darkened for an instant. He whirled Miss Rutherford suddenly in his arms. She gasped and laughed delightedly.

At the close of the dance, Arabella allowed Sir Darien to take her back to her mother. Lady Ann said complacently, "It appears that Elsbeth is quite popular tonight. And as for you, my dear, I saw you speaking with Lady Crewe. Whatever did you have to talk so long about with her?"

"Oh, nothing of any importance," she replied carefully. She quickly changed the subject. "Sir Darien grows so frail, Mama. I worry about his health."

Dr. Branyon said, "Nothing wrong with him, to speak of. It's merely age, my dear, merely age." He was vaguely aware that his future daughter-in-law was behaving in a perfunctory manner. He saw her eyes scanning the dance floor, and said with a smile, "I believe Justin is fetching a glass of punch for Miss Eldridge, Bella. If Miss Talgarth has her way, I fear you will have no chance to dance this evening with your husband."

"It does not matter, sir," she said, and turned away. She heard Suzanne's bright laughter from among the throng of young people.

Arabella felt suddenly disgruntled. Everyone, including her husband, appeared to be having such a gay time, while she . . . What you need is a deep breath of fresh evening air, my girl, she told herself. "Excuse me, Mama, Dr. Branyon," she said. "It is so close in here, I think I shall step onto the balcony for a moment.

It took her several minutes to reach the long, narrow windows, pull the latch, and slip into the moonlit night. She drew a deep breath, savouring the fresh cool air upon her face. She gazed out over the neatly scythed front lawn, and then to the east side of Talgarth Hall, where Lady Talgarth had most adamantly insisted upon designing a parterre of more noble proportions than the one at Evesham Abbey. Her result had not been a felicitous one. The trimmed rows of yew bushes seemed thin, the daffodils, roses, and other flowers bedraggled and faded.

She glanced away from the parterre and found her attention caught by a cloaked gentleman walking quickly to the side of the hall toward the stables. There was something familiar about the way he moved, an almost cocky gait that jarred her memory. She watched him now with more than idle interest.

As the man neared the east side of Talgarth Hall, he turned abruptly to look behind him. The moonlight fell directly onto his face, and Arabella felt her heart jump. It was Gervaise. In that moment he turned again and disappeared around the side of the hall. How furtively he was acting! And he was on his way to the stables! She felt excitement mingle with fear that made the hair bristle on the back of her neck. She turned and rushed back through the open window. She searched the dance floor but did not see the earl. The minutes, precious minutes, dragged by, but still she could not find him. With sudden decision she turned away and scanned the width of the ballroom. She knew she would never make her way through the throng of guests without more interminable delay. She slipped back onto the balcony, leaned over the side, and mentally measured the distance to the ground. It was much too great to risk jumping. Her eyes fell upon a knotty old elm tree whose wispy branches touched the far edge of the balcony. Without a thought to its sturdiness, she ran to the end of the balcony, bundled her skirts above her knees, and reached out for the branch. She clasped it firmly in her gloved hands and swung out away from the balcony, dangling for a moment in the air before her feet connected with a knobby outgrowth in its trunk. She felt the branch groan under her weight. She paid it no heed, easing her hands along the branch until, without too much risk, she was able to drop to a lower branch. Her skirts tangled about her legs. "Damnation!" she growled aloud. "If God would mete out justice, he would give me a sturdy pair of breeches!"

She looked down at the smooth grass below, took a deep breath, and kicked free of the tree. She fell lightly on her feet, then set off at a run toward the stables, clutching her bothersome skirts high above her ankles. She heard from a distance, to the other side of the hall, the loud laughter of the servants who had accompanied their masters and mistresses. Suddenly she heard the steady pounding of horse's hooves.

She quickly lowered herself to her knees behind a yew bush and waited. But a moment later, horse and rider passed her, and she saw Gervaise's pale face in the moonlight.

She forced herself not to move, counting down long seconds, until he was out of her sight. She surged to her feet and ran to the stables. When she drew up, winded, at the lighted stable door, she found herself facing a bewildered groom, who seemed unable to do anything but stare open mouthed at her.

"My lady?" he asked uncertainly, recognizing her as Miss Deverill, now the Countess of Strafford.

Arabella drew two more panting breaths, took in the patent uncertainty on the groom's face, and reverted instantly to an arrogant, haughty Miss Deverill who demanded unswerving obedience. "What is your name?" she demanded imperiously.

"Allen, my lady," the groom replied promptly.

"Very well, Allen, I wish you to saddle Miss Talgarth's mare, Bluebell, this very instant? Be quick about it, for I have no desire to kick up my heels here in this stable!"

"But, my lady . . ." The groom faltered, wishing there were someone to tell him whether or not to give Miss Talgarth's mare to the countess.

A black brow flared disdainfully and cold gray eyes swept over the hapless groom. "Come, now, Allen, you would not wish to lose your post for the want of simple obedience." She said nothing more, merely fixed her eyes upon the groom until he turned to do her bidding.

She grinned at his back.

Arabella eyed the gentle Bluebell with distaste. If only she had Lucifer! He would gallop like the wind. "Well, you comfortable old hack," she said as the groom tossed her into the saddle, " 'tis off for a moonlight ride for us.

"I thank you, my good fellow," she said to the groom, her eyes alight with mischief. "Assure Miss Talgarth that her horse will be returned safe and sound!" Before the groom could further protest, Arabella dug in her heels and wheeled Bluebell down the drive.

Her elegant hairstyle became loose masses of streaming hair even before Bluebell gained the main road. She pressed the mare to a steady gallop, promising her a large pail of oats when they reached Evesham Abbey. Yes, she thought, without a doubt Gervaise is riding to Evesham Abbey. It was about the only thing she was certain of at the moment.

She knew that what she was doing was perfectly outrageous. She really had no clear idea at the moment of what she was going to do. Follow him? Confront him? Again she felt a tingling of fear. It was foolhardy not to have found Justin, no matter what the delay. She knew it, but now it was simply too late. "Come, my girl," she said stoutly, "no recriminations." She lowered her head and kept her eyes steady on the road in front of her.

As she turned Bluebell onto the graveled drive in front of Evesham Abbey, Arabella was not at all surprised to see Gervaise's horse tethered to a bush just to the side of the front steps. She reined in the panting Bluebell and slid from the saddle. Everything was eerily quiet. Only a few candles were shining from the first-floor windows. There was but one light glowing from the second floor—it was from the earl's bedchamber.

She raced up the front steps and pushed the great doors open. The entrance hall was empty. She frowned. Where were the servants? she wondered.

She chewed on her lower lip, trying to decide what she should do. She thought of her small pistol, safely placed in the night table beside her bed. Well, it was simply impossible to think of fetching it, with Gervaise either in or near the earl's bedchamber. Her father's gun collection in the library! She sped silently through the entrance hall, past the Velvet Room, and quietly slipped into the library. Her father's favorite brace of pistols lay in their velvet case atop the mantelpiece. She gingerly grasped the butt of one of the pistols and drew it down. She felt again tingly with excitement as she probed the barrel with the loading rod. Finally the pistol was loaded and primed.

Slowly she mounted the staircase, the gun tucked in the folds of her skirt. It was Gervaise who had chosen the time and place where she could confront him. She wondered if she were not trying to prove something to Justin.

The door to the earl's bedchamber stood slightly ajar. She saw the flicker of a single candle weave itself into bizarre shapes and dancing patterns on the opposite wall. Slowly she pressed against the door.

The earl's eyes swept the crowded room as they had at regular short intervals throughout the evening. He soon spotted Miss Lucinda Rutherford, standing quite alone, looking for the world like a homely friendless little pug. "Damn!" he said under his breath. But a short time ago he had seen Gervaise leading Miss Rutherford into a quadrille. Satisfied, he had left the large ballroom with Lord Talgarth leaning heavily on his arm. "Enough of this nonsense," his gouty lordship had said.

He looked down distractedly into Miss Talgarth's upturned face. "Do forgive me, Suzanne, but I must take you to your mama."

Suzanne's lovely eyes widened. "But—" she began.

"I am sorry, but there is no time to explain."

Her blond curls bobbed over her ears as she cocked her head to one side. "Very well, my lord"—she pouted—"but I think it monstrous ungallant of you."

The earl offered Lady Talgarth and Suzanne a perfunctory bow before retreating quickly to the ballroom entrance. His eyes searched the room once again for Gervaise. He was not there. He had taken the bait, and Justin knew that if he did not hurry, he would lose all, through naught but his own carelessness.

"Justin!" He whirled about at the sound of his name. He saw Dr. Branyon beckoning to him. He was loath to waste a precious minute. "Arabella was searching for you," Lady Ann called. "I thought she had intended to go to the balcony, but now I cannot find her. Have you seen her, Justin?"

"No, I have not," the earl replied. "You must excuse me . . ." He turned abruptly and wended his way through the chattering guests from the ballroom. It was only when he stepped out into the clear moonlight that the force of Lady

Ann's words broke upon him. He felt a moment of murderous fury. Arabella was gone, fled with Gervaise.

He had thought himself so very clever, bending all his energies upon trapping the Frenchman. He had even thrown her in his company all the afternoon, while he had carefully looked for the proof he needed in Gervaise's room.

He gained the stables in a trice. The groom stood in the doorway, fidgeting nervously. He was not certain whether he should have sent a message to Lord Talgarth that the Countess of Strafford had taken Miss Talgarth's horse.

The earl burst in upon the groom. "My horse is the bay stallion already saddled in the far stall. Bring him to me at once."

The gentleman's peremptory command emptied the groom's mind of his other worry. Somehow the gentleman looked familiar to him.

But a few moments later, as he watched the gentleman bound upon his horse's back, he remembered who he was. "My lord, her ladyship, your wife . . ." The words died on the groom's lips. The Earl of Strafford was plunging down the drive astride his stallion. He did not look back.

Arabella stood motionless in the open doorway, the heavy pistol held firmly at her side, hidden in the folds of her skirt.

She watched Gervaise as he stood before *The Dance of Death,* a candle raised high in his hand. The image of Josette flashed through her mind. The old servant had stood just as Gervaise stood now, her eyes searching the macabre carving.

She saw him carefully probe with his left hand into the slight hollow recess just beneath the skeleton's raised shield. She thought his fingers closed over something, perhaps a small knob. As if by magic, the lower edge of the skeleton's heavy dark wooden shield suddenly slid away and exposed a hidden compartment, no wider than a hand's width.

"It is a very clever hiding place, monsieur. Perhaps Josette would have found it if I had not interrupted her." She was pleased at the cold preciseness of her voice.

Gervaise leaped back from the panel, surprise and then anger distorting his patrician face. His flashing eyes swept past her. He had expected the earl. When he realized that she was alone, he felt his anger melt away, and he smiled almost genially at her. His hand relaxed away from his pistol and fell to his side. "Ah, my lovely Countess. Would it be foolish of me to ask why you are here?"

"Not at all, Gervaise. I was on the balcony and saw you going to the stables. I followed you."

"A wild moonlit ride," he mused. "And in your ball gown. How very enterprising of you, *chère madame*."

"But not so enterprising as you, monsieur," she said composedly. "Do not, I pray, let me disturb your search."

He paused a moment, then shrugged indifferently. "Very well. You can witness my legacy." He slipped his fingers into the small compartment. A bellow of fury erupted from his throat. "They are gone! It is not possible! No one knew, save Magdalaine."

Arabella drew back from his sudden rage. "What is gone, monsieur? What did Magdalaine hide in the compartment?"

He seemed almost unaware of her presence. "The Trécassis emeralds. Worth a king's ransom! Gone!"

For a fleeting instant Arabella pictured the smudged lines of Magdalaine's letter to her lover that she had not been able to decipher. She felt a sudden knot of anguish in her stomach. Her father had sent Magdalaine to France, in the midst of the dangerous revolution, to bring him the emeralds. That was what Magdalaine must have meant in her letter to her lover about their becoming rich from her husband's greed. Magdalaine and her lover had sought to gain freedom from Arabella's father. Had Magdalaine been fleeing from Evesham Abbey, with perhaps Elsbeth in her arms, to meet her lover at the old abbey ruins? Had her husband caught them? Murdered Magdalaine's lover? In his fury, had he also murdered Magdalaine?

Gervaise had regained control of himself. He said meditatively, "My dear Arabella, I find it most curious that you are so greatly apprised of my affairs. Perhaps it is you who found the emeralds?" He took a purposeful step toward her.

"No, monsieur, I did not find your emeralds," she said quietly, her thoughts still on her father and the violent deaths of so long ago.

"Somehow I do not quite believe you, *chère madame*." His hand shot out to grab her arm.

Arabella jumped back and drew the pistol from the folds of her skirt. She cast him a glance of contempt. "I am not such a fool, monsieur, as to face a murderer without protecting myself."

A somewhat unpleasant note entered his voice. "Murder, *madame?* Come, you speculate wildly."

"No, Gervaise, I know that you helped poor Josette to her death. It seemed more than peculiar to me that she should be wandering about Evesham Abbey in the middle of the night without any light to guide her. It was careless of you not to have left a candle near her. Why did you kill her, Gervaise? Was it because I caught her in the earl's bedchamber, her hands roving over *The Dance of Death?*"

He made no answer. She added in a still-cool, precise voice, "Or perhaps she threatened to expose you, monsieur, to tell everyone that you were a bastard, that you were Magdalaine's son? Did she tell you that your seduction of Elsbeth violated the very laws of nature? I only pray that Elsbeth does not ever discover that you are her half-brother."

His face had gone chalk white in the dim candlelight, his dark eyes so blind with bitterness and anger that they showed as would black chunks of coal against the whiteness of new snow. His voice was harsh and grating. "No, Elsbeth does not know! I did not realize it myself until that wretched old woman told me! Were it not for your damned interference, *madame,* and that of your husband, I should be away now, free, with what is rightfully mine!"

"Yours, monsieur?" she spat contemptuously. "You are no Trécassis, Gervaise. If the emeralds do exist, they would belong to Elsbeth."

He stood staring at her, his face now flushed angrily.

She pressed. "Did it not occur to you that the skeleton in the old abbey ruins was your father? I know it for a fact, for after you so obligingly entombed me in that chamber, I found a letter in his breeches pocket. There is no doubt, Gervaise."

"Damn you, your father killed him!" He lunged at her in a frenzy, taking her off her guard. His fingers tightened painfully about her wrist, and the pistol went spinning from her hand and thudded to the floor.

He flung her back, and she grabbed at the back of a chair to keep from falling. Arabella watched him pick up the pistol and lay it on a table beside him. Still she felt no fear of him, only anger at herself for being so foolish as to allow him to catch her unawares.

"Now, my dear Arabella," he said with a curl to his lips, "I shall know the truth from you."

"I cannot help you, Gervaise," she said levelly.

She saw a sudden transformation in him. His dark eyes widened with a calculated gleam. He smiled at her unpleasantly. "You know, my dear Countess, you are really quite a lovely woman. Perhaps it would not be a bad thing at all to have you for my companion, at least until your wealthy husband provides me with ample compensation. Of course, I would prefer the emeralds, but if you will not tell me where you have hidden them, I shall not repine. You will enjoy Bruxelles, Arabella."

She drew up to her full height and stared at him coldly. "I know nothing about your emeralds, Gervaise. Do not imagine that your forcing me to accompany you would be an easy task. Ah, I can see that the thought of dragging me screaming and kicking from here gives you pause."

"Your search has ended, monsieur! Are these what you have sought so ruthlessly?"

Arabella whirled around to see the earl standing quietly in the open doorway, countless bright green glowing stones nestled in his outstretched hand.

"Justin!" she gasped. "Oh, how did you know? How came you here?" But as she spoke, she realized that she had blundered into a trap set by him.

The earl scarce heard her questions. He had overheard what Arabella had said to Gervaise. She had never intended to flee with the Frenchman. Indeed, now, at least, she wanted nothing to do with him.

He smiled at her gently, then turned to Gervaise. "You took the bait, just as I thought you would, monsieur. I must thank Arabella for holding you here, else I alone might have missed you. Did you think me a fool, Gervaise? I knew weeks ago that you were not the Comte de Trécassis. Although my informant was uncertain as to your true heritage—well, it is not important now, is it? No, monsieur, I sought more knowledge of you. I searched your room, you know. Without the exact instructions Magdalaine wrote to Thomas de Trécassis of the hiding place of the emeralds, I knew I should never know what it was you sought. With the instructions, it was all quite simple. The frustration you must have known all these weeks!"

"The emeralds are mine!" Gervaise shouted, his eyes never leaving the bright gems in the earl's hand.

The earl shook his head. He turned to Arabella. "Now you see him as he really is, Bella, a ruthless, scheming thief."

Gervaise gazed at the earl. It was all so very easy. There, the earl, all his attention riveted on his wife. Gervaise pulled the pistol from his waistcoat and gave a crow of triumph. "The emeralds, my lord!"

The earl reluctantly looked away from Arabella and regarded the Frenchman with almost detached interest. "As you will, monsieur. They are really not important now. I have achieved what I wished—Arabella now sees the truth about you."

"Justin . . ." she said, now understanding his motives. He waved her to silence and with cold indifference tossed the necklace to Gervaise. He slipped it into his pocket and stood, his head tossed back, gloating his victory.

"You know, my lord," Gervaise said conversationally, "it should have been so very simple for me to fetch the emeralds. But no, you must needs meddle. You forced me to go to desperate lengths, my lord, to retrieve what was by all rights mine! The old servant Josette was an encumbrance, with all her righteous rantings about conscience and duty. 'Twas a pity, her death. It really does not matter now that you believe me, but I will tell you. I sought only to speak to the old woman that night, but she fled from me—afraid, she was, so afraid that she ran down the dark corridor, tripped, and fell down the stairs. As to causing the rocks to collapse in the old abbey ruins, I had no wish to harm you, Arabella, merely to empty Evesham Abbey of his lordship's interfering presence. Well, the game has taken a complicated turn, my lord, but I shall contrive."

He paused, then continued in a meditative voice, "You know, my lord, I have never liked you. Arrogantly proud you are, just as was the old earl. Of course, I could not come for my birthright while he lived. Thomas de Trécassis cautioned me to wait, to be patient.

"Though I am not by nature a murderer, unlike *your* father, *madame*," he spat, "I do not think, my lord, that I shall be overly troubled at your unfortunate demise. It is an eye for an eye, as you English say."

The earl swiftly measured the distance between him and

the Frenchman, saw the pistol had yet to be cocked, and dived his hand into the pocket of his cloak for Arabella's small gun.

"I hope you rot in hell with her father," Gervaise cried. He whipped back the hammer and stepped forward.

"Damn you, no!" Arabella shouted, and threw herself in front of her husband.

A deafening roar rent the silence of the room. Arabella felt a great force hurl into her body, its impact flinging her backward. She was vaguely aware that Justin's arm was about her waist, supporting her upright. She saw Gervaise frantically leaping for her pistol on the table, his face distorted with frustrated rage. She felt Justin's arm jerk up, saw her own small pistol in his hand, and heard its staccato report. How odd Gervaise suddenly appeared! He clapped his hand to his arm and sank forward to the carpet on his knees.

She felt a strange lassitude.

It was as if through a darkening mist that she saw her husband's face above her, and said only, "Justin . . ."

She felt suddenly weightless, only dimly aware that the earl had lifted her into his arms. She thought she heard him speaking to her, but she could not be certain.

She tried to focus her eyes upon his face, but saw instead a movement from the corner of her eye. Deep cold fear brought her momentarily back to her senses. Gervaise was staggering to his feet and moving, swiftly now, across the room to the open door.

"He is escaping," she cried, the effort to produce the words spinning her down into molten pain. She felt the bed under her and saw her husband's face above her. "It is all right, Bella. Let him go. 'Tis no longer important."

She accepted his words and was silent. Yet there was something else that was important, something she had to tell him. She struggled to keep the blackness from pulling her away. "Justin . . ." she whispered.

"Do not talk, Bella," he ordered. She felt his hands on her gown, ripping it open.

"Justin, please listen," she pleaded, trying to bring her hand to his arm. "You must not tell Elsbeth that Gervaise is her half-brother. You must not tell her. It would destroy her."

She did not hear his sharp intake of breath. She let the

darkness close over her mind and take her away from the pain.

The earl ripped away her bodice and the silk chemise below, to bare the wound in her shoulder. The ball had entered high above her left breast. If she had not thrown herself in front of him, he thought grimly, the bullet would have gone straight through his heart. He worked with the efficiency that the years in the army had taught him, all of his energy focused on stanching the flow of blood. He wadded his handkerchief into a thick pad and pressed it over the wound. The blood welled up over his fingers. Even as he heard the servants' hurried footsteps up the stairs, he did not look up or lessen the steady pressure.

He had ordered all the staff belowstairs for the evening. The sound of gunfire had, thankfully, made them disobey his orders. Giles stood panting in the doorway. "My lord!"

The earl looked only momentarily into the footman's white face "Quickly, Giles," he rapped out, "ride to Talgarth Hall and fetch Dr. Branyon. Her ladyship has been hurt."

He heard Crupper's familiar wheezing behind Giles. "Giles is bringing Dr. Branyon. Crupper, have Mrs. Tucker tear up clear linen and bring hot water."

"Yes, my lord," Crupper croaked.

When the hot water and clean linen were assembled by the bedside, the earl curtly dismissed Mrs. Tucker and Crupper. He could not bear the dazed looks on their faces, knowing that they must reflect his own.

He cupped his hand under Arabella's breast to feel her heartbeat. It was rapid, but, he thought, steady. He looked down at her pale face, the heavy black lashes lying still against her cheeks. If his clever plan to expose Gervaise cost her her life, he knew there would never be forgiveness for himself.

However long ago, he did not know, Arabella had learned the truth about Gervaise. Had she not spoken with scorn and anger at the thought of him taking her with him? He found that he cared not about the past now. They would begin anew, forget about her father's ridiculous will, her infatuation with the Frenchman, all the vicious misunderstandings that had kept them at dagger points.

He slowly lifted the pad from the wound. He breathed a sigh of relief, for the bleeding had slowed to a trickle. The wound was deep, he knew, and Dr. Branyon would have to remove the ball. He prayed that she would not regain consciousness until it was over.

As he waited, he thought of her final words to him before she lost consciousness. He realized that she had known many things about Gervaise that he himself had not discovered. So Magdalaine was Gervaise's mother. Arabella had known, yet she had not told him. He shook his head regretfully. There was much they had to talk about when she was well again.

He frowned suddenly, recalling her words about Elsbeth. Why should Elsbeth not know that Gervaise was her half-brother? Certainly it would come as a shock, but still . . . And she had said something about "it would destroy her." Surely that made no sense. He leaned over and gently smoothed a lock of tangled hair from Arabella's forehead.

The earl did not again look up until Dr. Branyon hurried into the room. "Good God, Justin! What has happened?"

The earl gently lifted the wadded pad from Arabella's shoulder, his eyes meeting Dr. Branyon's.

Dr. Branyon abruptly turned and held up his hand for Lady Ann and Elsbeth to stop. He said curtly, "Ann, I do not want you in here. Take Elsbeth and go downstairs. I will come to you as soon as I can."

"No," Lady Ann cried, advancing.

"Do as I tell you, Ann," Dr. Branyon said sternly, not softening his tone. "You would only be a hindrance. Send Giles up when he arrives with my instruments."

"Please, Ann," the earl added more gently, "trust me. I swear that she will be all right."

Elsbeth was looking dazedly at the scene before her. Arabella was shot. Gervaise was gone. She knew the answer to her question even before she spoke. "My lord," she whispered, "did Gervaise do this terrible thing?"

"Yes, Elsbeth," the earl answered simply. "He is gone now, and I am certain that he will not return here."

Elsbeth lowered her head and allowed Lady Ann to take her arm. "You . . . you will inform me as soon as you have taken care of her?" Lady Ann asked Dr. Branyon. He nodded to her, knowing that it cost her a great deal to leave her daughter. She turned, and he saw that she leaned heavily on Elsbeth's arm.

"Tell me what happened, Justin."

As Dr. Branyon cleaned the wound and probed the area to determine the depth of the ball, the earl related all he knew, his voice low, his choice of words placing entire blame upon himself. He omitted any mention of Gervaise's and Arabella's relationship, and for some reason he could not be certain of, he said nothing of Gervaise being the son of Magdalaine.

"Is that all?" Dr. Branyon asked when Justin had finished his recital, his eyes hard upon the earl's face.

"No, but it is all that I may tell you," he replied.

Dr. Branyon straightened. "You know that I must remove the ball when Giles arrives with my instruments. You have had experience with wounded men in battle, Justin. Will you assist me?"

"Of course," the earl said tersely. He realized that he was clasping Arabella's hand. He did not release it.

Arabella moaned.

Both men stiffened at the sound, their eyes meeting over Arabella's still figure.

"It is not fair, Paul," the earl said harshly. "It is too much for her to suffer the operation."

For an instant Arabella felt only a great weight upon her chest. With an effort she forced her eyes to open and focus upon the faces above her. She felt bewildered. "Justin . . . Paul?"

A white-hot pain flashed through to her mind. She pressed her head back against the pillow as hard as she could, arching her back upward, trying vainly to still the agonizing pain in her shoulder. She felt a damp cloth being daubed against her forehead, strong hands clasping her shoulders, holding her steady.

Slowly she began to gain control over the dizzying, scalding pain. She bit down on her lower lip until her mind focused itself where she wished.

"Bella, can you understand me?"

She forced her eyes to meet the face that spoke the words. "Justin?" she murmured.

"Yes, my love. You will have to be brave, Bella. The ball in your shoulder must be removed. Do you understand me?"

His low, deep voice was so very vibrant with concern. Vaguely she realized that he had called her his "love." Suddenly she felt above all things that she must know if he really cared for her. She swallowed down a cry of pain and rasped, "Do you mean it, Justin? Please . . . I must know if you mean it."

For a moment the earl thought she had fallen into delirium. He responded only to the frantic urgency in her voice. "Of course I mean what I said, Bella," he said gently.

"I . . . I am so very glad. I thought that you still hated me." The few words cost her dearly. She turned her head slightly on the pillow and closed her eyes against tears of pain.

A glint of understanding lit the earl's gray eyes. He gently kissed her on the cheek.

She was no longer aware of him, only of the vast molten shroud of agony that encased her.

The earl did not look up from her face until Giles entered on tiptoe bearing Dr. Branyon's surgical case. He gazed at the sharp, slender scapel and the array of other equally unpleasant instruments and said in a shaking voice, "God, how I wish we could spare her this." He had seen so many men in battle, crying out their pain until their voices were unintelligible rasping sounds in their raw throats.

Dr. Branyon's voice was curt. "Justin, you must hold her firmly. I shall remove the ball as quickly as possible." He added more gently as the earl hesitated, "Your pity cannot help her, only your strength."

The earl placed his hands upon her shoulders, unwilling at first to bear his weight upon her. He thought perhaps that she had fallen again into unconsciousness until Dr. Branyon, in a sudden sure movement, dug the scapel into the wound.

She writhed suddenly beneath his hands, a choking cry torn from her throat.

"Damm it, hold her!" Dr. Branyon shouted above her cry.

Amid the blurring, horrible agony, she suddenly saw herself whirled away, back into time, years ago. Her father stood above her, his lips curled derisively, his voice mocking. "A simple fall and you shed tears and cry out your foolish pain! I am disappointed in you, Arabella!" Strangely, Justin's face took on her father's features, and she found herself biting ferociously down upon her lower lip, choking back her tears. She licked her dry lips and tasted a drop of her own blood.

She gulped convulsively and gritted her teeth. She whispered to the face above her, "I will not be a coward."

The earl looked down at her helplessly. Her eyes were enormous gray pools of suffering. Yet she made no sound.

"There! I've found it. Hold her firm, Justin, I must draw out the ball."

As the curved knife closed under the ball, Arabella felt a shattering explosion in her head. She was plummeted into a vortex of searing, unbearable agony. She tried desperately to jerk away from the excruciating pain, yet she could not move. She gazed hopelessly into the blurred face above her, choked back a sob, and slid away into merciful blackness.

"Arabella!"

"She is not dead, Justin, merely unconscious. It is amazing that she bore the pain for so long."

The earl forced his eyes from his wife's pale face and gazed at the ball. "It did not splinter?" he asked in a shaking voice.

"No, my little Bella is very lucky." Dr. Branyon gingerly placed the blood-covered ball and his knife upon the table beside the bed. He straightened and ran his hand over his perspiring brow.

The earl wet a strip of linen and gently bathed away the blood from around the wound, and then with a grimace washed away the purple rivulets from between her breasts.

"Hand me the basilicum powder, Justin. Then we will bandage her and fashion a sling for her arm."

The earl did as he was bid, surprised that his hands went so calmly about their tasks. Soon the bandage was in place around her shoulder and her arm supported in a sling of white linen. Dr. Branyon rose and placed his hand upon the earl's arm. "Well done, Justin. All we have to fear now is a fever."

The earl suddenly became aware that Arabella was still naked to the waist, her gown in shreds around her. "Her nightgown, Paul. I do not wish Lady Ann to see her like this."

"No, I think not yet." Dr. Branyon shook his head. "Putting her into a nightgown might cause the bleeding to begin again. Help me remove her clothing, then we will place only a light coverlet over her."

"I shall take care of her, Paul. If you would speak with Ann and Elsbeth . . ."

"As you wish, Justin. I will bring Ann up to see her presently."

The earl nodded and turned his attention to his wife.

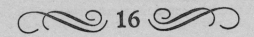

## 16

The earl took a deep drink of the strong black coffee. He raised weary eyes to Lady Ann. "You look fagged, Ann. Why do you not retire? I shall stay with her, you need have no fear on that score."

"No, Justin," she replied firmly, eyes traveling to the motionless figure in the middle of the large bed as she spoke.

"How very odd that it is morning," she said, and rose to fling open the long velvet curtains. Sunlight flooded into the earl's bedchamber.

She turned to let the warm sunlight shine upon her face. "You know, Justin, Elsbeth has surprised me. I had thought that she would be quite upset, for she is very sensitive, yet she was strangely calm. Until Paul came down, she sat in front of the fireplace gazing silently into the flames. When he told us what happened, that Gervaise had come to Evesham Abbey to steal the emeralds, she looked up at us and said something about it being all her fault, that she was to blame for what happened. I could get nothing more out of her. I finally convinced her to let Paul give her a sleeping draught."

The earl merely grunted, his mind too fogged with fatigue to think about anyone else save Arabella.

Lady Ann took a turn about the room to stretch her stiff muscles. She poured herself a cup of tea, disliking the black coffee, and walked to the bedside to look down upon her daughter. She placed her hand lightly on Arabella's brow. "Thank God," she breathed, "there is still no fever. I would dread Paul bleeding her, for she has lost so much blood already.

"You know, Justin," she continued, turning back to the earl, "Paul must have reminded me three times before he fell asleep that Arabella has the constitution of a horse."

The earl said more to himself than to Lady Ann, "She was braver than most men I have seen wounded in battle. She cried out only once."

Lady Ann said slowly, a reminiscent smile in her eyes, "She was always brave. I shall never forget the last time she was seriously hurt. Her father was in a black rage, ranting at her for falling like a clumsy churl from her perch in the barn."

The earl, who she had thought was not paying any particular attention to her maunderings, suddenly looked up, a queer glint in his eyes. "The barn, Ann? What do you mean?"

"Did Arabella not tell you, Justin? I thought you knew all of her favorite haunts." She smiled at his bewilderment. Although it did not seem particularly important, she continued, "Arabella has a special hideaway in the very top of the barn. As a child she would climb up the narrow crawlway whenever she wanted to be by herself. I shall never forget that day—she could not have been more then ten years old—when one of the boards gave way and she fell some twenty feet to the ground, breaking her leg."

The earl was gazing at her intently. "Where is her special hideaway, Ann?" he asked softly, disregarding the rest of her recital.

Lady Ann felt a tug of surprise. "Why, Justin, I am not really certain. All I know is that there is a small ladder, just inside the front barn door, that leads up to the crawlway. She used to say that it was the most perfect spot for being alone—even better than the old abbey ruins—for no one could see or hear her, and the stable hands could be milking cows and chattering away on the lower floor without her ever hearing any of their racket."

"I begin to see," the earl said slowly. He rose jerkily to his feet and strode to the door. "I shall be back shortly, Ann. I . . . I must attend to an important matter," he said over his shoulder, and strode from the room.

The barnyard was bustling with early-morning activity as the Earl of Strafford, dressed only in breeches and open, rumpled shirt, made his way with single purpose to the barn. Stable hands were busily forking clumps of fresh hay into the wide wooden bins, while the farmhands led out the fat, sleek cattle to pasture. His presence in the doorway called an abrupt, uncomfortable halt to all chatter.

He did not even notice that he was being eyed with nervous uncertainty. He slipped inside the barn and saw immediately the small spindly ladder just to the left of the door. He set his foot upon the first rung, and ignoring the creak of the slender wooden rods, climbed swiftly to the top, and stepped carefully onto the narrow ledge that wound around to the far corner of the loft. He came presently to a tiny closed-off area, almost a small room, that looked out over the rolling hills behind the north pasture. It was a private place, a place for thinking private thoughts, a place for dreaming. Lady Ann said that Arabella came here only when she wished to be alone. He stood silently for only a moment longer. He could only faintly hear the sounds of the cows and the racket of the servants.

Slowly he made his way back down the ladder and out of the barn. He looked bleakly at the giant gnarled oak tree where he had stood so long ago, witness to what he had been certain was Arabella's betrayal of him. He felt again his anger, his bitterness and the overwhelming emptiness. He saw Arabella on their wedding night, her face alight with anticipation until he savagely raped her.

He walked, deep in thought, to the oak tree and sank down to the ground. Who, then, if not Arabella, had been with Gervaise on that afternoon? Suddenly he remembered his wife's words, so urgently spoken before she fell into unconsciousness: "You must not tell Elsbeth that Gervaise is her half-brother. It would destroy her." Could it have been Elsbeth with Gervaise? Elsbeth and Gervaise. Arabella had found out, yet she had told no one. She had thought only to protect Elsbeth. He looked deep within himself and found only bitter recrimination.

He rose slowly and walked back to Evesham Abbey. He

heard conversation from the Velvet Room and paused a moment. His eyes fell upon Elsbeth and Lord Graybourn.

Lord Graybourn took in the earl's disheveled appearance and the look of suffering in his eyes as he rose hurriedly from his seat beside Miss Deverill. "Do forgive my intrusion, my lord," he said earnestly. "I thought to stay with Miss Deverill a while to . . . to lighten her anxiety."

The earl forced a slight smile to his lips. "You are most welcome, sir. I think it kind of you to take Elsbeth's mind off her sister." He turned as he spoke and gazed at Elsbeth with new vision. He felt no anger at her, only a great pity. She was such an innocent child, wanting desperately to please, to be loved. Now she must bear the knowledge that the man to whom she had given her love and her body had left her. He was no more than a liar and a thief.

He said to her gently, "Arabella will come around, Elsbeth. She is made of stern stuff, you know."

She did not reply, but averted her face and pressed a small handerchief against her lips.

"Now, Miss Deverill," Lord Graybourn cajoled, "you really must not . . ."

The earl did not wait to hear the remainder of Lord Graybourn's speech, but trod quickly back to the earl's bedchamber.

"Justin?" Lady Ann queried, rising from her chair.

"Lady Talgarth's viscount is visiting with Elsbeth downstairs. It cannot but be good for her," he said significantly. He walked to his wife's side. "She is still the same?" he asked quietly.

Before Lady Ann could answer, there was a gentle, almost childlike moan from Arabella.

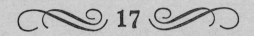

# 17

"Justin, really! You are being quite ridiculous! I am certainly strong enough to walk across the bedroom!" Arabella's vehement protest was greeted by a tolerant grin from her husband. When she realized that he was not to be gainsaid, she found that she rather enjoyed being carried in his strong arms to the comfortable settee beside the window.

"There, madam," he said, depositing her gently. "You cannot say that I am not an excellent, quite trustworthy beast of burden."

"If you mean by beast of burden a *bully*, then I have no disagreement with you, my lord," she replied impishly. "I suppose one simply must tolerate your overbearing nature."

"I believe that a bully and a she-devil are well suited. Though, I daresay," he continued meditatively, placing a pillow behind her head, "that if you are not soon on the mend, I shall be lost to all appeal, having had my way without your colourful interference these past three days."

"I shall do my utmost to counteract your tryant's influence as soon as you release me from this room." She pulled the knit coverlet more closely about her. The simple movement made her wince.

"Slowly, Bella," he said gently, and removed the coverlet from her fingers.

"At least you have finally allowed me a nightgown," she said waspishly.

"If you would as soon be without it, I shall be delighted to oblige you," he countered with a wolfish grin.

"I thank you, no, sir!"

Silence fell between them, and Arabella watched her husband's grin change into a very serious expression. During the past days and nights, a bond had grown between them, yet he had not allowed her to speak of all that had passed between them. When she had tried to ask him about Gervaise, he had shaken his head and put his fingers to her lips. "Later, Bella," he had said. "You must think now only to get well again."

But now she was stronger, the pain only a light throbbing in her shoulder, her mind no longer clouded with laudanum.

He rose abruptly, took a quick turn about the room, and returned again to sit beside her. She watched the firm line of his jaw harden. She rushed into desperate speech, afraid now to let him be the first to speak.

"Justin, please do not be angry with me. I know that I should have found you at the Talgarths' ball, told you about Gervaise. But somehow . . ." She faltered a moment. "Somehow I wanted to prove something to you. I know it was foolish of me, yet I thought if I trapped him, you would realize that there was never anything between us."

He looked at her, startled. She had seen his anger at himself and thought he was angry at her. "Yes, you were foolish to follow him by yourself, but that is not important now. I know, Bella . . . I know now that there was never anything between you and Gervaise."

"You . . . you know?" she stammered. "You believe me now?"

He nodded, clasped her slender hand in his, and brought her fingers to his lips. "I have no anger at you, my dear, only at myself. You see, I know now that it was Elsbeth." He paused a moment at the widening of her eyes in silent query. He heaved a deep sigh and continued, "It is difficult to begin, for mine is the fault from the beginning. Because I saw you with my own eyes enter and then leave the barn but the day before our wedding, with Gervaise not many steps behind you, both your appearances leaving no doubt in my mind as to what you had done, I would not listen to you. I believed that you wanted to defy your father's orders, that you saw our marriage as being forced upon you. I wanted revenge upon you for what I thought was your betrayal of me. I wanted to make you suffer for making me pay so dearly for my inheritance. I gloried in the thought of my revenge upon you. Yet, when I raped you, I felt loathing for myself.

"I made inquiries about Gervaise, but learned only that he could not be the son of Thomas de Trécassis, that indeed de Trécassis' wife had died before Gervaise was born. When Josette died, I believed him to be involved, but I had no proof. Fool that I was, it never occurred to me that you could be in any danger from the man I believed to be your lover. You see, that day you were trapped in the old abbey ruins, I was busily searching his room for anything that would tell me what he was up to. I should have forced him to leave that very day, yet I was still uncertain that you did not perhaps still care for him. I feared that if he left, I might lose you. That is why I did not wish to speak to you that day of the Talgarths' ball. I wanted to set a trap for him, expose him for what he really was, prove to you that he was not worthy of your love. When I overheard you tell him that you would never go willingly with him, the stupid emeralds, my elaborate plan—none of it was of further importance. Again, I made a mistake, for I did not know of his violent hatred for the Deverill family, particularly your father. But you, Arabella, you saved my life."

He spoke more rapidly now, his eyes never leaving her face. "Your mother, quite by accident, told me about another injury you had sustained many years ago. It was a fall from the barn, she said. I have been to your hideaway in the loft, Arabella."

Arabella said quietly, "How very ironic it is. The day you saw me coming from the barn, but the day before our wedding, I wanted to be by myself, away from Gervaise and Elsbeth, away from everyone, to think about our marriage. I did not believe that ours would be a marriage of convenience. Indeed, that afternoon I was thanking Father for being so very wise." She closed her fingers tightly about his hand.

"There has been so much that has happened," she said finally. "What do you intend to do now, Justin?"

He looked down at her searchingly, realizing all too well

the enormity of what had passed between them. He saw no clue to her feelings. He said heavily, "I could understand if you could not forgive me, Arabella. I shall do as you wish now. If you choose, I can be gone from your life as soon as you are well again. Perhaps to rejoin my regiment."

It was she who searched his face now, the wrenching in his voice more painful than the wound in her shoulder. There was so very much he had yet to learn of her, and she about him. She felt his wounded pride, his mortification. She saw the deep regret mirrored in his gray eyes.

She said simply, knowing that their future together rested with her words, "I forgave you the night I asked you to stay with me, Justin. I wanted you as my husband, and I desire you above all men. I gave you my love that night, my lord."

She turned her face against his shoulder and whispered, "If you were to leave me, Justin, I should not want to go on."

Dr. Branyon slipped into the room without knocking, fearful of waking Arabella. He stood on the threshold and stared silently at the scene before him. His indomitable Arabella lay nestled in her husband's arms, her head cradled against his shoulder. He sensed that he had inadvertently intruded upon a precious moment. He quietly began to edge out of the room.

The earl raised his head. "Do not go, Paul. As you can see, I have our patient well in hand."

Dr. Branyon grinned and shook his head.

"Come, sir," Arabella said with a serene smile on her face, "if you are to be my new papa, you certainly must not be backward in your attentions."

"Actually, Bella," he admitted ruefully, "I thought you would be asleep. It was Justin I sought."

Justin looked down at Arabella, kissed her lightly on the tip of her nose, and said gently, "Love, there is something else we must speak about. Paul, do sit down."

The earl disengaged his hand from Arabella's and drew a small folded piece of paper from his waistcoat pocket.

Arabella gasped sharply. The small paper was the letter she had found on the skeleton in the old abbey ruins!

She shook her head back and forth. "Justin, please do not—"

Dr. Branyon interrupted. "Come, Justin, what have you there?"

The earl patted Arabella's hand reassuringly, then turned to Dr. Branyon. "It is a letter, Paul, a letter written some twenty years ago from Magdalaine to her lover." He handed the letter to Dr. Branyon. As he read the letter, Justin said gently to Arabella, "I undressed you that night, love, and it fell from one of your slippers. There is naught for you to worry about, Bella, I promise you. You must trust me.

"Arabella had fitted more pieces of the puzzle together than I had, Paul. It would seem that the earl sent Magdalaine to France in 1789 to fetch the Trécassis emeralds, promised to him, I would imagine, as part of Magdalaine's dowry."

Arabella said dully, "It was obviously a bribe. Magdalaine had given birth to a son—Gervaise—before she met my father. To avoid the scandal, the Comte te Trécassis must have promised my father a vast sum to wed her and remove her from France."

Justin said evenly, "Bella, a marriage of convenience such as theirs was not at all uncommon. No dishonour can attach itself to your father."

Dr. Branyon looked up from the letter. "There is no mention of the emeralds here, Justin. How did you find out about them?"

The earl looked a bit rueful. "Well, actually, Paul, I spent two afternoons searching in Gervaise's room. I finally found the instructions to their hiding place in the lining of one of his valises. It was in a letter from Magdalaine to her brother, Thomas de Trécassis."

Dr. Branyon looked thoughtful. "I often wondered, you know. 'Twould appear that Magdalaine returned to England with her lover only to fetch Elsbeth."

"Yes. The earl must have discovered their plain to escape and shot Magdalaine's lover, Charles. The skeleton Arabella found in the old abbey ruins was, of course, this Charles. She found the letter in his clothing. Is that not right, Arabella?"

She nodded, then raised herself painfully from the pillow. "Please, Justin, no more," she pleaded, a catch in her voice.

The earl gently pressed her back against the pillow. He turned to Dr. Branyon. "Paul, you have not spoken all these years. Arabella kept the letter from us primarily to protect her father's name. It is time you told her the truth. What really happened to Magdalaine?"

"Bella," Dr. Branyon said gently, "your father did not kill

Magdalaine, although from reading this letter I can readily imagine how you drew such a conclusion. No, she killed herself. I was with her when she died. She must have hidden the emeralds and written their hiding place to her brother before your father knew her intentions." He paused, then drew a deep breath. "I cannot lie to you, my child. Your father bore no love for her, but he did not kill her."

A single tear gathered at the corner of her eyes and trickled down her cheek. It was as if an incredible burden of doubt and uncertainty had suddenly been lifted from her heart. She gave a watery sniff and with a trembling hand dashed away the salty tear. She gazed wonderingly at her husband. "But how did you know, Justin? How could you be so certain that my father did not kill her?"

He said simply, "Your father told me several years ago, not any of the details, of course, merely that his first wife had taken her own life. I could not be certain that you would believe me, so I asked Dr. Branyon to tell you."

The earl said to Dr. Branyon, "There is but one secret that I must ask you to keep, Paul—even from Ann. No one must know that Magdalaine was Gervaise's mother."

Dr. Branyon looked puzzled. "Can it matter so very much, Justin?"

"Yes, Paul. I vow it matters a great deal."

"As you will, then," he replied after a moment's consideration.

Arabella cast her husband a look of profound gratitude that was not lost upon Dr. Branyon. He strove to maintain a look of puzzlement on his face, yet understanding lurked deep in his eyes. He rose and turned, handing the letter back to the earl. "I think it time you destroyed this letter, Justin. I believe that Ann, Elsbeth, and for that fact, all our neighbors should only know that Gervaise was a desperate young man who had somehow discovered the existence of the emeralds. Indeed, to dampen curiosity, Ann and I have already circulated to the proper quarters that the gun went off by accident."

"Well done, Paul," Justin said.

Dr. Branyon smiled down at Arabella. "Now, young lady, you need your rest. No, do not gainsay me, for now I have a formidable ally in your husband!" He passed the palm of his hand over her cool brow. "Yes indeed, the constitution of a horse." As he turned to leave, he thought to ask the earl, "Justin, there is but one other question I have for you."

The earl raised an inquiring eyebrow.

"The emeralds. Why did you so readily give them to Gervaise? Surely he had no right to them."

Justin replied, unperturbed, "'Twas an easy decision, Paul. You see, the emeralds were paste."

"Paste!" Arabella gasped.

"Yes, my love, paste. All these years, a worthless necklace of green stones lay carefully hidden in *The Dance of Death* panel. It is probable that the Comte de Trécassis never intended to give your father the real emeralds. But he readily bestowed upon his daughter a supposed heirloom to appease your father, at least for a time."

"But, then, where are the real emeralds, I wonder?" Dr. Branyon asked.

The earl replied with an indifferent shrug of his shoulders, "We shall probably never know. The de Trécassis family was killed in the revolution. The comte must have taken the secret with him to his death."

Arabella shivered suddenly. "I wonder what Gervaise will do when he discovers that the emeralds are paste?"

The earl said dryly, "I think you need have no fear that he will return to Evesham Abbey. He is probably now in Dover booking passage on a packet back to Brussels."

"Lord," Dr. Branyon exclaimed, "it is all too fantastic! Save for the ball in your shoulder, Bella, we at least managed to survive all of Gervaise's machinations."

Arabella said quietly, her eyes gentling as they rested on her husband's face, " 'Twas not the only wound, Paul. But it is the only one that has yet to heal."

Dr. Branyon gave a little chuckle. "I do not understand your words, my child, but I am quite certain that I have become suddenly *de trop*! Now, if you will excuse me, your very lovely mother awaits me downstairs. I shall have her nearly all to myself, for Lord Graybourn occupies all of Elsbeth's attention."

As Dr. Branyon quietly closed the door behind him, the earl gathered Arabella once again into his arm. He remarked appreciatively, "A most perceptive man, my new father-in-law-to-be."

"Yes," Arabella agreed softly, "most perceptive." She

smiled up at him longingly, and he gently leaned down and kissed her. He was thinking himself the luckiest of men, when suddenly she drew away and sighed.

"Good God!" he exclaimed ruefully. "I had hopes of a very tender encounter, my love. Here you have turned me off after but a kiss!"

She forced a smile. "I am sorry, Justin, but I was thinking of Elsbeth. I . . . I am concerned for her, I cannot help it. There is so much that she must bear now."

"I have not seen her much these past three days. But, you know, somehow I believe that she is made of sterner stuff than we imagine. Lord Graybourn, too, is giving her a comfort that neither of us could provide. Time, Arabella—it must be a matter of time."

"I trust that you are right, Justin."

"We shall see. Now, wife, if we could return to more pressing matters." He pulled her gently to him and kissed her long and deep.

"Oh, Justin . . ." She sighed in his ear as he nibbled her throat. "You should not have allowed me a nightgown after all. I vow the sleeve is beginning to pain me."

"A stupid mistake, my love, that I shall remedy this very minute," he said promptly.